Praise for
Kay Hooper

"A multi-talented author whose stories always pack a tremendous punch." —Iris Johansen

"A master storyteller." —Tami Hoag

"Kay Hooper's dialogue rings true; her characters are more three-dimensional than those usually found in this genre." —*The Atlanta Journal-Constitution*

"Kay Hooper is a master at painting the most vivid pictures with words!" —*The Best Reviews*

"Not to be missed." —*All About Romance*

Kay Hooper

Enemy Mine

JOVE BOOKS, NEW YORK

THE BERKLEY PUBLISHING GROUP
Published by the Penguin Group
Penguin Group (USA) Inc.
375 Hudson Street, New York, New York 10014, USA
Penguin Group (Canada), 90 Eglinton Avenue East, Suite 700, Toronto, Ontario M4P 2Y3, Canada
(a division of Pearson Penguin Canada Inc.)
Penguin Books Ltd., 80 Strand, London WC2R 0RL, England
Penguin Group Ireland, 25 St. Stephen's Green, Dublin 2, Ireland (a division of Penguin Books Ltd.)
Penguin Group (Australia), 250 Camberwell Road, Camberwell, Victoria 3124, Australia
(a division of Pearson Australia Group Pty. Ltd.)
Penguin Books India Pvt. Ltd., 11 Community Centre, Panchsheel Park, New Delhi—110 017, India
Penguin Group (NZ), Cnr. Airborne and Rosedale Roads, Albany, Auckland 1310, New Zealand
(a division of Pearson New Zealand Ltd.)
Penguin Books (South Africa) (Pty.) Ltd., 24 Sturdee Avenue, Rosebank, Johannesburg 2196, South
Africa

Penguin Books Ltd., Registered Offices: 80 Strand, London WC2R 0RL, England

This is a work of fiction. Names, characters, places, and incidents either are the product of the author's
imagination or are used fictitiously, and any resemblance to actual persons, living or dead, business es-
tablishments, events, or locales is entirely coincidental. The publisher does not have any control over
and does not assume any responsibility for author or third-party websites or their content.

ENEMY MINE

A Jove Book / published by arrangement with the author.

PRINTING HISTORY
Published in 1990 in Great Britain by Mills & Boon Ltd.; 1992 by Silhouette Books
Included in *The Real Thing* published by Berkley Sensation November 2004
Jove mass market edition / November 2005

Copyright © 1989 by Kay Hooper.

Cover design by Rita Frangie.
Cover photos: "Young Woman Running Up Red Dirt Hill" by Jonathan Kim/Getty Images; "Australia,
Victoria, Maits Rest Rainforest Walk" by Photodisc Green/Getty Images.

ISBN: 0-515-13926-2

JOVE®
Jove Books are published by The Berkley Publishing Group,
a division of Penguin Group (USA) Inc.,
375 Hudson Street, New York, New York 10014.
JOVE is a registered trademark of Penguin Group (USA) Inc.
The "J" design is a trademark belonging to Penguin Group (USA) Inc.

PRINTED IN THE UNITED STATES OF AMERICA

10 9 8 7 6 5 4

To Leslie,
Who waited very patiently for this,
And for Eileen,
Who never wailed at me,
even though I'm sure she wanted to

chapter one

"*PENDLETON!* OH, GREAT, that's just great. It had to be you!"

"Nice seeing you again, too, Tyler. Damn it, will you get your foot off my—"

Tyler found a bit of purchase against his upper thigh and managed to boost herself higher. "Go to hell!" she snapped, holding on to an all too narrow ledge.

"We're both likely to get there any minute now," he told her, a little winded but entirely his normal insouciant self. His left hand groped and discovered a murderously narrow crack in the rock about two feet below her shoulders; wedging his long fingers into that, he hung by one hand long enough to remove her foot from his thigh and place it on an almost nonexistent ledge she couldn't see.

Tyler would have choked thanking him, but she felt more secure.

Kane Pendleton worked his other hand into the crevice and pulled himself higher, the strain bunching powerful muscles beneath his khaki shirt and cording his forearms. Rock splintered a scant few inches from his shoulder, but he paid no attention even when the crack of the rifle echoed down the ravine.

His boots scrabbled for a foothold, discovering one finally, and he was hanging on to the same ledge, showing her white teeth as his tanned face split in a grin. "Fancy meeting you here," he said cheerfully.

Tyler ducked instinctively as another rifle shot chipped rock above her head, but her voice was as steady as it was fierce. "What're you doing here, Kane?"

"The same as you, I'd bet. Work your way along the ledge; the one you're standing on gets wider a couple of feet to your left. Come on, honey, move—that guy can't keep missing us forever."

"Don't call me honey!" she muttered, but began moving cautiously to her left. The ledge beneath her feet was soon wide enough to lend considerable security, and her tense fingers eased somewhat, no longer forced to bear most of her weight.

Since Kane was occupying himself in finding a more secure perch, she risked a glance at him. She didn't know whether to be relieved or annoyed to see that he had changed not at all in the several months since their last encounter. Only his face, throat and forearms were

2

bared to her sight, and she could see no scars, no recent marks on his flesh.

He was, as always, darkly tanned, his big, broad-shouldered body unnervingly powerful, those beautiful long-fingered hands of his still filled with their amazing strength. He wore no hat despite the heat, and his thick, shining black hair was, as always, a little long and somewhat shaggy.

A black-maned lion, she had always thought, proud and strong in the summer of his life.

Annoyed with herself, Tyler returned her full attention to the task of moving along the ledge, seeking some shelter from the sporadic gunfire far below them. She sent mental advice to the part of her that wanted to look at him, reminding herself that nothing would be different this time, nothing at all.

They were after the same thing—again—and neither would stop until the chalice was found and claimed. By one of them.

It had been a beaten gold necklace last time, she remembered, working her way along the ledge slowly and carefully. And before that—What had it been before that? Oh, yes . . . An uncatalogued Rembrandt offered for sale by a private collector in France.

Three years since their first meeting under the burning sun of Egypt, where they had met and fought for a golden figurine. And during those years they had clashed a dozen times all over the world. Mexico, Budapest, Hamburg, Madrid, the Sudan, Athens, Venezuela, Madagascar. To date, she thought wryly, the honors were evenly split. In twelve face-to-face confrontations, she had come away with the prize six times—and so had Kane.

Tyler found it incredible that she and Kane worked for bitter rivals, two indecently wealthy men who thought nothing of sending their representatives halfway around the world in a hurried and often dangerous search for certain carefully chosen rare art objects, antiquities and artifacts. She still found it hard to believe that those two men enjoyed a mutual bitter delight in their games of one-upmanship, each spending vast amounts of money to get the objects each coveted—and to get them first.

She could hardly complain that her own part in the games had not been both exciting, adventurous and profitable—all three being reasons she had taken the job in the first place. Her employer had found her in a small antique store in London, where her reputation for possessing an unerring instinct for detecting genuine antiquities over faked ones had grown so that even some museums kept her on a retainer.

Robert Sayers had introduced himself, talked to her for less than an hour and then offered her a job. Tyler had been twenty-three and restless; she had spent most of her life in following her archaeologist father into some of the most remote parts of the world, and her settled life since his death had taught her nothing if not that the gypsy in her was still strong.

She had been ripe for Sayers's offer.

Her mind in the past, Tyler stepped off the ledge and

into thin air. Her fingers scrabbled for a hold and she felt Kane's hard arm lock around her waist.

"I'd hate to lose you now," he remarked, his deep voice showing none of the strain he must have felt; he was leaning outward from the cliff face to support her, one hand jammed in a crevice above them—and she was not a little woman.

She managed to regain her fingertip hold on the ledge and get her feet beneath her again. "You can't lose what you've never had!" she snapped, turning her head to glare at him. "And I thought you said the ledge widened."

His remarkably vivid green eyes were amused. Ignoring her second comment, he responded to the first. "Now that's a provocative thing to say. A challenge, no less." His arm tightened around her waist before releasing her. "One of these days—when we have time—we really should explore that. I wonder if I *would* lose you once I had you."

Tyler showed him a smile that was all teeth and no humor. "Don't hold your breath, pal," she advised.

Kane laughed softly. "Right. The ledge *did* widen by the way, and it widens again, on the other side of this spur. But we'll have to go around the tip."

She looked in the opposite direction and winced, grateful that he couldn't see her expression. Unnoticed by her, the ledge they'd traversed had swung outward to follow the spur that protruded into the ravine like some granite giant's elbow. They couldn't climb higher since the cliff face was sheet-smooth, and they certainly couldn't descend into the ravine where that gunman waited with his trusty rifle. They had to go on.

"Great," she muttered.

"Give me your hand," he instructed, "and stay pressed against the cliff. Try to stretch your foot around to the other side; the ledge should be within reach."

Tyler usually trusted Kane Pendleton about as far as she could throw a bull elephant, but she didn't hesitate to give him her hand and follow his orders. If she had learned nothing else of him during their past encounters, she had learned to trust him in times of danger. He might well pull every trick he could think of in order to beat her to whatever they both sought, but he would no more abandon a bitter enemy in trouble than he would his best friend.

She fell somewhere between.

And the strength of his big hand was comforting as she braced one foot on the ledge and stretched the other around the spur, keeping her body pressed to the rock. She searched blindly with that extended foot, holding her breath, feeling the rock dig into her painfully. She was no mountain climber, but this wasn't the first time she'd been forced to broaden her horizons out of the need to escape something or someone. The survival instinct, Tyler had learned, was a great motivator.

Her foot finally located the ledge, and she was pinned there momentarily while her hand searched for something to hold. Then she was sliding cautiously around the point of the spur, knowing that Kane wouldn't let go until she felt secure.

"Got it," she called breathlessly, all of her once more on one side of the spur. She moved along the ledge, pausing once she was a couple of feet away from the point to watch Kane work his way around. Within seconds, he appeared, moving far more easily than she. But then, he *was* a mountain climber. Among other things.

Securely on her side of the spur, he nodded toward what looked like nothing more than a crooked gash in the face of the cliff. "There's a cave, and it's invisible from the bottom of the ravine; if we get inside fast enough, our friend with the gun may lose us."

Tyler didn't waste time in working her way toward the cave, but she wondered silently how Kane could possibly know of it. Still, she didn't doubt his knowledge. Kane, damn his black-hearted soul, was always right. *Always*. It was enough to give a woman a complex.

She slid into the narrow opening of the cave easily and stood staring, discovering that he could still surprise her.

"Hey, you're blocking the door."

Casting an irritated glance over her shoulder, Tyler moved farther into the cave, muttering to herself. Obviously he hadn't planned to be absent long, because he'd left a lantern on. The welcome scent of coffee filled the small cave, and Tyler's jaundiced eye took in the creature comforts that Kane always—somehow—managed to scrounge from what anyone else would consider barren wilderness.

A double-sized, double-thick sleeping bag was unrolled welcomingly a short distance from a small fire burning brightly in the center of the roughly ten-by-twelve-foot cave. A backpack leaned against the wall near a rifle, with two plastic jugs of water close by. A camp chair was set up on the other side of the fire, and it was here Tyler sat, frowning at the lantern.

It shouldn't have surprised her, she thought. Kane had an absolute genius of making himself comfortable wherever fate happened to drop him. He would, she knew, abandon most of his stuff before he moved on, but he'd find more later when he got tired of roughing it. He always did. She had once seen him find the only sleeping bag within two hundred miles. And he'd made it look *easy.*

"Coffee?" he asked, folding gracefully into a cross-legged position before the fire.

Even though she was thirsty, Tyler was in no mood for pleasantries. "What're you doing here?" she asked tautly.

Kane poured coffee into a gaily decorated ceramic mug and sipped, gazing at her with thoughtful, shuttered green eyes. "The chalice, of course," he said, calm. "You didn't come way the hell out here without a rifle, did you?"

Tyler gritted her teeth. "*No,* I didn't come here without a rifle. I dropped it in the ravine when that maniac started shooting!"

Kane shook his head pityingly. "That was hardly the best time to lose your only means of defense," he pointed out.

8

"You didn't have your rifle, either. You left it in here like the rawest tenderfoot."

"Touché," he murmured.

She saw the hidden smile and realized he had side-tracked her—again. It was a favorite ploy of his, and one she was ridiculously prone to accept. Determinedly she reclaimed her major grievance. "You won't get the chalice. *I* talked to the man who found the cache, and he—"

"Told you he'd give you the chalice if you brought the rest of the stuff back to him," Kane finished smoothly. He smiled a little as surprise and rage widened her fine amber eyes. His had been a guess, but her reaction was proof enough; they'd both been suckered. "Funny. He told me the same thing."

Kane sipped his coffee and watched her while she absorbed the implications. Tyler St. James was nothing if not quick, and Kane enjoyed the play of emotions across her delicate, expressive face. He remembered those tense moments on the cliff face and kept a grin off his own face with an effort. How many women, he wondered, could have spit curses at a man while dangling from a cliff by her fingertips? With someone shooting at her?

Not many.

She was one in a million, Tyler was. A strong, intelligent woman with the beauty to launch ships and the courage to follow them into battle. Kane could recall a number of past occasions when he'd been glad to have her at his side when things had gotten sticky. Tyler never waited for the cavalry to come charging to the rescue, but instead grabbed a big stick and started swinging.

She'd very nearly brained him once or twice.

That memory helped alter admiration to uneasiness. Apparently history was about to repeat itself yet again, and the duration promised to be bothersome. A hunter by choice and by nature, Kane certainly had no objections to Tyler's company on this particular hunt—in theory, that is. He wouldn't have minded another opportunity to discover what made the lady tick, for one thing. And, as partners went, she was far better than most at this sort of thing, and unlikely to panic if things got rough—and they almost always did at some point.

The trick, he thought, would be to come to some sort of understanding with her. They were rivals, after all, both after the chalice and both determined to have it. Still, with unknown dangers lying ahead of them and the gunman—who might or might not be after the cache, as well—possibly tagging along, two stood a better chance than one of making it.

Kane met that amber gaze, reflecting that he'd never met another woman who hid her thoughts so well. She made no secret of her emotions, but the thoughts behind them remained enigmatic. One in a million.

Her musical, deceptively gentle voice was even. "We both have the same information. The same directions to where the cache is hidden. So it's a race."

"Is it?" Kane freshened his coffee, frowning a bit. Apparently going off on a tangent, he said, "I was out reconnoitering when I saw you coming along the ravine. Then that shooter chased you up on the cliff face. Since you and I were obviously both after the chalice, I thought it'd be smarter if we teamed up."

"Really?"

Kane kept his gaze on the coffee; he wasn't sure that his ability to hide his thoughts was as good as hers. "Why not? We make a good team. When we aren't trying to con each other six ways from Sunday, that is. This clearly isn't going to be a piece of cake, not with a trigger-happy unknown likely dogging our steps and after the same thing."

"How do you know he is?"

"I don't," Kane replied promptly. "But I think we'd better assume he is. We're in the middle of nowhere with no reason to draw gunfire, unless you consider a hidden cache of antiquities. So what else could he be after? And since our cagey friend back in Panama obviously decided to hedge his bets by sending two of us after the cache, it's probably safe to assume we'll run into trouble somewhere along the line."

"Trouble that a team would stand a better chance of surviving than either of us alone?" she asked dryly.

"Stands to reason."

"And when we find the cache—assuming we do—and get it back to Panama—assuming we do? And assuming that our *friend* Tomas holds up his end of the bargain and gives us what he promises? Who gets the chalice, Kane?"

He ran a thumb along his jaw, half frowning and half

smiling. "We draw straws? Flip a coin? Arm wrestle? Split the thing down the middle? I'm open to suggestions, Ty."

"I've told you not to call me that," she said, more or less automatically.

He looked vague. "Did you? I don't remember."

Tyler gave him one of the looks reserved especially for him, a combination of intense suspicion and total mistrust; Kane was, she knew, about as vague as a defense computer. And about as likely to raise the flag of surrender. He was up to something.

"Well? Look, Ty, we can waste time and energy in racing each other to the cache, or we can team up until we get the stuff back to Panama. Then, when we're on solid and relatively safe ground, we can decide about the chalice. Maybe we could even make like Solomon and call our respective bosses, asking which would prefer to hand the chalice over to the enemy rather than get only half."

Gloomily Tyler said, "They'd both say split it, you know they would. And neither of us could do that."

Kane was a little surprised that she knew that about him, but obscurely pleased as well. "We'll come up with something."

Tyler studied his face, keeping her own expressionless. All things considered, she'd rather he was within sight until the chalice was found and carried safely out of Colombia; it was simply *safer* to know what Kane was doing whenever possible. And if there was danger to be faced, he was the next best thing to a loaded gun and a mean dog to have at her side.

She smiled despite herself at the comparison, and saw Kane's green eyes drop to her mouth. And that slight flicker of his gaze brought home to her vividly the danger of spending any amount of time at all with him. Risky as it was to count him a partner for the duration, it was nothing less than insanity to place them both in the peculiar intimacy of a situation where they would be forced to depend on each other, possibly for their very survival.

Their past encounters had consisted of a series of brief meetings between fiercely competitive surges of independent action as they'd each fought to claim the coveted prize first. All told, they'd spent little time together—being mostly occupied with finding ways to trick each other—but even that had been taut with a tension that was far more intense than mere rivalry could have accounted for.

She could, Tyler thought, barely keep him in line now; what would happen if they turned *that* corner? And how did she feel about the possibility?

"Ty?"

For a moment she couldn't seem to breathe, but then her mind had neatly assigned Kane his proper place in her life. He was a rival. Usually an enemy. Sometimes a partner. Occasionally the strong arm that would prevent her careless dive off a cliff. Nothing more.

Her breathing resumed, steady and even. "I don't see a choice myself," she said calmly. "It looks like we're partners—for the duration." She ignored her mind's gentle siren song. *Seduce an enemy and earn his loyalty.*

No. Not Kane. Seducing Kane for the wrong reasons would mean more than playing with fire; it would mean a blithe trek into a live volcano just to see what molten rock looked like.

"Then we've agreed," he said in a brisk tone. He glanced down at the broad watch on his wrist. "Nearly sunset. Our friendly gunman out there can't get close without alerting us, so we'll stay in here tonight and get an early start tomorrow. That okay with you?"

"Fine."

"When did you lose your backpack?"

If Tyler's teeth gritted again, at least it was a silent indication of annoyance. "When I lost the rifle."

Kane didn't seem disposed to make sarcastic comments on her ineptitude. Perhaps he was mellowing.

"Well, my sleeping bag's big enough for two." He met her gaze, his own mild. "Unless you object?"

There was, Tyler decided, a middle ground strewn with land mines between assertive feminine independence and the coming decidedly chilly night. She swallowed her instinctive objection, determined to be rational about things. "Fine."

Kane seemed not to notice her struggle. He poured more coffee into his mug and handed it to her. "Have some. I haven't eaten yet; how about you?"

"Not since this morning."

He reached for his backpack and opened it, digging in and producing a wide array of packaged and canned foodstuffs. Tyler watched him retrieve his Swiss Army knife from his pocket, and when he looked quizzically at her, responded haughtily.

"Caviar, of course."

Kane grinned, but opened the can and arranged crackers on a tin plate. "Ought to taste good with coffee," he murmured.

"You mean you don't have champagne?" she demanded, offended.

He reached into the backpack and produced a bottle.

Tyler's mouth fell open. "Damn. And I thought I had you."

"I like champagne," he responded simply.

Annoyed by her inclination to giggle, Tyler set her mug aside and watched him neatly open the champagne and pour the foaming liquid into two tin cups. (For some obscure reason she'd never had the nerve to question, Kane always carried a variety of plates, cups, and utensils rather than just enough for himself. As if he always expected a party, no matter how unlikely.) She accepted a cup from him, wondering if he would propose a toast. Being Kane, he did.

"To our partnership."

She tapped her cup against his, a wry smile curving her lips. "Right. And let's hope we don't kill each other."

"I'll buy that," he murmured.

Silence fell as they sipped champagne and munched caviar and crackers. Tyler avoided looking at him, asking herself fiercely why on earth she had agreed to this.

If asked to name the ten people she trusted least, she would put Kane Pendleton's name at the top of the list, underscored and in bold print. In fact, his name would probably occupy the first three places on that list. It was insane to agree to even a temporary partnership.

She could grudgingly admit that the man had a basic core of integrity, some kind of private code of honor he adhered to, but she knew nothing much else about him. Oh, she knew he'd garnered survival training somewhere in his past, and that he was a sharpshooter with any handgun or rifle. That he was physically powerful and blessed with singular endurance. That he had a quick temper and quick humor. That he was smart, tough and ruthless when he had to be. That he loved antiquities even as she did, and possessed a certain rare, intuitive "feel" for them, even as she did.

From their past encounters, she knew he was not cruel even to enemies, but did not hesitate to employ rough tactics if information was needed or if escape or survival depended on quick action. She knew he slept like an animal with every sense alert and that he was cool to the point of iciness under stress.

But what did she *really* know about the man? He might well have sprung full-blown into life, there on the sands of Egypt, for she knew nothing of his background. She had no idea of where he lived or what he did between assignments.

The silence was bothering her. In a casual tone, she said, "Tomas has a buyer for the cache, don't you think?"

Kane nodded. "I'd say so. As a matter of fact, I think

he'd lined up more than one buyer, and that he's beginning to feel the pressure. He was jumpy as hell when I talked to him."

"Drugs," Tyler offered.

"No, I think his vice is gambling. I got the feeling he needed a lot of money very quickly. Maybe that's why he sent the both of us after the cache; he figured one of us was bound to make it."

A silence fell again.

Tyler glanced across the fire at him, studying him beneath her lashes. Her interest in Tomas was fleeting; she couldn't keep her mind off Kane. There was in him, she thought, something just barely tame, a cloak of civilization hiding what lay beneath, and women always seemed to sense that; Kane drew women like a magnet drew ore. And he was attractive, possessing aside from his rough good looks a sexual aura that was almost a tactile thing. Her stomach tightened, and Tyler ordered her body to ignore that. Not that it did. He was the most physically compelling man she'd ever encountered, and in a world where various types of liberation sought to overhaul the male nature, she found his toughness of spirit and blatant sexuality more than a little attractive.

Damn it.

In the past she'd found her thoughts turning speculatively to him because of that. In another age he would have been a warrior, a conqueror, even a king if there had been kingdoms to be won; in this day and time he appeared on the surface to be just that slight degree out of step with the times. A throwback to a more dangerous age. And yet he never treated Tyler as if her sex made her weaker than he, as if she needed his protection.

The man was an enigma.

"Ready for bed?"

She blinked and stared at him. "What? Oh—right."

"We should move out of here before dawn if we want to lose our trigger-happy friend," he observed mildly. "So we'd better get some sleep."

"Uh-huh." She shook off the uncharacteristic passivity, adding with spirit, "I hope you don't snore."

"I don't. How about you?"

Tyler gave him a look, set her cup aside and went over to the sleeping bag. She sat down and hauled her boots off, muttering to herself, then wiggled into the bag and tried to get as far over to one side as possible. Conscious of his watching gaze, she kept her face expressionless and hoped the heat she felt suffusing her skin wasn't visible to him. Turning her back to him, she resolutely closed her eyes, wishing she could have removed her bra; she hated sleeping in it. She listened to the faint sounds of Kane's movements, stiffening when she felt him slide into the sleeping bag beside her. He was a big man, and even the double bag was cramped with both of them inside it.

She felt a weakness in her limbs when his hard body brushed hers, her breath catching despite herself. Zipped into the bag, she felt trapped, helpless, and her own vulnerability shocked her as a wave of panic swept over her. How could she defend herself? She could barely move—

A hard hand grasped her shoulder, turning her over onto her back, and Kane's head blocked out the flickering firelight when his lips found hers unerringly. His kiss was rough, overpowering in its male demand, and Tyler pushed against his chest fiercely in a panicky rejection that was mental rather than physical. The banked heat inside her flared at the touch, and she almost moaned aloud in frustrated anger when she realized her mouth was opening to him, responding to him in the face of all reason and despite the cold mental panic. Her fingers curled, digging into his chest, and a dizzying wave of raw desire swept over her.

Abruptly Kane broke the kiss and turned away from her. "All right," he said dryly, "I've made my move. The attempted ravishment you were worried about. Now we can go to sleep. Good night, Ty."

Tyler nearly smothered trying to hide her ragged breathing, staring at him uncomprehendingly. And this time when her fingers curled, it required a supreme effort of will to keep herself from raking her nails down his back. Mentally calling him every violent thing she could think of, she turned her back to his. "Good night, Kane," she managed evenly. She thought she heard a faint chuckle from him, and spent a good ten minutes silently plotting to get even. Soon.

FAR BELOW THEM in the ravine, the watching man saw only a dim flicker of light at the cave entrance. He stood undecided for a moment, then shrugged to himself and moved silently away. Some distance down the ravine he found the woman's backpack and rifle, and gathered them thoughtfully. He made camp out of sight and hearing of the cave, eating and then settling down to sleep. His powerful body relaxed totally in sleep, but like his quarry he slept like an animal with every sense alert.

He didn't stir until nearly dawn.

TYLER HAD PECULIAR dreams. She was in a straitjacket and moved irritably to free herself, muttering in disgust at the feeling of confinement. The straps were cutting into her back and beneath her breasts, and her shoulders were chafed. She complained about the matter to her shadowy companion, whispering her grievance in annoyance. Then she felt one of the straps give and sighed in relief as the ones on her shoulders were smoothed away. Her arms were constricted for a moment as the elastic straps were worked free of them, and then there was an odd tickling feeling of something sliding away beneath her shirt, leaving her breasts free. Content, she murmured wordlessly and snuggled down in the warm pocket surrounding her, barely aware of something hard and warm at her side. The dream faded away.

The delicious scent of coffee woke her, and Tyler stretched luxuriously before opening her eyes. The rough ceiling of a cave met her startled gaze, and it was several confused moments before she remembered where she was. And whom she was with. Sitting up abruptly, she remembered her dream. But it hadn't entirely been a dream, she realized, because she was definitely—

"Where the hell's my bra?" she demanded, glaring across a cheerful fire at a man with quizzically raised brows.

Kane gestured toward a small mound of folded material lying near the sleeping bag. "There. I took it off," he explained casually. "You weren't comfortable, and you wanted it off."

"How do you know?"

"You told me in your sleep."

She stared at him, trying to remember. No, she didn't think he'd removed her khaki shirt to get the bra off. Had he? She was wearing it now, buttoned correctly. Granted, it was short-sleeved. And it was entirely possible to remove a bra without first taking off a shirt, as long as the straps were elastic; she had done it often when she'd wanted the thing off but hadn't been ready to change her outer clothing. But she certainly didn't remember asking him for help. Had he—?

"I didn't see anything, if that's what's worrying you," he murmured.

Glaring at him, Tyler reached out and snagged her bra, then slid down a bit so that the material of the sleeping bag hid her chest from his steady, faintly amused gaze. Given a choice—and another companion—she would have gone braless, but she was full-busted and preferred to wear support when she was active. The trick, however, was getting her bra back on without removing her shirt or otherwise giving Kane an eyeful.

Putting a bra *on* under a shirt was a bit more difficult than taking one off.

She wasn't overly modest, and her own behavior in Kane's company bothered her; why didn't she just turn her back to the man and wrestle the bra into place? Somehow she couldn't respond to the awkward situation with simple directness.

She had to remain sitting in order to get her bra back on, but the flap of the sleeping bag kept dropping to her waist. Finally, annoyed by the ridiculous picture she knew she was presenting, she gripped the material in her teeth and glared at Kane, daring him to say a word, while she managed to slip her arms from the sleeves of her shirt and get the bra on beneath it.

He watched her quite steadily, but in silence, and if he was amused he hid it well.

Decently attired at last, she scrambled from the bag and got to her feet, tucking her shirttail into the snug waistband of her jeans. Her long hair, having come free of its braid during the night—it always did—swung about her shoulders and persisted in falling forward over her face. Muttering, she pushed it back, only then noticing the comb Kane held out to her.

For only an instant Tyler hovered between stubbornness and need, then sighed and accepted the offering, sinking back down onto the sleeping bag to begin the task of restoring some order to her unruly hair.

Kane set the ceramic mug filled with coffee near her, then sipped coffee from his own tin cup while he watched her. Silence never bothered him, not even the prickly silence generally to be found in her company, and he enjoyed watching her tame her long, thick mass of red-gold hair. She was concentrating entirely on what she was doing, and Kane found his gaze dropping to her full breasts when her lifted arms drew the khaki material taut across them.

He should have tossed the bra into the fire.

chapter two

THE SHOOTER WAS nowhere in sight, and no gunfire greeted their cautious exit from the cave. Kane suggested that they climb rather than descend just to be on the safe side, and much as she wanted to, Tyler couldn't really disagree. The ravine below was narrow and appeared miles long, meaning that it was a dandy place from which to be ambushed, should their friend with the gun have that in mind. The cliff face above them, Kane pointed out, was climbable.

Tyler stood outside the cave on the narrow ledge and gazed upward, controlling a shiver. Tearing her eyes from the fifty-foot expanse of jagged rock rising above her head, she watched Kane crouch on the ledge and dig a long nylon rope from his backpack. He had, as she'd expected, abandoned most of his equipment, settling on the backpack and sleeping bag, two canteens, and his rifle. Tyler carried one of the canteens, the strap slung bandolier-fashion across her chest; Kane had arranged the rest for himself to carry, but now he piled the gear on the narrow ledge.

Kane slung the rope over one shoulder and across his chest, then stood gazing upward with narrowed, measuring eyes. Then he sat down on the ledge and, unperturbed by the sheer drop below him, began unlacing his boots. "I'll go up first," he told her, "and drop a line for you and the backpack. Tie the pack securely. Keep the rifle with you, and when you're ready to come up, *don't use the rope to climb*. Just hold on and I'll pull you up slowly. All right?"

"I— Yes." Tyler watched him stow his boots in the backpack, and felt her throat tighten when he rose to his feet. "I know you've done this before. You *have* done this before?"

"Sure."

"So you're just going to climb using nothing but your fingers and toes. Right?"

"That's the plan."

"I thought this was a democratic partnership."

Kane looked at her, half guarded and half amused. "It is—as much as possible."

She ignored the qualification. "Then I vote we go down into the ravine. The shooter's gone."

"And maybe waiting up ahead for us. It's an easy climb, Ty, and we need to move to higher ground anyway. We should climb toward the coast and then head south."

Tyler didn't have to ask if Kane knew what he was talking about; he did. He probably had a map of Colombia imprinted on his brain, and she knew he spoke Spanish like a native. But Tyler wasn't exactly ignorant of the geography herself, never mind that she knew little Spanish. "Why the coast? It'll be murder traveling through those swamps and forests. Why not stick to the mountains and just head south?"

He studied her for a moment. "I get the feeling you're arguing the way a kid whistles in a graveyard—just to hear yourself."

His perception annoyed her. It also disturbed her in a way she didn't want to think about. She fought a brief silent battle with her pride and lost. "I'm not very good with sheer drops, that's all." She looked at him defiantly, daring him to make some smart crack about her phobias.

Kane glanced down at the drop below them, then back at her. "You hide it well, I must say."

In a put-upon tone, she said reasonably, "I'm standing on a ledge of rock; it may not be much, but it's solid. You expect me to dangle at the end of a rope. I don't like ropes. I don't trust them."

Matching her tone, he said, "Look, Ty, if we go down, we'll have to either take our chances there isn't an ambush ahead, or else follow the ravine about eight miles north before we can get to higher ground the easy way. In this terrain, that'll cost us a day at least. You really want that?"

After a moment Tyler sighed, picked up the rifle and

held it ready for anything, and then leaned back against the rock. "All right, damn it. Climb."

He winked at her, solemn, then began climbing.

The morning air was chilly; Tyler told herself that was why she shivered as she watched him scale the cliff with the ease of a mountain goat. He never seemed to put a foot wrong, testing the placement of each finger and toehold with exquisite care before allowing his weight—and his life—to depend on it. He obviously knew what he was doing. And Tyler watched, her head tilted back against rock, her eyes fixed on him always.

Her mouth was dry and her heart seemed to have lodged in her throat, choking her with its pounding. She wasn't worried about him, she assured herself fiercely. After all, he thought too much of his own hide to risk it unnecessarily; he wouldn't have begun climbing if there had been any great danger. No, it was just that it was getting lighter, and they didn't know where their friendly gunman was.

It was eerily quiet, as it always was in the dawn hours, and Tyler's anxious sense of urgency grew as the light strengthened. Even in his khaki shirt and jeans Kane was obvious against the cliff, she thought, his thick black hair shining in alien darkness against the light-colored rock. If the shooter was still around, and chanced to look up . . .

She jerked her gaze from Kane and began searching the ravine, eyeing each jumble of rock suspiciously. Nothing moved, and there was no sign of anyone save themselves. It didn't reassure her particularly. The ravine was deep and wide. Rocks, brush. There were so many places someone could hide—

A rock nearly as big as her head bounded downward suddenly, striking the ledge not a foot from where she stood. Forgetting the gunman, she looked swiftly up to find that Kane had nearly reached the top; he seemed to be having no difficulty at all, but the khaki shirt showed damp patches indicating his task wasn't nearly as easy as it appeared.

Tyler felt dizzy as she watched him pull himself up over the top, realizing only then that she had held her breath, and her lungs were aching. She allowed herself to breathe normally now, faintly irritated by her reaction to his danger. She certainly wasn't worried about the man, it was just that this was a lonely area and it was nice to have someone to talk to, even if the someone was Kane. If he hadn't made it, she would have been forced to talk to herself.

But once she got up there . . . It occurred to her only then that she herself would be a dandy target while he pulled her up—and that neither of them would be able to hold the rifle ready to return any gunfire.

The nylon line snaked downward, and she knelt to tie the backpack securely, her mouth twisting ruefully as she remembered who had taught her to tie a decent knot. Kane. In North Africa during their first meeting— and first clash.

She watched the backpack ascend, then slung the rifle across her back as the line dropped down again. She tied the end around her waist loosely, making certain not to use a slipknot, then waved to Kane to signal she was ready. The line tightened immediately, and she kept her feet braced against the cliff, "walking" upward as he pulled the rope. She didn't look down. She didn't look at anything at all, in fact, and realized that only when Kane hauled her over the top and spoke.

"You can open your eyes now."

He was laughing, and all Tyler's misgivings about the situation suddenly exploded within her. Her reaction, she knew, was excessive, but knowing that did nothing to lessen it. She dropped the rope and swung at him furiously and accurately, missing his jaw only because he ducked with a fighter's lightning reflex.

"Damn it, woman—"

Tyler lunged at him, both fists doubled and her legs tangling with the rope trailing from her waist. She told herself that rope gave him the advantage, told herself it was because of that Kane was able to wrestle her to the ground. Her pride wouldn't admit how pathetically easy it seemed to him.

He didn't make the mistake of allowing her to get a knee anywhere near him; she had used that trick before. Roughly pinning her hands to the ground above her head, he threw a leg across her and sat astride her hips, his two hundred pounds easily holding her still despite her best efforts to throw him off.

And she tried, bucking beneath him furiously, her impotent rage and sudden panic growing because he was holding her down and she felt smothered, helpless.

She never wanted to feel like that again. Never. "Damn you, you son of a—"

"Tyler!" He glared down at her, his handsome face less humorous than she'd ever seen it, his mouth hard. "Just what the hell is wrong with you?"

"You laughed at me!" she practically screamed, panic clawing at her mind. "I hate that, I hate being laughed at!"

His flying brows drew together. "And that's why you attacked me like a wildcat? For God's sake, Ty, I wasn't laughing *at* you. You might have been scared to death, but you climbed the damned cliff. I happen to think that took a hell of a lot of courage."

"You laughed," she insisted between gritted teeth, fighting to hold the anxiety at bay.

He was still frowning. "Honey, I was laughing because I admired your guts."

She didn't want to believe that, but his steady green eyes were honest. And she believed him. Her rage drained away, leaving her shaking and oddly bereft.

With anger gone, there was nothing left to insulate her from those other disturbing feelings. He was sitting on her and she was more helpless than she could bear, but the clawing panic was fading with astonishing speed. The rifle beneath her jabbed into her back, but she hardly felt it. Instead she felt the warmth of him, the heavy weight of him, and he was leaning down so close she could see his oddly expanding pupils blocking out the green, and smell the musky male scent of his big body. Her wrists were held together by one of his hands, while the other lay on her shoulder just inches from her breast, warm and heavy.

The abrupt urge to feel that big hand close over her breast washed over her in a dizzying wave, and she could feel the tight prickling of her nipples in response to the astonishing burst of desire. Her belly knotted, and beneath his heavy weight something flamed inside her, heating her loins.

Her own response shocked her, not the least because helplessness had always been a fear and she knew only too well that sexual helplessness was the greatest fear of all. How could he make her feel this way? *How?*

She almost moaned aloud, and her teeth gritted while she tried frantically to control the insane impulse of her body. Dangerous. Dear God, it was dangerous!

"All right," she said in a small, husky voice. "I believe you. Now let me up."

"I'm not sure if that's a good idea," he said whimsically, his eyes darkening even more. "You're an unpredictable lady, Tyler St. James. And I've had cause to be sure of that. I remember it well. After North Africa— and Budapest—I ached for days."

Tyler could feel heat sweep up her throat, and with an effort she kept her gaze on his face. "That was your fault. You tricked me. You made me furious; I struck out without thinking. And I could have done worse."

"I suppose you could have used that knife you carried. Instead of being bruised and sick, I would have been a total eunuch. I've heard about places in the world where a woman does that to her man in revenge for betrayal."

"You're not my man. Get off me!"

"I'm comfortable," he murmured wickedly. "I may make a day of it. D'you still carry that knife, by the way? You didn't have it on you last night when I took your bra off."

Tyler gritted her teeth in helpless rage, welcoming the return of anger because it overwhelmed those other feelings. "Maybe I'm just hiding it more carefully these days!" she snapped.

"Shall I search you and find out?" he asked softly.

She watched his gaze move considerably over her chest, where khaki material was pulled taut by her position and the rifle and canteen straps cut diagonally between her breasts. The khaki was thin, like the silk of her bra, and neither hid the jutting response of her nipples.

A different kind of panic swept over her. In a desperate, mindless need to stop this before something irrevocable happened, she fed her anger wildly, and a snarl tangled in the back of her throat. In such a situation as this, unable to match his strength, she knew that only words could serve as her weapons. And Tyler had learned in a number of very hard and dangerous situations to use every weapon available to her.

Keeping her voice low and even, she said, "Is this the way you get your kicks, Kane? The old macho domination routine? Well, you weigh nearly twice what I do and you're strong even for your size, so I'm defeated from the start. I can't possibly win. Satisfied? Or d'you want me to cry and beg? I'm not very good at begging, Kane, but if that's your game, I'll play. Because I'm *very* good at surviving." And the flat, fierce truth of that was in her voice like a knife pulled from its sheath to gleam starkly in the sunlight.

Curiously blank green eyes met her wild amber gaze, and Kane was still and silent for a long moment. His mouth was hard again, his face expressionless. Without a word, he freed her wrists and lifted his weight off her, leaving himself vulnerable to an avenging knee for just an instant.

Tyler didn't take advantage of that. She sat up and untied the rope at her waist with shaking fingers, then got to her feet as he coiled the line and returned it to the backpack. He didn't look at her as he sat down on a boulder to put his socks and boots back on. Then he shrugged into the pack, his face stony, and started moving east into the forest.

Tyler followed. Her breasts felt heavy and achy, and she could still feel the imprint of him against her lower stomach and hips. She could feel his hand on her wrists, and looked at them vaguely, wondering why there were no marks. There should have been marks. Absently she adjusted the rifle so that she carried the strap on one shoulder. She had the feeling that Kane had deliberately allowed her to keep the gun. To make a point? She didn't know.

Her legs felt shaky and she had the curious urge to cry. Her eyes were hot, and she thought something had torn loose inside her. She didn't know what it was. Gazing steadfastly at the middle of Kane's broad back, she trudged along behind him.

HIS MOOD DIDN'T bother her at first, but Tyler soon discovered that Kane's silence was inexorably stretching all her nerves as taut as bowstrings, and she wasn't a nervous person. It would take days for them to find the cache even if there was no trouble; the thought of days filled with his brand of silence was enough to make her forget the childish determination not to be the first to break the deadlock.

"How far to the coast?" She addressed his back, since he was still leading the way.

Kane said nothing.

"He's obviously mad at me," Tyler told the surrounding forest, keeping her voice light. "I must have bruised his pride." No reaction from Kane. She gripped the rifle's carrying strap more tightly. "So now I'm getting the silent treatment." Nothing. Tyler began to feel seriously alarmed. She hadn't realized it until then, but in the days it had taken her to get this far, she had missed the sounds of human companionship.

Even the voice of an enemy was welcome, she told herself miserably.

Falling silent, she stared at his back and thought about their confrontation. So he resented what she'd said? Because she'd hit too close to home, or because what she'd said had been an insult to him? Curiously enough, she thought it was the latter. Kane wasn't the type to sulk because his ego was bruised.

No, his reaction was something else. Did he believe she had meant what she'd said? Had his perception failed him this once so that he hadn't realized she had said the most hurtful thing she could think of—

She felt an odd jolt. The most hurtful thing? Had she been that certain of him? Some men would have taken her own words and used them to taunt her, proving their truth. But not Kane. *And she had known that.*

She wondered then, uneasily, if that was why her usual panic at being helpless had been brief. Had she known instinctively that her fears would always be groundless where Kane was concerned? Was she sure of him in a way she had never been sure of any man for ten years? She didn't want to think about that, didn't want to consider what it might mean.

Swallowing hard, she said, "I'm sorry, Kane. I didn't mean— I knew you weren't trying to dominate me."

Kane paused for a moment, consulting the compass that was a part of his multifunction watch. Then he continued. Silently.

Tyler bit her lip and followed.

By midday they were descending, leaving the mountains behind as they moved toward the coast. The forest grew more dense, slowing them; at times they had to force their way through underbrush. Kane halted at last near a narrow stream, and Tyler sank thankfully onto the trunk of a fallen tree. She took the rifle from her shoulder and leaned it against the tree, watching him shrug off the backpack.

"We're moving again in half an hour," he said flatly.

At least he said we. Sighing, Tyler moved to the stream and followed it a little way until she was out of sight. She knelt on the bank and pulled a big linen handkerchief from her pocket, wetting the cloth and wringing it out before washing her face and neck. It was when she was wiping her hands thoroughly that she noticed the *KP* monogram on one corner. She stared at it for a moment, shaking her head unconsciously. His. *His,* and she hadn't realized she had it?

She stood up, waving the handkerchief gently to dry it. It was hotter now; they were closer to sea level, nearer to the hot, flat land of the eastern plains. The linen dried quickly, and she watched it, bothered by the small indication of his persistent presence in her life.

But—no. That was nonsense, of course. She just happened to have his handkerchief, and she'd kept it and carried it only because it looked like one of her own large linen squares. Would he laugh, she wondered vaguely, if she were to confess that she carried large handkerchiefs always because of an old and popular movie? Would he think it amusing that a thirteen-year-old girl had gazed at a huge screen and listened to the hero tell the heroine that never in any crisis of her life had she had a handkerchief while he dried her tears with his own?

Odd the things one remembered. Tyler loved *Gone with the Wind* now, but then she had only despised

Scarlett because she hadn't had a handkerchief and hated Rhett because he'd shot the pony.

And she was determined to always dry her own tears.

Shaking her head again, Tyler folded the dried linen square neatly and returned it to her pocket. Then she headed back to Kane. Back to her silent enemy.

He was sitting cross-legged on the ground, eating from a package of trail mix. He tossed another package to Tyler, watching her with unreadable eyes. She sat on the fallen tree again and began eating, enjoying the mixture of granola, dried fruit, and nuts partly because she was hungry and partly because she liked the stuff. She returned his steady gaze as long as she could, then looked away.

"Damn it, Kane, I apologize! How much longer will I get the silent treatment?"

"Sorry." He didn't sound it.

She took a deep breath and released it slowly. Without looking at him, she said, "Doing the kind of work we do, I've run into plenty of men who used muscle as a—a sexual weapon. If you had been that kind of man, you would have loved my recognition of that. It would have been a turn-on. But you aren't that sort of man, Kane. And I knew that. So *I* used it as a weapon, because I felt helpless and vulnerable. It's—it's almost a phobia with me, feeling like that. I can't take it, and I strike out. Do you understand?"

After a moment he said, "Yes. I just hope you really believe I wouldn't do that, Ty."

She almost slumped with relief at the shortened version of her name. "I—I do." She managed a twisted smile, looking at him finally. "And I won't be able to use that as a weapon again, will I? You'll know it for what it is—a bluff."

"There's always your knee," he murmured.

Tyler matched his tentative smile, but her heart sank momentarily when his face abruptly went hard. Within a few seconds, though, she heard the faint sounds that had alerted him.

"Take the rifle," he said softly, rising. "Move about twenty yards downstream and wait for me. If that's our gun-happy friend, he's going to stop right here."

She rose, as well. "But, you'll need—"

"*Move,* Ty! Go on. I'll be fine."

There was no time to argue; the sounds were getting closer. She snatched up the rifle and moved swiftly and silently downstream, tense and worried.

Alone, Kane dropped the backpack behind the fallen tree, annoyed with himself because he hadn't thought to have Tyler take it with her. He wore a hunting knife on his hip, and loosened it in its sheath now as he moved across the tiny clearing and got behind a shielding thicket of low-growing bushes. He could just barely see the clearing, and fixed his eyes at the point where he expected to see their visitor emerge.

But what burst through the underbrush a few moments later was hardly what he expected to see. It was a woman, her long black hair flying around her face in wild tangles, her brightly colored peasant blouse torn and her jeans filthy. She looked absolutely terrified, and Kane moved almost instinctively toward her, drawn by the helpless fear in her big black eyes.

For once, all his survival instincts failed him.

She was babbling incoherently in Spanish, her eyes widening even more when she saw him, and though Kane understood the language he couldn't get a word of hers. He stepped toward her, making soothing noises, removing his hand from the haft of his knife when she backed away shakily. He wanted to reassure her that he meant her no harm. But then, in the blink of an eye, a curious transformation took place. She straightened, smiling, and the fear in her eyes became a sultry wickedness.

Bemused, Kane's instincts were just that fraction of a second slow in reacting. And that was all it took. The cold male voice came from behind him, speaking steadily in all-too-understandable English.

"No sudden moves, señor. I have a gun."

Kane turned very slowly, hoping that someone besides Tyler was well-versed in the art of bluff. The hope died a small, resigned death. It was no bluff.

TYLER WAITED FOR ten minutes, tense and uneasy. She had heard voices, at least one of them speaking Spanish—a feminine voice. It had definitely been a man shooting at them yesterday, she knew. She hesitated, worrying. Then, silently marshaling arguments in case Kane got mad, she crept back upstream until she reached the clearing. The deserted clearing. She found the back-pack, but no Kane.

She had taught herself years before never to give in to panic in a crisis. There was, after all, time for that once the crisis was past. So she didn't panic now.

Her mind went still for an instant, then began working coolly. She searched the clearing, foot by foot, her eyes trained on the ground. There was little to see, few signs available. But Tyler had learned to follow tracks as a child, and she knew what to look for. It took nearly half an hour, but she was finally able to distinguish a faint trail leading from the clearing.

North.

KANE VERY NEARLY found the situation amusing. He'd been caught off guard, pure and simple, and both the woman, Valonia, and the man, Silvio, were delighted that their trick had worked. Kane was almost amused because a pair of black eyes might well have sealed his fate.

They talked freely as Silvio's gun nudged Kane through the woods to higher ground. They were bandits, they explained, hiding in the hills after their last raid in Bogotá. And boredom had nearly driven them mad. Happily they had heard Kane passing not far from their shack and had followed him. Clearly they hadn't realized he was not alone.

This ingenuous explanation might have disarmed another man, but Kane wasn't about to let his guard down twice in one day. The gun in his back was damned real, and Silvio had the lifeless eyes of a shark. And if Kane was any judge, Valonia was a woman who would definitely castrate a man who had betrayed her. Or even one who had annoyed her.

Kane had heard of recent raids in Bogotá and other areas, and those accounts came back to him as he was herded through the forest. There was no romantic Robin Hood myth clinging to these bandits; reportedly they were educated and well-off, and simply raided because they enjoyed it. They didn't bother to spout political or social rhetoric; they merely attacked in cities, towns and remote villages, destroying property, stealing whatever they fancied and killing anyone who got in their way.

Comforting thoughts.

This wasn't the first tough situation Kane had found himself in and, as always, his mind was working, seeking a solution. He had an ace up his sleeve in the shape of Tyler; he doubted she'd abandon him to his fate. She was adept at tracking, and would likely be able to follow them. What worried him was that Tyler was apt to jump into danger with both feet and damn the consequences.

He had to get himself out of this before Tyler could act. The thought of what cruel men could—would—do to her didn't bear thinking of. But he did think of it, of course, and his guts clenched in a tight knot of fear for her. It never occurred to him to think along those same lines regarding himself, but other possibilities did present themselves.

Torture. They'd maybe torture him just for fun. Or curiosity. See how much the guy can take. What'll make him scream? How do you break a strong man?

Something like that had happened to him once before, and he still bore the scars to remind him. If he'd needed reminding. He didn't. Bile rose in his throat as he remembered. Still, he had survived. It was something to keep in mind.

When they emerged from the forest, Kane realized that these bandits had been here for a while. Three crude shacks had been thrown together and looked it. In front of one, three men were restlessly playing cards on a rickety table, and all looked up with brightening faces when Kane and his escorts approached.

Kane kept his own face immobile, his eyes roving constantly as he measured his opponents and looked for a means of escape. He barely listened as Valonia and Silvio explained how they had captured him, the laughter of the men rolling off him easily because he didn't give a sweet damn what they thought. But when they began discussing ways and means of enjoying their captive, he paid a bit more attention. An argument broke out over the subject, one man holding out for slow torture while another was determined on more exotic pursuits.

Stalling for time and only dimly hoping for success, Kane told them in fluent Spanish that he was on the trail of a vast cache of treasure, and if they'd only come with him—

It didn't work. He hadn't really expected it to. These

bandits didn't give a damn about riches even if they had believed his tale. They just wanted to have fun.

"I want him," Valonia told the men.

It seemed the lady was the leader of these bandits, for her statement instantly halted the arguments. Even Silvio, his shark eyes blank, nodded obedience.

Recklessly Kane directed a few exquisitely polite and choice obscenities toward the woman. Spanish was such a wonderfully fluid language, filled with lots of pretty flowers—and lots of sharp thorns. He was clubbed beneath an ear for his trouble, and there was red-hot pain for an instant before blessed darkness claimed him.

He woke with an aching head to find himself tied securely to a narrow cot. He was alone, and he lay there for long moments just trying to clear his sluggish mind. Once that had been accomplished, he attempted to free himself and found it impossible. He was tied with leather thongs and the cot's frame was stronger than it looked. Flat on his back, he couldn't get enough leverage to wrench himself free. He was trapped and helpless. For the first time he truly understood what Tyler had done earlier in the day, and why. It was an unnerving feeling, helplessness, and one he wasn't familiar with.

He wondered, then, if she *would* come after him. Why should she, after all? She wanted the chalice, and "losing" him would remove at least one rival for it. Certainly Tyler wasn't afraid of possible trouble; she didn't need a man for protection. The lady could take care of herself, in all honesty. And she'd survived twenty-some-odd years without his help. Of course, North Africa might well have ended her career if he hadn't been there. But if he *hadn't* been there, she never would have fallen into that pit while trying to steal the figurine back from him.

She didn't need him.

It was a curious, unwelcome shock. Not that she didn't need him, but that he minded. Kane avoided emotional baggage in his life, and his thoughts of Tyler looked suspiciously like just that. But it was absurd, of course. He was only thinking about her, regretting that he'd never see her again in all likelihood, because she had never, however briefly, belonged to him.

During the past occasions when they'd fought each other for antiquities, he had been always conscious of her as a woman. He would have had to be blind and senseless to have not been conscious of her that way. Kane was neither. And he had wanted her. In the midst of bitter arguments, he had wanted her. In the midst of trickery, he had wanted her. In triumph and defeat, he had wanted her. But Tyler was . . . Tyler. Different from any woman he had ever known. Somehow beyond his reach. And desire was all the more strong and bittersweet because of that.

Last night in the sleeping bag, he had ached with wanting her. And unfastening her bra, slipping it off beneath her shirt while she had murmured pleasurably, he had very nearly gone out of his mind.

But she was Tyler. Sometimes enemy, sometimes partner and even friend. A fiery hellion who would fight at his side or guard his back with that intriguing explosive determination of hers. A woman who *was* a woman, one hundred percent feminine; yet she had a bedrock-solid core of strength and clearly felt no need to prove herself to anyone, man or woman.

Tyler. He wanted to see her again.

It grew dark as hours passed, and Kane bore the passing time stoically. He blanked his mind and waited, knowing that they would come for him. But when a lantern was carried into the one-room shack, he saw that Valonia held it.

He had been told, by a number of ladies in various parts of the world, that he had a charming smile and charming ways. He had been told he possessed the gift of being able to persuade a woman even against her own nature. But when he looked into Valonia's black eyes, he felt a primitive shock tingle down his spine. Because there was nobody there. And on the beautiful face that housed that soullessness was a smile never meant to be worn by a woman. A smile never meant to be worn by anything human. A smile of pure evil.

"You have a name?" Her voice was soft, gentle, her Spanish investing the question with a curiously erotic sound.

"Kane." She had cleaned herself up, he saw, and was wearing only a man's shirt that reached halfway down her thighs.

She set the lamp on an upended crate that served as a table, then turned to face him with her hands on her rounded hips. "Kane. Have you ever been at the mercy of a woman, Kane?" She laughed when he was silent.

"No, I see you have not." She approached the bed and bent down, beginning to unbutton his shirt. Her own shirt gaped away from her breasts, giving him a view all the way to her navel.

He moved suddenly in resistance, realizing what she had in mind. And his mind balked violently. She was right; he'd never been at a woman's mercy before. Not like this, not physically. Not even emotionally. He didn't know if she planned to tease him sexually or simply torture him, but given her scanty outfit he thought the former was most likely. And the excitement gleaming in her eyes was purely sensual. She intended to . . . But he couldn't believe she meant to—

"A man can be raped," she purred, running a hand down his chest and curling her fingers under his belt. "But I want your full cooperation, lover." Laughing, she backed away from him and began moving slowly, sensuously, in a dance expressly designed to arouse a man. She unbuttoned the shirt, dropping it teasingly off one shoulder, then the other, her hips moving in a rhythmic gyration. Twirling on bare, light feet, she danced close to the cot and then away, her hair flying, the material of her shirt baring and then concealing golden flesh.

In all his varied adventures, Kane had never before had a woman dance to arouse him. He wondered if he could be aroused totally against his will. Somehow, he didn't think it would happen. Not this time, at least. His mind was blank, his body chilled. Valonia literally radiated sex, but it was a hungry, grasping thing. Like a black widow, she would consume her mate once his duty was done, whether or not he performed to her satisfaction. And though everything male in Kane acknowledged her beauty and sensuality, his instincts icily rejected the attraction and a hard inner core of self-preservation kept a wary guard on his senses.

Even when she danced close enough to stroke his chest and teasingly unbuckle his belt, Kane felt only a deep, cold distaste, a grinding revulsion so strong he could hardly keep it out of his expression. Her flesh was hot, burning, the red-painted nails curved like the talons of a bird of prey.

He watched her dance, his face immobile, his eyes detached and dispassionate. He wondered what kind of rage her failure would unleash.

TYLER HAD BEEN forced to bide her time after trailing Kane and his captors to their camp. Reckless in some ways she certainly was, but she wasn't fool enough to storm a camp containing four armed men and a woman who, unless Tyler didn't know her own sex at all, was more dangerous than the rest together.

It was dark when she managed to move closer to the shacks. She flitted silently from one patch of darkness to another, using cover wherever possible, careful to remain downwind. Peering cautiously between the warped boards of the shacks, she managed to place all four of the men in one; they were sitting around a fire talking, laughing. One was jabbering away in his own language and making graphically obscene gestures as he talked.

Tyler was glad her Spanish was almost nonexistent; she really didn't want to know what that one was saying.

Slipping away, she headed for the third and last shack. It stood apart from the others and seemed in better shape structurally. It was lighted from inside, and Tyler was cautious as she circled it far enough to find a few warped boards. She looked inside. For a long moment she remained frozen. Then, moving silently back, she searched until she found a piece of wood a little over a foot long and fairly heavy. Hefting it, she started around the shack toward the door.

KANE FOUND HIMSELF looking up into black eyes holding nothing but mindless, animal fury. His entire body grew taut, expecting that anger to explode into action. Deadly action. She was hissing obscenities as she whirled toward the door, groping almost blindly for his hunting knife where she'd left it on the upended crate.

As she turned back toward him, jerking the knife from its sheath, the door opened silently behind her. She barely had time to step toward him, arm raised to begin the vicious downward plunge, when a thick board cracked across the back of her head. She went down instantly.

Tyler eyed her for a wary moment, then knelt to check her pulse. Muttering to herself and completely ignoring Kane, she methodically shredded Valonia's abandoned shirt, bound the naked woman and gagged her. She picked up his knife, then rose to her feet and looked at him expressionlessly.

"I thought you were probably having fun, but the lady seemed a mite upset. If you'd rather, though, I can untie her and come back later—"

"Just untie me, if you don't mind," Kane managed. "I got tired of the party a long time ago." Like Tyler, he kept his voice soft.

She used his knife to cut the thongs binding his hands, then sliced the ones at his ankles while he sat up and buttoned his shirt. Still expressionless, she said, "Well, I owed you one. You saved my skin last time in Hong Kong. And just like this—from a fate worse than death. *Would* it have been a fate worse than death? I'm just curious, you understand."

Kane grabbed her arm and pulled her down across his lap, holding her tightly and completely ignoring the knife she still held. He kissed her quickly, hard, and said in a rough voice, "Yes, it would have been—except that *that* lady didn't turn me on and *this* lady tracks better than Daniel Boone. Let's get the hell out of here."

"Sounds good to me," she murmured.

chapter three

THEY RETRIEVED THE backpack from where Tyler had hidden it, and within half an hour they were back at the clearing by the stream. Kane led the way from there, moving downstream swiftly to put as much distance as possible between them and the bandits. Around 2:00 A.M. they left the stream, heading due west. The night air was warm and sticky, and the forest grew even more dense.

By 4:00 A.M. Tyler decided that enough was enough. "Hey, let's stop, okay? I knocked that she wolf silly, and from the look of them, the men weren't about to interrupt her little games. We've got hours before they even know you're gone."

There was no moon visible, and it was almost pitch black in the forest. Tyler had been walking directly behind Kane, at his very heels, in fact, and when he stopped she banged into him. She grabbed at his shoulders to keep her balance, but almost instantly rebounded away from him nervously. Damn it, *why* did she react to just *touching* the man? She hadn't been aware of it before this encounter.

Kane spoke calmly, apparently not noticing her reaction. "If I know where we are, there's another stream about twenty minutes' walk from here. You game?"

"You've been here before?"

"No. I once met a man who'd traveled all through this part of the country."

It figured; Kane had a phenomenal memory. She sighed. "All right, but walk a little more slowly, will you? My night vision is practically nil."

Kane took her hand in a firm grasp and began walking again. She was beside him, a little behind, and didn't want to admit to herself that she felt more secure with her hand lost in his. Nor did she admit to the tingling warmth of his touch; what lay behind that was too frightening and dangerous to think about.

But she found herself comparing this adventure to the ones that preceded it. This was different not only because they were wary partners almost from the moment of encountering each other, but also because their surroundings were completely unlike the others. In North Africa they had maneuvered in baking cities and tumbled ruins, outguessing and outfoxing each other half a dozen times before temporarily joining forces to outwit a sophisticated gang of art thieves. Most of their other clashes had been equally harried and brief, with little time available to dwell on anything other than the goals they had shared, and they had rarely been alone together.

In Hong Kong, their most recent adventure several months before, it had been an all-out race for an elusive necklace. In that extremely crowded, overpopulated city, they had each won and lost the necklace, tricking each other a number of times before teaming up to smoothly con an expatriate American of Chinese descent who had a nifty racket going in stolen antiquities.

Kane *had* saved her from a fate worse than death on that occasion. He'd had the necklace and could have just left her to the tender mercies of the Tong leader. But he had come back for her, bursting in mere hours before she would have been shipped to parts unknown where her new life promised to take place inside a house with a red light at the door.

Dangerous circumstances, those. And even Tyler's innate craving for adventure had wavered from time to time. Still, she had found a fierce enjoyment in sparring with Kane, and her anger at his various tricks and betrayals had contained more than a nugget of reluctant and somewhat rueful admiration for his cunning. She had missed his presence on the few occasions that one or the other of them had located what they sought first and departed; as galling as it had been for her to admit he had beaten her to something, she'd found little pleasure in winning herself—unless it had been a face-to-face contest with both of them on the scene.

And their sparring in the past had been just that: a

contest, a game with both working to win. Always on the move and generally surrounded by other people, with foes to outwit alone or together, foes they both recognized.

Now, this. The surroundings were curiously elemental, the circumstances new ones. They had teamed up for the duration. And there was a mutual enemy or two—they thought. The bandits had been unexpected, but fought successfully. The gunman lay behind them or before them, and they didn't know his face or his reasons for being involved in this.

They were virtually alone, moving cautiously through a lonely wilderness that was ever changing. First the cool grandeur of the mountains, and now the sticky, cloying heat of the approaching lowlands. The dense forest was gradually becoming marshy, the ground giving spongily beneath their feet.

"Wait here." He released her hand.

"Kane?" The question was instinctively uttered before she could get her bearings. She saw they had reached the stream; it was little more than a glittering ribbon of darkness whispering softly.

He touched her shoulder lightly. "I'm just going to check out the area. Stay put."

Tyler remained there, absently pulling the material of her shirt away from her skin. She was uncomfortable. It was hot and misty, and she felt dirty. She could tolerate any amount of dust, but the sticky dampness of heat and high humidity combined was something she hated. But not even that distraction could pull her mind from thoughts of this strange new relationship with Kane.

They could sharpen their wits on each other, face-to-face, both wary and a bit uncomfortable with this new arrangement. Like stray dogs they circled each other uneasily, both just on the point of lunging but holding back because territorial rights were maddeningly undefined. They had declared themselves partners, but their background was not such as to lend certainty or trust to the partnership.

And there was that other thing, that sexual awareness between them. It hovered just beneath the surface of words and looks and touches, as much mistrusted as their ability to depend on each other. And as likely to explode in some confrontation neither was ready for.

Tyler realized then that her misgivings about the situation had little to do with her ability to trust Kane; she hadn't trusted him before, yet they had been able to work together at the need. What had disturbed her instinctively was the intimacy inherent in a partnership in this place and time. They were too alone, too much together in surroundings that would spark primitive emotions between a man and woman.

Even if the seeds of those emotions had not been sown thousands of miles away and many months in the past.

She started when she felt him beside her again; she'd expected him to move silently, but was nonetheless unprepared for his lithe soundlessness. In a city he could move like a shadow; here in the forest, he moved like a jungle cat.

"We'll stay here," he told her. "I'll start a fire." He faded away again, and very faint noises indicated he was gathering wood nearby.

Tyler stood still until she saw the flickering of his lighter, then stepped toward him. The firelight shadowed and highlighted his lean face, and with his head bent as it was he looked curiously savage. His flying brows and hooded eyes gave him a devilish appearance, and the broad shoulders looked even more massive than they actually were. Tyler thought then that it would be easy to be afraid of him, and wondered why she wasn't.

He glanced up at her as she approached the fire, then reached to dig into the backpack he had laid aside. "How d'you feel about creepy-crawlies?"

Tyler shrugged a little. "Well, I don't like them. But I'm not deathly afraid of them, either."

"How about snakes?"

"The same."

Kane pulled a bundle of material from the backpack; it appeared to be a woolen blanket. "This is a ruana," he told her, indicating the slit in the middle of the blanket. "Put your head through here, and then you can belt it around your waist."

She glanced toward the stream, realizing what he had in mind.

"I'm going to build a lean-to," he continued, producing a plastic-wrapped bar of soap from the pack, "because it'll likely rain by dawn. If you want to rinse out your things, they'll probably be dry by then."

Tyler accepted the ruana and the soap, but stood

her ground. "Why'd you ask about snakes and creepy-crawlies?"

"We're on the edge of the swamp, can't you smell it? Fair warning, Ty; you may share your bath with a snake. But this is a mountain stream, so maybe not. There's a deeper pool just around that bend; it looks pretty good. It's up to you."

She hesitated, then said, "We'll turn south when we head out again, won't we? Through the swamp?"

"Around it, if possible. But this may be your last chance for a decent bath for a couple of days. Is that what you wanted to know?"

"That's what I wanted to know." She turned away, then glanced at him over her shoulder. "If I yell, it *won't* be because the water's cold!"

"Gotcha," he murmured, smiling a little.

Tyler found the pool, discovering that the forest thinned out here and that dim light was able to show her the way. She eyed the peaceful water suspiciously, but laid the ruana on a rock and sat down to pull off her boots and socks. Her jeans felt stiff and damp, and she had to roll them over her hips and down her legs. The shirt, too, was damp, and her bra and panties had to almost be peeled away from her flesh.

She hesitated for a moment, feeling ridiculously like a wood nymph standing there naked. A glance over her shoulder showed her that she could barely see the camp-fire, and she could faintly hear Kane at work building the lean-to. She freed her hair from the braid, slipping the rubber band around her wrist since it was her last

one, then unwrapped the soap and fished the handkerchief from the pocket of her jeans.

Stepping cautiously into the water, she shivered at
the delicious coolness. The pool was waist-deep in the
middle, the water moving sluggishly, and the bottom
was sandy and fairly firm. Tyler ducked completely under the surface, straightening with a gasp and blinking
away water. It seemed lighter suddenly, and she looked
up to find that the moon had peered through a break in
the clouds.

She held the handkerchief in her teeth and worked
up a lather with the soap, washing her hair quickly but
as thoroughly as possible. When it was clean and rinsed,
she moved toward the bank until the water reached her
knees, then soaped the handkerchief and left the bar on
a rock while she washed every inch of her skin.

There was still no sign of a snake, but Tyler wasn't
anxious to push her luck. After a brief debate, she
washed out her shirt, socks and underthings, reasoning
that they would be the most likely to dry before she
needed them again. The jeans were damp, but fairly
clean, and too heavy to dry quickly if she attempted to
wash them.

She returned the soap to its plastic and pulled the ruana over her head, realizing only then that she had nothing to belt it with; she never wore a belt with jeans. The
light woolen material hung in folds to the middle of her
thighs, and felt faintly scratchy against her flesh; it
wasn't an uncomfortable sensation.

Shrugging, Tyler gathered her jeans and wet clothing

together, picked up the soap and her boots and headed back for the campfire. The small clearing was deserted, but the lean-to had been completed and a small tin pot filled with some kind of stew simmered over the fire beside another pot of coffee. The lean-to was built near the fire, and she hung her wet things and the jeans over the line Kane had strung with his rope just beneath it.

Where was he? Bathing himself downstream? She looked at the soap she still held, then went to the stream's bank and called softly, "Kane? If you need the soap—"

"Downstream," he called back immediately.

Tyler followed the stream, seeing him just a couple of minutes later. He was submerged to his waist, and his chest and shoulders gleamed in the faint moonlight. He looked like something pagan, a part of the forest. A part of the wilderness. She glanced down at the pile of his clothing at her feet and swallowed hard.

"If this is our only bar of soap, do I dare throw it to you?" she asked him, striving for lightness.

Unlike Tyler's, Kane's night vision was excellent; in fact, it was too good at the moment. He could see her all too clearly, especially since the ruana she wore wasn't belted and tended to gape open at the sides. The darkness had stolen the fiery color from her hair, and it hung about her shoulders gleaming wetly and curling as though it were living. And despite her shapeless garment, the thrusting mounds of her firm breasts were as obvious to him as though she were naked.

He cleared his throat softly and tried not to think

about her naked. "I don't think I should come out and get it," he returned, managing to keep his voice equally light.

After a moment Tyler stepped into the water and waded out until she was knee-deep. "Catch." She tossed the bar carefully, relieved when he caught it.

"Thanks, Ty."

"Sure." She retreated to the bank. "Oh, d'you mind if I use a piece of that rope? I don't have a belt for this thing."

"I noticed," he murmured. "Help yourself."

Tyler realized then that she hadn't exactly been holding the poncho securely; it covered front and back completely, but the sides were open. She wrapped it about her and headed hastily for the camp, further unsettled. Once there, it took several minutes' work with the rope to get herself decently covered, and even then she reminded herself not to bend over or move suddenly. She found his comb and used it to untangle her wet hair, then returned it to the backpack.

She unrolled the sleeping bag and used it as a cushion to sit on, then scrabbled in the backpack until she found the mug. She poured some coffee, wrinkling her nose at the first hot, strong sip. Black, and strong enough to raise the dead—she hated it that way. But she'd learned to drink it in the past, and since Kane always drank it like that, he wouldn't bring sugar or milk along as one of his little luxuries.

Kane returned to the camp a few minutes later, wearing only his jeans and carrying his wet shirt. His hair was wet, gleaming, and the thick mat of hair on his chest drew her eyes like a magnet. She looked away, angry with herself. What was *wrong* with her? She was too aware of him, too conscious of his every movement, and too apt to watch.

He hung the shirt on the line beside her things, and she glanced at him again without being able to stop herself, her gaze fastening on to the faint scars on his back. How had he got those? She'd seen them before but had never asked him about them. She wondered if he'd tell her if she did ask. Then she saw him finger the handkerchief with his monogram.

"I didn't know you still had this," he murmured.

Tyler could feel herself flushing, and looked hastily back to her coffee. "I don't remember how I came to have it," she said casually.

"Don't you?" He sank down beside her, cross-legged, reaching to dig into the pack for another cup and to return the bar of soap. "North Africa. The figurine was wrapped in it the first time you stole it from me."

Tyler could feel her hackles rising. It took a supreme effort of will to keep her eyes off him, and she was deeply disturbed by that. Anger was safe, and she allowed it to build. "You mean when I *rightfully* took it back after you tricked me to get it in the first place?"

"I suppose that's one way of looking at it." He sipped his coffee meditatively. "And it doesn't matter now, does it?" He was all too aware of her warmth beside him, and his eyes were drawn again and again to the bare length of her golden legs. Hard to think of the past—hard to think of anything at all when he looked at her.

"Maybe it doesn't matter," she was saying tightly. "Maybe I should keep it in mind. You've tricked me before; you'll trick me again. I can't trust you out of my sight, can I, Kane?"

He frowned a little, staring into the fire. "You'll have to make up your mind about that. There's nothing I could say to convince you."

"Is your word any good?" she asked bitterly.

Kane had the certain feeling that she was whistling in a graveyard again, deliberately starting an argument to divert herself—or him—from something else. But even with that feeling, he was aware of a slow, curiously bitter anger coiling inside him, tangling with the hot, building desire he felt for her. She always got under his skin. Somehow, she always got under his skin.

"Is yours?" he snapped back. He could feel her stiffen, feel the tentatively open doors between them slamming shut.

"I don't lie," she said shakily. "*You* made up the rules in this little game of ours—anything goes. I should have left you to the mercies of the she wolf and gone after the damned chalice alone!"

"Then why'd you come after me?" He gave a small, hard laugh. "The she wolf, as you call her, would have cut my throat in another few seconds. You would have been rid of me for good. So why'd you come after me, Ty?"

She swung around on the sleeping bag, her eyes glittering at him. "Beats the hell out of me!"

Kane didn't know whether to laugh or goad her until they both found out just why she'd gone after him. He wasn't given the chance to decide, however, because her fierce scowl faded abruptly and quick concern darkened her amber eyes.

"What happened?" She reached out, her fingers brushing aside his hair and lightly touching the bruised swelling just behind and below his left ear.

Bemused, Kane stared at her, highly conscious of her cool, gentle touch on his aching flesh. "One of the bandits." He cleared his throat. "I said something nasty to her majesty and one of her boys conked me."

Tyler set her mug aside and scrambled up in a flash of golden legs; she snagged the handkerchief from the line, going over to the stream and wetting it in the cool water. Returning, she knelt beside him and applied the folded pad to his head. "You should have said something," she told him irritably. "You must have a horrible headache."

Kane was gazing down at her upper thighs where the ruana had ridden up, and he barely felt the tin cup give a little under his tightening grasp. He closed his eyes briefly, then yanked his gaze upward. And that was a mistake, because the woolen material of the ruana had molded itself lovingly to her full breasts. Her nipples showed plainly, either because of the cold mountain stream or the friction of woolen cloth, and Kane couldn't take his eyes away. God, she was beautiful. . . . He could almost feel her against his fingers, his palms, feel her satiny flesh swell and harden to his touch.

The throbbing in his head spread slowly throughout his body and his loins ached with the hot surge of desire for her. It was a fire inside him, blazing rapidly out of control. He wanted to push her back on the sleeping bag and rip away the woolen material hiding her body from his. He wanted to look at her, touch her and taste her until she held no secrets, until he knew her body as well as he knew his own. He wanted to settle himself between her long, beautiful golden legs and fuse his body with hers, lose himself in her until he shattered with the pleasure of it.

He could feel her hand on his shoulder as she steadied herself, and was only dimly aware of the cool cloth pressed to his head. His gaze skimmed upward slowly, pausing to watch the pulse beating in her throat then lifting to examine the flawless pale golden flesh, the delicate features of her face. Her amber eyes were intent on her task, frowning slightly, and she was biting her lower lip with small white teeth.

God, that really got to him. It always had. It was a habit of hers whenever she was concentrating, and he thought it was the most provocative gesture he'd ever seen. He'd never noticed another woman doing it, just Ty. And it never failed to send a sharp jolt of desire through him.

Under his skin. Damn her, she was under his skin, like a thorn buried too deeply to get at. What would it take to get at that maddening thorn, to get her out of his mind, what would exorcise memories of her that had haunted him since the first time her amber eyes had blazed at him in a wild temper?

Always before, physical possession of a woman who attracted him had been enough. The first sexual excitement satisfied, boredom or restlessness had crept in. And it would again, he decided. If he took Tyler, she would no longer have the power to haunt his dreams. It was just desire, and the unusual circumstances of their past meetings had kept that desire simmering.

Unfortunately he couldn't believe that Tyler would make it easy for him. He was reasonably sure she felt an attraction to him, but there was something . . . stubborn in Tyler, something guarded and aloof.

And she wouldn't lie down with an enemy, except to reluctantly and warily sleep.

Tyler became conscious of the silence then, and when her eyes met the heat of his something turned over inside her. The skin of his shoulder burned her hand suddenly, and she drew away, almost dropping the folded linen of his handkerchief. "If—if we had some ice or something . . ."

"I'm fine," he said in an oddly still voice. "Thank you for saving my life, Ty."

It seemed a strange thing for him to say, not because he didn't owe her gratitude, but because there was little of that between them. Just acceptance or rejection, with few words about the matter. And his thanks bothered her, because his eyes were still hot.

She cleared her throat. "Don't mention it." She looked

away from him, and when her eyes fell on the pot of stew her stomach growled audibly. She laughed unsteadily. "Somebody just rang the dinner bell. Is that stuff ready?"

"It's ready." He was casual again, digging into the backpack for tin plates and forks. He dished out the stew and handed her a plate, then began eating himself.

They had avoided it. Tyler was dismayed and unsettled when that thought occurred to her, because she couldn't avoid the realization that both of them were all too aware of the fact that there was a point of danger, a point of no return, and that they had retreated from it again with wary care. But what disturbed her more than anything else was that it was happening more often, this electric sensual awareness.

Enemy, she reminded herself with a surge of bitterness she was hardly conscious of. *He'll trick me if he can. When this partnership no longer suits him. He'll trick me again. Maybe he's tricking me now.*

And she had to be on guard against that.

Halfway through the meal, Tyler realized that she was exhausted. It came over her suddenly, in a wave, leaving her feeling decidedly shaky. Trailing Kane and his captors, and then waiting tensely for an opportunity to get him out of there, she'd felt no tiredness even though they had been on the move since dawn. And while they were putting distance between themselves and the bandits she'd been conscious of nothing but relief that the episode had ended in their triumph.

But now she was utterly tired, her eyes heavy. Dawn had lightened the sky and a few birds greeted the day merrily, but thunder rumbled a soft warning in the distance. She thought about that muzzily, remembering how much she liked to sleep when it was raining. And she started when Kane reached to take her empty plate away from her.

"Time for bed," he told her, unusually gentle. "Let's get the sleeping bag back under the lean-to."

Tyler moved off the cushioning softness, yawning uncontrollably, and the moment Kane had the bag positioned she was crawling into it. The lean-to provided a canopy of branches and leaves above her head, and she gazed upward sleepily while she listened to Kane moving about the camp. He was cleaning up, she realized, washing the pots and things, packing them away again.

Ready to be on the move again, instantly, at the need.

Tired as she was, she couldn't fall asleep until he joined her, and she was too sleepy to think about that. She waited, yawning, listening to him. The first patter of raindrops came before he did, but then he was sliding into the bag beside her. Tyler felt the rough material of his jeans brushing against her bare legs, pleasurably scratchy, and wondered vaguely if the ruana had ridden up to her waist the way it felt as if it had. Probably. Not that she cared.

"Will this thing leak?" she asked drowsily.

"Let's hope not. Get some sleep, Ty."

She fell asleep with the suddenness of a child, while Kane lay awake and stared at the branches overhead and listened to the rain. She had left her hair unbraided; he could feel strands of the silky stuff beneath his shoulder.

And his mind taunted him with visions of what he would see if he were to throw back the top layer of the sleeping bag; he knew damned well her woolen garment had been pushed up to her waist when she'd slid into the bag.

She hadn't turned her back to him this time, and he could feel her warm curves pressed against his side. He wondered what she'd do if he began kissing her, touching her. Respond, probably, and there was no vanity in that thought. Tyler sleepy and tired was sweet and vague and vulnerable; he'd noticed that about her before. She never got cranky because of weariness, and all her prickly barriers came crashing down.

He was tired himself, and inclined to be reckless with the throbbing need of his body to taunt him, but he couldn't take advantage of her vulnerability.

He'd be just what she thought he was.

And why did that bother him? Why did he care, as long as the end result was achieved; she'd be out of his system then, out of his head, and the tormenting desire would be sated. He could take her now, right now, drive her as crazy as she drove him and watch her face as passion made of it something elementally beautiful. He could feel her warmth sheathe him, push his body and his senses to the edge of madness and beyond. He could steal an interlude of pleasure from her, just as he'd stolen a golden figurine and a few other antiquities. With trickery and treachery.

She'd hate him afterward. Hate him because it would be stealing, allowing her no chance to give. Hate him for a basic dishonesty that had nothing to do with their "anything goes" games. But she'd be out of his system then. Wouldn't she? The partnership would be null and void, and there would be no Tyler to ever again fight at his side.

Kane linked his hands together behind his neck, moving carefully so as not to disturb her. The rain was beating steadily against the branches of the lean-to and thunder rumbled, but Kane was listening to his own thoughts.

He should have been thinking about the chalice and the hefty fee Joshua Phillips would pay him to bring it back to New York. That fee would make the last payment on the ranch, and the place was self-sustaining now; he could retire. Could he do that? Yes, he thought he could. He'd spent ten years roaming the world, and it was getting harder now to leave home.

How did Tyler feel about ranches? Could she ride? She could ride a camel, he remembered, and smiled despite himself as he recalled that occasion. But his smile faded.

What in God's name was wrong with him? Thinking of Tyler on his ranch . . . that was absurd. And only moments before he had thought about stealing from her because it didn't seem possible she would give to him . . . not that. Not Tyler.

She moved then, murmuring in her sleep, turning to snuggle close to him, her cheek on his chest, one hand sliding upward to touch his neck, warm and boneless. Kane felt everything in him go still for an instant, and then he lowered his arm until it curved around her shoulders, and rested his chin in the fragrant silk of her hair.

Something inside her trusted him, even if she didn't know it consciously. And he couldn't take advantage of that.

The rain droned steadily on, and it was growing hotter and more humid, but Kane didn't notice. Tension seeped from his muscles as he held her, felt her soft breath, and he fell asleep without even realizing he was going to.

TYLER FELT VAGUELY bothered, and she realized only gradually that it was because of the rain. Or, more precisely, because the rain had stopped. The steady sounds, the pattering and the splashing, had helped to make her sleep deep and dreamless. But now the sounds were only faint and sporadic, an occasional splash, a minute thud, and she felt she should awake.

She moved restlessly, and the faint, pleasant scratching of something against her cheek woke her fully. Bewildered, she opened her eyes to see a thick pelt of curling black hair. She stared for a moment, then jerked her head off Kane's chest. She felt his arm around her then, and heat suffused her face as her eyes met his wide-awake gaze.

"You sleep like a cat," he murmured, his free hand lifting to smooth a strand of her hair back. "A trusting cat. Utterly boneless. Maybe you trust me more than you know."

She couldn't read his face. What was he thinking? Why was he talking to her like this? She wanted to push away from him and quickly get out of the bag with what grace and dignity she could muster, but another part of her was conscious of a suspended waiting, a deep, churning uncertainty.

The point of danger. Again, the point of danger. She could feel herself quivering like some wild thing scenting peril. But she couldn't find the strength or the will to draw back.

Kane's free hand slipped over her back to her waist, rubbing lightly. "You weren't bothered by the bra this time. You sleep in the buff when you're alone, don't you, Ty?"

"That's—none of your business." But she was shaken because he'd guessed right.

"I suppose not." The hand at her shoulder moved, his fingers curling around her neck beneath the heavy weight of her hair and drawing her slowly downward. He took his time, giving her the opportunity to pull away if she wanted. But Tyler stared into his eyes, her own startled and wavering, and though the nape of her neck was tense, she didn't resist him.

He had kissed her twice before, once roughly and half in anger because she had expected him to try, once very briefly in relief and thanks because she had saved his life when she could have left him to shift for himself. This time, Kane intended to leave her with a memory. He might never be granted this opportunity again, and he meant to make certain that Tyler faced the fact that there was something between them, something more than rivalry and mistrust.

He molded his lips to hers, guiding her head firmly, watching until her lids fluttered and then closed. Her mouth was cool and stiff beneath his for a long moment, but his tongue glided insistently between her lips and a helpless shiver went through her. He could feel her fingers curl against his chest suddenly, the oval nails digging into his skin, and then her mouth warmed, opened to him.

The wet heat of her mouth sent shudders through Kane's big body, but he concentrated only on the fusion of the kiss. His tongue touched hers silkily, demanding a response, receiving it instantly but tentatively. His hands roved to her waist, where he could feel the bunched material of the ruana, and the thought of the scant covering over her nakedness maddened him. The material had slid apart at her sides during the night, and his thumbs found the sensitive satin flesh, stroked it.

Tyler felt that touch as if it were fire, and when dizziness swept over her she didn't even try to fight it. He was taking her mouth, she realized dimly, possessing it and branding it his own, and she had never felt anything like that before. The roughness of his morning beard was a heady caress, and her skin tingled with the contact. He was seducing her, slowly and inexorably, kindling a fire where none had ever before blazed. She was hardly conscious that her hands had curled around his neck, barely aware that she had drawn one leg up over his, frustrated by denim when she wanted to feel his flesh against her own.

Then he was moving her, lifting her with his easy strength until she lay fully on him, the close confines of the sleeping bag pressing her tightly against his big, hard body. Her legs parted instinctively to lie on either side of his, and her body responded wildly to the swelling response she could feel from him. The denim between them was a rough caress and a curse, and his every faint movement was a searing jolt to her senses.

She felt no panic, no smothering sensation of helplessness and vulnerability. There was no hard shadow over her, blocking out the light and holding her down. There was only heat and a building tension that was restless and a strange, unfamiliar combination of pleasure and pain.

Kane hadn't meant for this to go so far; he hadn't expected such a total response from her. But her response was total, and his hunger for her had burst out of control. She was soft and warm as she lay on him, her breasts pressed to his chest, and he was drunk with the feel of her, the taste of her, the heady feminine smell of her. His hands slipped down over her hips until the firm mounds of her buttocks filled them, and he moved beneath her, driven, feeling he'd explode if he didn't take her, didn't roll over and bury himself in the warmth of her body.

But it was then that some ever-vigilant sense warned him of danger, and Kane forced his eyes to open and his lips to leave hers. Instantly, without thought, his hands jerked from beneath the quilted bag and shot upward, bracing the heavy branches of the lean-to a scant few seconds before the structure would have collapsed on them both.

Tyler was unaware of it at first. She was trembling, her breathing shallow and her body aching with an emptiness she'd never felt before. His chest rose and fell raggedly beneath her breasts, and she felt a blind, mad urge to find his mouth again because she desperately needed that heated touch.

But sanity penetrated the veils of her emotions, and her dazed eyes finally absorbed the rigid posture of his strong arms. Logic told her then that the rain had soaked an already marshy ground, causing the lean-to's support posts to sink, and that the structure was heavy enough to have given them a nasty jolt.

Tyler moved without thinking about it, her actions dictated by some rational corner of her bewildered mind. She twisted, reaching for the zipper of the sleeping bag, trying frantically to ignore the screamingly aware nerves of her body as well as the rough sound he made as she moved on top of him. She could feel her face flaming. Unzipping the bag, she managed to squirm off Kane and get out, yanking the ruana down as she scrambled to her feet.

"Can you hold it a minute?" she asked him huskily.

"I can hold it." His voice was harsh, and his green eyes were blazing.

Ten feet away, Tyler found a sturdy limb with a forked end. She brought it back and kneeled to jam it under the crosspiece of the lean-to, bracing the other end firmly against the ground. The structure wobbled a bit, but it held.

Silently Kane crawled from the sleeping bag.

Tyler was holding the limb with both hands, staring at her fingers with a baffled expression. Then she looked at him, and the perplexity in her amber eyes was almost pain. "Another trick, Kane?"

He didn't pretend to misunderstand. Yanking his shirt from the line, he shrugged into it and growled, "You know damned well it wasn't. And you could have stopped me with a word, Ty. Think about that."

She was still frowning, trying to fit the action to the man she thought she knew, unwilling to examine her own participation. "You must have had a reason," she murmured almost to herself. "Something to gain by it."

He stared at her for a long moment, truly recognizing only then the gulf that lay between them. "Oh, I had a reason," he told her bitterly. "I wanted you, Tyler, pure and simple. And you wanted me, whether you'll admit it or not. But we're just enemies under a flag of truce, aren't we? I should have remembered that." Turning abruptly, he strode off through the woods.

Tyler stared blankly after him.

chapter four

SEDUCE AN ENEMY and earn his—her—trust?

Had that thought occurred to Kane as well as to her? It was the only reason that made sense, and Tyler accepted it with a flash of pain that surprised her. She still refused to think about her own participation. Fiercely she reminded herself that he was adept at trickery, and ruthless. She didn't doubt his desire, but told herself that he was an innately sexual man; other men had found her attractive, and Kane apparently did, as well.

Physically at least.

She ignored the pain that she didn't understand, concentrating instead on this situation. Partners. Fine, then. Partners for the duration. And she wouldn't be seduced, wouldn't allow this insane attraction she felt for him to lower her guard.

By the time he returned to their camp nearly an hour later, Tyler was dressed, her hair braided, her control and her guard firmly in place. The sleeping bag had been rolled up and tied to his backpack. She had made coffee, and had unearthed, from that rather amazing pack of his, pancake mix and canned milk. A stack of golden cakes was piled on a tin plate, and she was paying strict attention to the task of fixing more when he approached.

"If you had told me there was canned milk," she said mildly without looking up, "I would have put some in my coffee last night."

"You didn't ask."

His voice was calm and guarded, she reflected, like hers had been. It seemed they had both decided to ignore what had almost happened between them. It was safer that way, she reminded herself. Much safer. But she felt cheated somehow, and a part of her recognized that both she and Kane were fighters, that it was unnatural for them and totally out of character to ignore this particular battle.

But this battle, she also recognized, was too dangerous to be fought. Not here. Not now. And not between the two of them. No matter who won or lost, the scars would mark them both for life.

She stole glances at him as they both ate breakfast silently. He had shaved, and she couldn't help but think of how sensual his morning beard had felt against her skin. Realizing where her thoughts had gone, she tried desperately to redirect them. But it was impossible.

Was it only the situation that was different this time,

the fact that they were too alone here, too intimate? Or had their relationship, sporadic though it was, always been heading toward this point? Was it possible, she suddenly asked herself, to feel so many strong emotions for a man, even though most of them were negative ones, without feeling also a primitive attraction?

They were alike, and she recognized that now. She and Kane were very alike, cut from the same stubborn mold. Adventurous, humorous, reckless, tough when they had to be, independent. They both loved artifacts, and both were, conversely, capable of great honor and integrity as well as great deviousness.

Tyler pushed the realization violently away. Alike they may be, she thought grimly, but they were still enemies, rivals. Infusing her voice with a mildly speculative tone, she said, "That shooter. Who do you suppose he is?" They had hardly had time to discuss the matter before now, and she grasped the subject as something safe and relatively unthreatening.

"I didn't get a good look at him." Kane was paying attention to his meal. "Did you see him clearly?"

"I was too busy diving for cover." He didn't offer her a smile or make a sardonic comment, and Tyler sighed to herself. She didn't like this minefield they were so warily crossing; at least in the past they'd been too busy snapping at each other and being sneaky to worry about mines beneath their feet.

"He's after the cache," Kane said.

"How can you be so sure of that?" she asked, even though she agreed with him.

"Because nothing else makes sense." He took his plate to the stream and began cleaning it. Over his shoulder, he said, "I caught a glimpse of blond hair, so it's doubtful he's native to these parts. As far as I could find out, the only likely valuables in the area would be the cache Rolfe smuggled out of Germany during the war and hid—for Tomas to find more than forty years later. Maybe Tomas talked too freely back in Panama about his discovery. Odds are, our trigger-happy friend is after exactly what we're after."

Tyler ate the last of her breakfast as she thought about it. Like many of the valuables their employers sent them after, the chalice's rightful ownership was a matter of speculation; it occupied a kind of legal no-man's-land. During World War II, much of Europe had been looted of its valuables, and many items had simply vanished, never to be found.

During the final days of the war, a number of men had taken what they could and jumped Hitler's sinking ship. Some of those men had hidden their treasures in various parts of the world, and for more than forty years items had surfaced from time to time, appearing on the black market or just changing hands privately. Interpol had traced many art objects and antiquities and returned them to their proper owners, but lists were incomplete and often contained inspired guesswork because too many records had been destroyed during the war.

The chalice that she and Kane were after now was one such homeless artifact. Ownership couldn't be proven legally because of the gaps in various records and, indeed, Tyler knew very little about it except that her employer was hell-bent to get it in his hands. Its intrinsic value was hard to estimate; it was believed to have been in the possession of a very old church in Italy a hundred and fifty years before, but was reportedly lost long before the church itself was destroyed.

Then the war had happened, and somewhere along the way the chalice had ended up in a cache of valuables hidden in the wilderness of Colombia. And their slippery friend Tomas had discovered it while—he *said*—visiting his family in the area, and had left it there until he could find buyers. He hadn't dared return for it himself, he'd told Tyler with a wide, artless smile. He hadn't explained why, and Tyler had been in too much of a hurry to ask.

Absently Tyler said, "Sayers didn't tell me how he'd heard about the chalice. Did your boss?" Kane's boss was Joshua Phillips, who lived in London as did his enemy Sayers.

"No."

She looked at him curiously as he returned and began packing his plate and fork away. "What do you know about it?"

"I know it's supposed to be cursed," Kane answered mildly.

Tyler didn't react with scorn or disbelief. She knew enough history to be aware of the reality of curses. Not that she believed inanimate objects could contain a malevolent spirit, but she *did* believe that events were sometimes tied to objects, connected in a sense, and that because antiquities had such a long and colorful history unlucky events were certain to have occurred near them and to have been connected in one way or another.

"I haven't heard of that," she said now, getting up and going to the stream to clean her own plate. "Tell me."

Somewhat surprisingly, Kane didn't seem to be in a hurry. He waited until she returned to the fire, then focused his eyes on the flames and spoke slowly.

"Most of what I know is pretty much speculative. Ironically enough, I stumbled across a reference to the chalice and the legend in an unpublished private journal years ago. Never thought I'd have the chance to hold the thing in my hand."

Tyler understood what he meant. One of the reasons she enjoyed this job so much was that it gave her the opportunity to see and touch objects whose existence was, in terms of history, almost mythical. She nodded now, and watched his profile as he gazed into the fire.

"It all started," Kane said, "with Alexander."

Tyler blinked. "Alexander the Great? But you're going back more than two thousand years! The chalice can't be that old."

"There's some confusion about that. Very little documentation has survived, what with various wars and all. There's probably little hope that the chalice we're after is the same one in this story. But you never know." He glanced at her, something both quizzical and oddly intent in his green eyes. "Sure you want to hear it?"

She was a little puzzled, but curious. "Of course. All I know about the chalice is that it disappeared from the church in Florence about a hundred years ago. And that there were supposedly two of them originally. Your story sounds more interesting than that. So tell me. It started with Alexander?"

Kane was gazing into the fire again. "Alexander. You may remember that he was barely twenty when his father was assassinated, and that he rounded up a number of suspects whom he very quickly had executed. All of them had claims to the throne. He also gave his mother the honor of dispatching his father's young wife and newborn son."

"I remember." Tyler grimaced faintly. "They sort of glossed over that part when I was in school, but my father told me what the books left out."

"Your father?"

"He was an archaeologist. Go on with the story." She felt a little disturbed at having made a personal reference; she and Kane never did that. The past they shared had begun three years ago after a confrontation in North Africa, and neither had ever looked further back than that.

Kane half nodded. "So Alexander became king, and an arrogant one at that. He got busy conquering the world. He also made two marriages, both political, to Asian princesses. One of those wives was the daughter of the king of Persia."

"King Darius. I remember," Tyler said.

"You may also remember that Alexander conquered Persia, and that Darius was killed, supposedly by one of his own generals."

"Yes."

"What his daughter felt about that is a matter for speculation, since it was more or less Alexander's fault." Kane shook his head. "But in any case, it's likely she found out that being politically married to a king who was continually off conquering the world wasn't much fun."

"I can imagine," Tyler murmured.

"Her name was Statira," Kane said. "And whatever she felt for her husband, she seems to have kept to herself. However, somewhere around 323 B.C. Statira and Alexander's other political wife jointly commissioned a pair of golden cups—chalices—to be fashioned in his honor. They sent the chalices to him, together in one package, with a message assuring him of their loyalty. He was busy making preparations to invade Arabia at the time."

"And?" Tyler prompted when he fell silent.

"And he was at the palace in Babylon when the package arrived. There was a celebration of sorts going on, lots of drinking and partying. Alexander opened the package and promptly used one of the cups to toast his loyal wives. He handed the second cup to his closest general, who also made a toast."

Tyler half winced. "Poison?"

"According to history," Kane said, "it was likely malaria. In any case, within a few hours of drinking from the chalice, Alexander fell ill. He was dead within three days. The general who had drunk from the second cup was fine. There was much talk, according to the legend, about which of the two wives had tried to poison

Alexander. But the chalices vanished, and with Alexander's empire coming apart nobody bothered to try to find out if he had indeed been poisoned."

"But the chalices were believed to be cursed?"

"Not just because of that. In 1478, Giuliano de' Medici was stabbed to death during mass by the Pazzi family. He was drinking from a gold chalice when he was stabbed; according to descriptions, it exactly matched one of the pair given to Alexander. And in 1791, when Louis XVI was captured at Varennes, two chalices were found in his coach—again, matching the description of Alexander's gold cups."

Tyler was frowning a little. "There are some big gaps in time in your legend. Where were the chalices?"

Kane shrugged. "There are just vague mentions of bad luck following the chalices, always connected in some way to betrayal and death."

"Is there a more recent history?"

"Just what you've heard. That one chalice was in the possession of a church in Florence around a hundred years ago and then vanished; there's no mention in existing records of the second one after about 1800."

After a moment Tyler said slowly, "The chalice we're after is just a piece of the loot Hitler collected; there's no record of where it was taken from, or any information about its history. What makes you think it's one of Alexander's?"

Kane shrugged again. "The description. According to what my boss gave me, the chalice we're after is the spitting image of Alexander's." A bit dryly, he added,

"And Joshua Phillips, at least, is so excited about it that he was almost stuttering when he sent me after it. The bonus, assuming I bring it back, is nothing short of staggering."

Tyler stared at him. She couldn't read his expression, but all her doubts about her ability to trust him were uppermost in her mind. The stakes this time were high. "My boss promised me a—staggering bonus," she confessed somewhat warily.

Kane suddenly rose and began making preparations to leave, pouring the last of the coffee in the fire and packing up everything. Casually he said, "Obviously neither of us was told all our employers know about the chalice; I think they both believe it was Alexander's. Or else why the secrecy? We've both known exactly what we were after before. Didn't you wonder why you weren't told more this time?"

Tyler had automatically followed suit in getting ready to leave, and stood, absently adjusting the strap of a canteen over her shoulder as she gazed at Kane. "Maybe I was blinded by dollar signs," she suggested. If she had meant it to be a pointed reference—and she wasn't sure about that—Kane either missed it or ignored it.

He slung the backpack over one shoulder, picked up the rifle and studied her deliberately. "No. You like the money, but that isn't the reason you do this. You do it for kicks, Ty. You do it because you love antiquities. And you do it because, for some reason I haven't figured out yet, you're driven to put yourself in danger."

She stood staring at him, conscious of her heart

pounding suddenly, of confusion clouding her mind. How could he have guessed that? *How?* And why did she abruptly feel vulnerable as she never had before? With an effort she curved her lips in a sardonic smile. "You don't say." It wasn't much as comebacks go, but Tyler knew him too well to arouse his hunting instincts by going overboard on the side of denial.

His smile was every bit as sardonic as hers. "Don't you ever get tired of it?"

"Tired of what?"

"Holding your guard up with me?"

Before she could stop herself, her gaze flickered toward the wobbly lean-to. Without waiting for him to comment on that tiny betrayal, she said sweetly, "It's just a matter of common sense, Kane. You should always carry a whip and chair when you walk into a lion's cage. And you should never turn your back to that breed of cat."

"Even one raised in captivity?" he asked in a light tone.

"Especially that one." She could hear the stony note of absolute certainty in her voice. "He knows how to purr. He even knows how to jump through a hoop when he has to. But he never forgets where the cage door is."

Kane looked at her for a long moment, then nodded almost imperceptibly. Softly he said, "But you won't stay out of the cage, Tyler. Think about that. Nobody forced you to step into it. You just won't stay out of the cage."

She followed as he left the camp, her movements

automatic. That strange, disturbing feeling of suspension was with her again, and the curiously stark analogy of lion and cage clung to her mind stubbornly. Kane was right; she couldn't stay out of the cage, even though nobody forced her to go in. Even knowing the danger of the lion.

The slight sounds they made as they went on covered her soft gasp, and she was grateful that he hadn't heard the evidence of her own shock.

Danger. *Danger*. Was that why she was so violently attracted to Kane, why she relished their rivalry? He was the strongest, most dangerous man she had ever known, and when she was with him the encounters demanded every ounce of her own strength and will. She had to push herself beyond her self-defined limits in his company, physically, mentally—and emotionally.

Could it be that simple?

Did some part of her fiercely enjoy their rivalry because he was the lion she needed to tame, the danger she needed to face and attempt to control? Three years before, she had accepted Robert Sayers's job offer out of boredom and curiosity, but on encountering Kane a couple of months later her determination to best him had been instant and implacable, and that ambition had never since wavered. And on each succeeding assignment, she had looked eagerly for him.

Tyler followed along behind Kane in silence as the hours passed, wrapped up in her own disturbing thoughts. When he finally called a halt in the late afternoon, she put the canteen aside and gazed around in vague surprise.

They had been circumventing the swamp for some hours, but she was only now aware of the rich, ripe scents and eerie sounds of the marshlands.

"We'll start back inland in another hour or so," Kane said, and tossed her a packet of trail mix. "We should make higher ground before dark."

She nodded, eating because she should and not because she was hungry. Her mind started ahead to the coming night, and she frowned at her own chaotic thoughts. She felt hot and sticky, and decidedly unnerved by the uncertainty she felt regarding the motives behind Kane's earlier desire for her.

Kane watched her, very aware of her silence and of the troubled frown on her delicate face. He had shocked her, he knew, by observing that she fought him by choice; he had been more than a little surprised himself at the realization. He thought he was beginning to understand her, at least more than ever before, and with that tentative knowledge had come something he had hardly been prepared for.

Want was such a mild word, or always had been, but now it was something alive and clawing at him. All day, he had been starkly conscious of her almost silent movements behind him, and he had glanced back often to see her bright hair and preoccupied face. And every glance had sharpened the ache of desire that was centered deeper than his loins, somewhere in his very bones.

He wanted her with a strength he had never felt before.

And not just physically. He wanted to understand

her. Always before, he had observed the enigma of her with interest and vague curiosity, with little time granted to him for probing. But this time he had caught several glimpses of what lay beneath her guard, either because of her own words or because he was looking harder. And what he had seen fascinated him.

He knew she mistrusted him, mistrusted even his desire for her. Maybe *especially* his desire. She suspected a trick, an attempt to get beneath her guard. He understood that; it was a reasonable suspicion given their past encounters. But what he was beginning to see was that Tyler herself was unconvinced by her own suspicions. She was wavering, looking at him one moment as an enemy and the next with puzzled uneasiness.

The question was, did her uncertainty argue well for a change in their relationship?

"We should reach the cave by tomorrow," he said now, casually, as he watched her. She looked at him almost blindly for a moment, but then her eyes focused and there was something in those amber depths he'd seen once before in the eyes of a doe, something wary and perplexed.

"Good," she responded in a taut voice.

"Assuming the cache is where it's supposed to be, we should be on our way right after that. We can head northeast to Bogotá and find transport out of the country. And since we have to get the cache to Tomas in Panama, our best chance of getting back to Europe is probably by ship from there. Agreed?"

Getting in and out of various countries with antiquities

whose rightful ownership couldn't be determined wasn't exactly illegal, but both Tyler and Kane had learned not to call undue attention to themselves in the process; both were usually pressed for time, and also wished to avoid possible thieves and other interested parties. So they tended to bypass airports with their terrorist-spawned and highly efficient security in favor of land or water transportation, where their accommodations were generally several notches below tourist class.

Tyler had often found it ironic that she traveled with an unlimited expense account and could also draw from banks in any major city in the world, and yet usually went from place to place in rickety buses or the cargo holds of leaky ships. Still, she was seeing the world from a unique perspective in this jet age, and wouldn't have traded even her most uncomfortable experiences for first-class travel all the way.

But she was thinking about that now, thinking of a long sea voyage in Kane's company. Presumably they would have the chalice in their possession. At least one of them would. There was still no solution for the problem of dividing one old, golden chalice for two separate employers.

"Ty?"

She drew a deep breath. "Agreed. Who gets the chalice, Kane?"

He reached for his canteen and unscrewed the cap, frowning just a little but not looking at her. "We don't have to make that decision for a while yet," he noted neutrally.

"And when *do* we decide? When we dock at Portsmouth or Liverpool, or wherever? When we get to London?"

"You think I'm going to try and give you the slip in Panama," he said after taking a leisurely drink from his canteen. He was looking at her now, steady and faintly amused.

"You've done it before," she reminded him evenly. "In Madagascar, you managed to have me detained by the police, and in Cairo you left me making arrangements for a ship while you hightailed it across the desert."

Kane grinned suddenly as a memory surfaced. "You got even, at least in North Africa," he offered. "Telling those Bedouins I stole one of their camels was a sneaky trick, Ty. By the way, what was the last offer from that sheik?"

She glared at him for a moment, but her sense of humor couldn't remain submerged for long and a reluctant gleam lit her eyes. "Once I told him I had an employer who valued me, he started sending his proposals to Robert. I told Robert I didn't want to know what the offers were, but he says he's keeping a file in case I ever change my mind."

"Or he ever needs a big favor from the sheik," Kane said somewhat abruptly. And when she stiffened visibly, he added, "Sorry. Didn't mean that."

Tyler's glare was back, this time holding a chill light. "I don't give a damn what you think," she said in a voice that shook slightly. "But I'll tell you this, Kane. Not everything's for sale. Even to the highest bidder."

Kane had gone too far, and he knew it. He didn't know why he had implied that Sayers would—or could—use Tyler's sexual favor as a bargaining chip, and was more than a little surprised at both his implication and the savage emotions it had inspired in him. His gaze fell before hers. "I know. I'm sorry, Tyler, really. I suppose I was thinking about how ruthless Sayers and Phillips are in this feud of theirs."

She got to her feet stiffly. "We'd better move on if we want to make higher ground by dark."

As he rose as well, Kane reflected wryly that this encounter between them was running true to form in one way; a verbal seesaw with each of them besting the other occasionally but neither getting the upper hand for long.

He led the way in silence as they circled the last of the swamp. They had made better time than he'd expected, partially because the swamp was smaller than he'd been told, and also because they'd been moving quickly. The sun was sinking behind them as they left the swamp and began making their way through the thickening undergrowth of a dense forest. They were heading east now, gradually climbing into the Andes, and the temperature was already falling.

There was still plenty of light when the rain began falling steadily, and Kane glanced back to see Tyler look upward with more resignation than annoyance.

"We're lucky the rain held off this long," he said over his shoulder.

Tyler accepted the olive branch, though her voice

was a bit stiff. "I know. But since we're almost into the dry season, I'd been hoping . . ."

"We usually have better luck," he agreed, turning to offer a hand to help her up a slippery granite outcrop. She came up beside him easily and without fuss, and remembering some of the feats demanded of them both in the past made him ask curiously as they went on, "Were you an athlete?"

She was silent for a moment as she followed him, then said, "If you mean in school, no. My father raised me, and since he spent at least six months of every year on a dig somewhere, I was lucky to just make decent grades."

"You went with him?"

"Yes."

He smiled a little at the brief answer. "So that's where you developed your strength and balance, climbing around ruins?"

There was another silence, and then she said, "Partly, I suppose. And, until I was sixteen, ballet."

Kane stopped on a rise to check the compass then looked at her with more than a little surprise. "Ballet?"

She smiled very faintly. "When I was fifteen, I was five-two and weighed eighty-five pounds. Between that birthday and the next, I grew five inches, gained thirty pounds, and, um—"

"Bloomed?" he suggested with a grin.

Tyler shrugged, unconsciously drawing his more intent scrutiny to the "blooming" that had turned her ballerina's slenderness into the rich curves of a woman.

"Let's just say my possibilities as a prima ballerina went down the tubes," she said wryly.

"Any regrets?" he asked, trying to keep his eyes on her face as the steady rain plastered her shirt to the ripe breasts beneath it.

She adjusted the strap of the canteen on her shoulder, returning his gaze with the same wary look in her eyes that had been present since this morning. Not the suspicion of a rival; it looked like the misgivings of a woman risking more than defeat in a contest.

It was really beginning to bother him.

"No," she said finally. "I was getting interested in antiquities by then and . . ."

"And?"

She fiddled with the strap on her shoulder again. "And shouldn't we be going?"

Kane frowned a little. She was unnerved, and he didn't know why. What had she been going to say about the year of physical changes that had altered her life? He was curious, but reluctant to disturb the fragile calm between them. So he went on, automatically choosing the easiest path as they continued to climb into the mountains.

It was still raining steadily, and the last of the light vanished as though a switch had been thrown. The footing was slippery in places, and Kane was beginning to look around for a place to hole up for the night when Tyler fell.

"Damn," she muttered irritably as he knelt beside her. "Of all the stupid—"

"Are you hurt?" he asked briskly.

"My leg." She shifted her weight slightly, then batted his hand away from her upper thigh. "Not that high, damn it."

"It's dark," he murmured, knowing by the sound of her voice that she wasn't in much pain.

"And you have eyes like an owl. My ankle—the left one. Just twisted a little; the boot protected it. If you'll give me a hand up, I can—" She gasped as Kane slipped one arm beneath her knees, the other around her back, and rose easily to his feet holding her against his chest. "Kane!"

Reasonably he said, "You shouldn't put any weight on that ankle until we can take a look at it, which is impossible here. There should be a level place at the top of this slope where we can build a fire." He was moving steadily up the slope, apparently untroubled by either the slippery footing or his burden.

Tyler knew very well that his backpack weighed every ounce of fifty pounds since she'd carried it herself while tracking him and the bandits the day before. He was also carrying a canteen and rifle by their shoulder straps. And carrying her. Up a slippery slope. In pitch darkness.

She had put her arms around his neck automatically as he'd lifted her, and now made a determined effort not to think about strong arms holding her. Clearing her throat, she said, "So much for my balance."

Kane chuckled softly.

That ambiguous response made her say aggrievedly, "I didn't fall on purpose, you know."

"You're whistling again," he said calmly.

Tyler frowned into the darkness, wondering when she had suddenly become so obvious to him. "I am not," she denied, even though she knew she'd been doing just that, just making noise to distract them both from unexpected closeness.

"Of course you are." His voice showed no strain. "We've always been a man and woman, Ty, but you're just beginning to realize it. And you're shying away like a timid deer."

She couldn't trust him, that's why she didn't want this! But she couldn't tell him that. So, as always, she worked up a flare of anger. "Don't flatter yourself!"

Ignoring that, Kane said, "I've been thinking about it most of the day. I know you don't trust me. Fair enough. To be perfectly honest, sweetheart, I don't trust you, either." He reached the top of the slope and stood gazing around for a moment.

Tyler, who couldn't see a thing except him even though her eyes had adjusted as much as they could to the darkness, stared at his arrogant profile and opened her mouth to spit the angry words still forming in her mind.

Kane turned his head suddenly, and his grin was a flash of white in the darkness. "But I want you," he said.

She closed her mouth, then said, "Put me down."

"Sure." He carried her several steps, then ducked

slightly to clear what was apparently an overhang and knelt to set her gently on dry ground. "Back in a minute," he said, shrugging off his pack and leaving it beside her. "I'll see if I can find some dry wood for a fire."

Tyler sat exactly as he'd left her, staring blankly into darkness. She was vaguely aware of hard rock at her back and dry dirt underneath her, and senses other than sight told her that a granite cliff curved protectively out above her. It couldn't be called a cave, but Kane had managed to find shelter.

She lifted a hand that shook and slowly wiped moisture from her face. She was wet and chilled, but she knew that the trembling she could feel in her body had little to do with either condition.

I want you.

She had heard the words, the implicit demand before, but not from Kane. When Kane said it, it was no overture, no testing of the waters before a relationship could take a next logical step. When Kane said it, it wasn't a simple statement of desire. When Kane said it, it was a challenge, a battle line drawn in the dirt between them.

After thinking it through, Kane wasn't willing to ignore this battle. He didn't trust her, or she him, but there was desire between them, and for Kane that was enough. He wouldn't pretend they were no longer enemies, that their rivalry was past. He wouldn't pretend to care about her.

Or at least, she hoped not. Bedroom lies were the one variety of deceit she would never be able to bear from him.

Tyler knew then that she wasn't ready for this particular battle. She shifted position in the darkness and began unlacing her left boot, trying to think clearly and finding it almost impossible. All she could bring to mind were memories of the tight, warm enclosure of the sleeping bag and Kane's hard body pressed so intimately to hers.

God, she couldn't let this happen. Her own body's response to him told her that not even her panicky feelings of helplessness and vulnerability could erect a guard between them, and with her mind in turmoil she had to doubt her intellectual will to resist him. It didn't matter that she didn't trust him, because her body didn't care about trust, and she doubted her mind's ability to control her body. Kane could make her want him, and he knew that as surely as she did herself.

She felt more than heard him return, but said nothing as he began building a small fire a couple of feet from her. The overhang provided a dry space four or five feet deep and about ten feet long, and he had placed the fire out near the edge of the hollow to give them as much room as possible.

"There isn't much dry wood out there," he said casually, "but I got what I could."

She watched the fire flicker as he fed it with sticks and then broke a couple of larger branches with his hands and one knee. The sharp cracking of the wood sounded loud in the silence.

"How's the ankle?" he asked, sitting back on his heels and brushing his hands together as he looked across the fire at her.

"All right." Her voice was steady. "Not even swollen."

He came around the fire, hunched a bit because he couldn't stand upright in the confined space and knelt beside her. His khaki shirt was soaked and plastered to his muscular chest and shoulders, his shaggy hair was wet, and his face glistened. She had removed her boot, and he took her foot in his hand and stripped off the thick sock, his long fingers probing her ankle carefully. He frowned suddenly. "Your skin's ice-cold."

Tyler wasn't surprised. "Give the fire time to work."

His frown lingered as he swept her still body with a searching gaze. "The temperature's dropped a good twenty degrees, and you're soaked to the skin. We have to get you out of those wet clothes before you catch your death."

"No," Tyler said in a brittle voice.

Kane's eyes narrowed. "Don't be a little fool," he said roughly. He half turned away to begin digging in his pack, opening a section she hadn't noticed before, then dropped a bundle of clothing into her lap. In a flat tone that didn't invite her to argue with him, he said, "Get out of your wet things and into those. Don't worry, you'll be decently covered. Then climb into the sleeping bag. I'm going to get some water and some wood."

Tyler stared after him as he picked up the pot he used to make coffee and vanished out into the rainy darkness. She wanted to resist him on this, if only because she needed to feel in control of the situation again, but she was too cold and wet to feel like putting up much of a fight.

He had left her a flannel shirt and a pair of sweat-pants, and she took a moment to speculate on his reasons for giving her the ruana instead of these last night. She didn't have to speculate very hard. She removed her right boot and set both of them aside with her socks draped over them, then got gingerly to her feet. Her left ankle twinged, but it was more of a grumble than a pain and she ignored it.

Minutes later she was draping her wet shirt and underclothes over a rock at one end of the shelter, having scrambled into the dry things very quickly, when it occurred to her that the fire lit her dressing room up very nicely for anyone watching from the darkness outside.

The shirt was ridiculously large; she had to roll up the sleeves to make them reach her wrists. And if the sweat-pants hadn't boasted a drawstring waist and elastic at the ankles, she wouldn't have been able to keep them on.

Dry and warming rapidly, she unrolled the sleeping bag and sat on it with her back against the wall. Her hair was still wet, but she didn't have the energy to unbraid it. Granted this interlude without Kane's disturbing presence, she needed very badly to think.

chapter five

HE RETURNED TO the hollow a few minutes later carrying an armful of wood and the water. He put the wood down and arranged the pot over the fire on a hook device he carried in his pack, then sat down a couple of feet away from Tyler and began getting out of his boots.

"Kane—" she began, but broke off when she realized how strained her voice sounded even to herself.

As if his earlier statement hadn't been followed by an interruption for other things, Kane said, "I meant what I said, Ty." He set his boots and socks aside, then sent her a glance that was both intense and faintly amused as he began unbuttoning his shirt. "But not here. And not now."

She was too curious not to ask. "Why?"

Kane looked at her again, hesitating for the first time.

She looked very small and fragile, swallowed in his clothing, the firelight flickering in her wide amber eyes. After a moment he said, "We have company."

It was the last thing Tyler had expected. "What?"

"Our friend the shooter."

She stared at him, her mind scrambling to make the shift from personal to professional. "He's been following us?"

"All day."

"How long have you known?"

Kane stripped his shirt off, exposing the broad, hair-roughened expanse of his chest. He tossed the shirt to lie across a large rock at his end of the hollow, and half turned to face her. Keeping his voice low, he replied, "When you fell. As I turned back toward you, I caught a glimpse of him." His mouth quirked suddenly. "Why do you think I charged out into the rain while you changed clothes? If we'd been alone, I would have stripped you myself."

Tyler decided to let that pass, although her face felt hot at the image his words evoked. "So you were protecting my modesty?" She managed to make her voice dry.

"Let's just say I made sure he couldn't get close enough to see anything."

Her eyes flickered as she glanced out beyond the fire. "He's out there now?"

"Yeah." Kane answered her next question before she could voice it. "I'm a little curious about our friend. Doesn't it strike you as a bit odd that he wasted all that ammunition in the ravine and didn't hit either of us? That kind of lousy marksmanship generally happens only in B movies."

Tyler felt slightly sheepish that she hadn't thought of that sooner, but chalked it up to having been unsettled since encountering Kane. "You're right. So why would he be trying *not* to hit us?"

Kane reached into the pack between them and pulled out a second pair of sweatpants, muttering, "God, I hate being wet." He rose to his feet in the confined space and began unfastening his jeans. "I have a theory," he added.

"Oh?" Tyler was searching through the pack for the coffee, keeping her eyes fixed carefully downward while he stripped off his jeans and changed into the sweatpants. She concentrated on swearing at herself silently for having used up all the canned milk for pancakes, now she'd have to drink her coffee black and she *hated* that, she really did. . . .

"You can look now," Kane said in amusement as he sat down again and cast his damp jeans over the rock where his shirt lay.

With an effort, she stopped herself from throwing the bag of coffee at him. Handing it to him with utter control, she watched as he dumped some into the can of hot water. "No wonder that stuff's strong enough to raise the dead," she said, because she wanted to say something she could sound annoyed about. "Don't you ever measure?"

"Only when it counts," Kane said.

Tyler drew her knees up and wrapped her arms around

them, scowling faintly as she stared at him. "What's your theory?"

Kane matched her pose and answered amiably. "Obviously the man is after the cache. Also obviously, he doesn't know where it is. Which is why he's following us. As to why he shot at us the other day . . . Maybe to hurry us along?"

"He isn't shooting now," she noted.

"We have to rest sometime."

Tyler shifted her gaze to the fire as she frowned in thought. Then she looked back at Kane, her eyes intent. "He's out there with a gun, and you aren't worried about it. Why not?"

She had been chewing on her lip again. Kane forced himself to be coherent. "I think I know who he is. If I'm right, it wouldn't do either of us much good to worry about him."

After a moment Tyler's mouth twisted and she said irritably, "Will you stop making me ask *why* every few seconds and just tell me what you know?"

"You're just so cute when you're in a snit," he explained solemnly.

"Kane . . ."

"Okay, okay. If I'm right—and that's a pretty big *if* since I hardly got a good look at him—our shooter is Drew Haviland. And you should know his name."

She blinked. "I think— Damn! He's a collector, isn't he? But he goes after antiquities himself."

"He certainly does. And he's beaten both of us more

than once. Remember that jade necklace about eighteen months ago? He got it."

"I thought you did," Tyler said, remembering her own disappointment at having missed both the necklace and Kane.

"No. As near as I could figure, Haviland got to Shanghai about two hours before I did. I was a step behind him for about twelve hours, then lost his trail."

A bit ruefully, Tyler said, "The trail was cold by the time I got there. I just assumed you got the necklace because I knew you'd been there." She sighed, then said, "So this time he's planning to let us lead him to the cache."

"Seems likely."

"So what're we going to do about it?"

Kane dug the tin cups out of his pack and poured coffee, handing one cup to her. Sipping the dark, strong brew, he said slowly, "We won't shake him off, that's a given. We could—" He broke off suddenly, his big body going taut like an animal sensing imminent danger.

"You could offer me coffee," a new voice commented helpfully.

Tyler heard herself gasp, and stared across the hollow as a patch of darkness moved in out of the rain and joined them.

He was wearing an enveloping slicker and carrying a rifle. He was a handsome man about Kane's age—mid-thirties—but where Kane was rugged Drew Haviland possessed the finely drawn yet hawklike good looks of an aristocrat. His vivid blue eyes were mild and perpetually amused, as if he found the world to be an excellent joke, and his voice was deep and calm. British by birth, American by inclination, he had no accent, but his voice carried the slight lilt of the cosmopolitan.

Without a word Kane dug into the pack again, pulled out the ceramic mug and poured coffee into it. He handed it to Haviland as the other man hunkered down by the fire on his left. It was the visitor who spoke first after sipping the coffee, his gaze flickering from Kane's expressionless face to Tyler's startled one.

"I thought it might be smarter if we teamed up," he said.

"Why?" Kane asked, his voice mildly curious.

"You two left that lady bandit in a hell of a bad mood," he told them. "She and her boys are a few hours behind us. They seem to know the area fairly well, so they may not have stopped for the night."

"I assume they're armed," Kane said politely.

"Heavily. And not inclined to discuss the matter, I think. It might be best if we moved on pretty soon."

"No doubt," Kane agreed.

Tyler was getting a little annoyed by this civilized discussion. Staring at Haviland and ruthlessly changing the subject, she demanded, "What are you after?"

Pleasantly Haviland replied, "The cache, of course. By the way, I have your backpack and rifle, Miss St. James; I left them outside, against the cliff. Sorry I caused you to lose them. That wasn't what I'd intended."

"Why did you shoot at us?" Kane was still being polite.

Haviland reached over casually to lean his rifle against the rock wall as an amused smile curved his mouth. "Curiosity, mostly," he admitted in a dry voice. "I wanted to see if you two would team up. Your partnerships in the past have been interesting to observe."

"You could have killed us," Tyler reminded him.

Coolly he said, "No, I think not. I'm a very good shot. And though there was certainly some danger of one or both of you falling, I had complete faith in your uncanny survival instincts—to say nothing of your abilities."

Tyler stared at him speechlessly for a moment, vaguely aware of Kane's low chuckle. "Rats in a maze," she muttered angrily, disliking the idea of having been under observation.

"I didn't build the maze," Haviland told her. "I just watch. During your past . . . encounters, I was only slightly interested in the antiquities you were after; it was much more enjoyable to tag along and try to guess what you'd do next. In case you weren't aware of it, Miss St. James—"

"Call her Tyler," Kane grunted.

Haviland nodded his thanks as if Tyler had given him permission herself. "Tyler, then. Ours is a relatively small community, and among those interested in acquiring antiquities the two of you have gained quite a reputation. Your . . . antics in trying to best each other are becoming legendary."

Tyler stared at him. "Mr. Haviland—"

"Drew," he insisted courteously.

A laugh sputtered abruptly from Tyler as her sense of humor overcame anger. "This is ridiculous. This is a ridiculous situation. We're *rivals,* all three of us, and neither of you seem to give a damn!"

Haviland chuckled softly. "Not as bad as that, Tyler. You and Kane are after, I believe, a gold chalice. I was promised the other valuables in the cache. I'm the buyer Tomas had found."

"Then why aren't you waiting in Panama?" Kane asked. "Is it us you don't trust, or Tomas?"

"I knew that whichever of you returned with the cache would keep your word to Tomas," Haviland said. "But I also know that Tomas was very nervous and needed money badly because of gambling debts, so I decided to keep an eye on him. Only hours after the two of you were sent on your way, he was killed."

"Because of the cache?" Tyler asked quickly.

"No. A senseless brawl in a bar. He was too quick to pull his knife—and not quick enough to use it." Haviland shrugged. "So I set out after you two."

He could have been lying, but Tyler believed him. Like both herself and Kane, Drew Haviland had the reputation of being honest in his dealings with others in the small "community" of people interested in art objects and antiquities.

"So you want the cache, but not the chalice?" she asked him intently.

"I'd like the chalice, as well," he said frankly with a

faint smile. "But since you two want only that, I'll settle for the rest. There are supposed to be several good bits of jewelry and at least two figurines that might be Egyptian. With any luck, at least a piece or two will lack rightful owners."

Tyler had heard that Haviland was more scrupulous than some collectors, choosing to return any traceable items to museums or universities in the countries that claimed them. Like Kane and her, he refused to participate in the worldwide black market of antiquities.

In the beginning of her relationship with Robert Sayers, Tyler had twice refused to go after artifacts whose ownership was legally established; after that, he had always taken pains to assure her that whatever he wished her to find for him was legally "available" to a private collector. She never took his word for that, a fact that she made no secret of and he was ruefully amused by.

On giving her this particular assignment, Sayers had been, as Kane had described his own employer, almost stuttering with excitement. Tyler, restless because it had been a few months since her last task, had checked her sources at Interpol and various museums very quickly, and had found no mention of a gold chalice that had been stolen from its country of origin or otherwise wasn't where it was supposed to be. Her Interpol contact had merely said, "If it's part of the loot Hitler raided, Tyler, God knows if it belongs to anyone. Let me know."

And she would. She wanted to believe that Kane would also relinquish the chalice if it turned out that some country or family could rightly lay claim to it. She thought he would.

Kane was digging in his pack again. "Well, I think we should have a quick meal and then get out of here. If Valonia wants my blood, she's going to have to work for it."

Unable to stop herself, Tyler murmured, "It isn't your blood she's after."

"I know what she's after," Kane returned politely but with a gleam of amusement in his eyes. "However, if she got close enough to use a knife, she'd get blood, as well. And I still say she's going to have to work for it."

REUNITED WITH HER backpack and rifle, Tyler was able to change into dry clothing that belonged to her. The men politely turned their backs while she changed, and she silently turned hers while Kane, grumbling, got back into his damp jeans. She had a slicker tied to her pack, and Drew produced an extra one for Kane, who, for some unfathomable reason, never carried one himself despite his dislike of getting wet.

"How's the ankle?" Kane asked her.

"No problem."

"That isn't what I asked," Kane said, staring at her. "You'd walk on it if it were broken. How is it?"

She returned his stare, ignoring Drew. "Fine, Kane. There's no swelling, and not even a twinge. Satisfied?"

He wasn't. With Drew an amused observer, Tyler irritably submitted to having her ankle thoroughly examined and then wrapped tightly in an elastic bandage which was, according to Kane, "Just to be on the safe side."

Within an hour they abandoned the hollow and continued on. Tyler walked between the two men, with Kane in the lead. They were climbing steadily through the rain and darkness, and the temperature dropped as they moved higher into the mountains. A bit ruefully, Tyler found herself grateful for the elastic binding her ankle; it had begun to throb dully not ten minutes after they moved out, and she knew the extra support was needed.

Kane was always right. It was annoying as hell.

They moved in silence, with only an occasional comment or direction such as, "Watch that branch," or "Careful, the rock's slippery here." Most of the comments were from Kane.

Dawn found them well into the mountains. The rain had finally stopped, leaving a cool mist behind it, and they encountered fewer obstructions as the forest thinned out. All three of them were experienced hikers and were blessed with the strong endurance that came from active lives, so their pace was steady. They halted once, briefly, for a quick breakfast, but didn't linger.

By 10:00 A.M. Kane was moving more slowly, his keen eyes picking out landmarks as he began searching for the cave where Tomas had promised the cache to be. Their position was about a hundred miles southwest of Bogotá.

Tyler almost bumped into Kane when he stopped suddenly. She sidestepped to peer around him, and instantly recognized the area from Tomas's description. They were standing on the edge of a narrow, inhospitable valley, the floor of which was thickly covered with tangled shrubs that had crept partway up the steep slopes. Kane double-checked his compass, sighting across the valley to a high peak recognizable for its odd shape, then looked at the others and nodded.

"This is it. The cave should be on the north slope, low down with the entrance hidden behind a boulder."

Tyler studied the north slope intently, then shook her head. "All I can see are bushes." With a sleepless night and hours of hard travel behind them, she was tired, but she also knew that she would press on as long as necessary. Still, an unconscious sigh escaped her as she eased the straps of her backpack and flexed her shoulders.

Kane looked at her steadily. "All right?"

"Fine. Let's go."

She was aware of Drew behind her as they moved cautiously down into the valley, but most of her attention was focused on Kane. He shouldered his way through the chest-high tangle of shrubs, making a path for the two behind him, moving steadily. They had all removed their slickers once the rain stopped because the gleaming black garments had made them too visible, and she fixed her gaze on Kane's khaki backpack and shining black hair.

To her surprise and vague uneasiness, she felt little excitement about being so near the chalice. Granted, they didn't have it in their hands yet and, granted, there was still a long way to go before they were safely out of

Colombia, and quite a trip after that back to England. But she didn't think that was why she felt this way. She felt . . . suspended, a part of her detached and waiting, another part disturbed and uncertain.

But not here. And not now.

That was it. Kane wanted her, and if she knew anything at all about him it was that he was a fighter. What he wanted, he went after with all the strength and will in his big, hard body and tough mind. The very thought of that kind of fight between them made her legs feel wobbly.

"Watch it." Drew caught her arm firmly from behind as she stumbled.

"Thanks." She didn't look back at him, afraid of giving her thoughts away even to a stranger. This was absolutely ridiculous, she told herself fiercely. Bandits bent on murder or something worse behind them, harsh terrain all around them, a hideous trip ahead of them, her very *life* in danger, and she was worried about being seduced.

She told herself to stop worrying about ridiculous things. Five minutes later, she told herself again.

It wasn't working.

NEARLY AN HOUR passed before they were able to reach the north slope of the valley. The cave entrance itself was easy to find once they fought their way through the bushes. What Tomas had called a "rock" guarding the opening was actually a slab of granite that might have fallen from above hundreds or thousands of years before and now leaned back against the outcropping at the base of the slope. It was possible to enter the cave from only one side of the slab, where a space about three feet wide and six feet high was provided by the slant of the granite.

"No wonder this place stayed hidden so long," Tyler ventured, studying the granite door and the profuse greenery that made even it invisible from any distance.

"A nice hiding place," Drew agreed. "If Tomas hadn't stumbled onto it, God knows when it would have been found."

Kane tossed a stone into the cave, and they all listened for a few moments to make certain no animal inhabitants would be waiting inside to greet them. They shrugged off backpacks and each produced a flashlight, then Kane led the way inside.

The cave was surprisingly dry, the humidity decreasing as they moved away from the entrance. The shaft slanted upward into the hillside, but it was a gradual rise, and they had plenty of room to stand upright since the ceiling remained consistently several feet above even Kane's head. The floor was dry and sandy underfoot, and there was no indication that there had ever been a cave-in.

She wasn't claustrophobic, but Tyler was no more fond of dark caves than she was of heights. Gripping her flashlight a bit more tightly, she asked, "Didn't Tomas say this shaft was about sixty feet deep? We've gone that far already."

Kane shone his flashlight in a wide are before them

as he walked steadily forward, and responded to her over one shoulder. "Not much more than that. I think— There."

Three more steps brought them to the back of the cave, and they shone their lights on a jumble of boulders among which an iron box sat with the firm air of having been there awhile. It was about two feet square and a foot deep, and there was a heavy hasp closure; about a foot away from the box lay a battered, rusted padlock half buried in the sand.

"Let's get it outside," Kane said calmly.

Tyler remained silent while the men each grasped a handle on the side of the box and lifted it, then followed them back toward the cave entrance. She had felt the first real jolt of excitement upon seeing the box, and even though her common sense warned that there could still be disappointment in store for them, she didn't listen to it. That particular caution wasn't very strong, because Tyler was coping with an unfamiliar and disquieting sensation in addition to her excitement.

There was still the trip out of Colombia, still the journey back to England, but if the box contained the chalice then there would be nothing left for her and Kane except to decide which of their employers would get it. It wasn't a decision she looked forward to, but even less did she anticipate a return to London. Because then they'd part again.

They reached the cave entrance before she could explore that unnerving realization, and Tyler was grateful for the small mercy. She joined the two men in kneeling beside the box, and it was she who flipped up the hasp and lifted the heavy lid.

Tomas hadn't lied to them. Inside the iron box were a number of bundles wrapped thickly in burlap. Tyler unwrapped them one by one, revealing two necklaces of sapphire and ruby, a diamond-encrusted gold bangle, several intricate gold chains, three golden figurines—two of which were obviously Egyptian with the third possibly Spanish—and a chalice.

Drew examined the other artifacts one by one, but Tyler and Kane had eyes only for the chalice. It was about ten inches high from its heavy pedestal base to the lip of the cup, and wrought of solid gold. The metal had been crafted with exquisite skill and astonishing delicacy, and gleamed dully. It had obviously been handled a great deal over its life, because the warrior-figures worked so skillfully around the bowl of the cup no longer stood out in stark relief as they must once have done, as if many hands and polishing cloths had gradually worn them almost smooth. The chalice had no handles, and was very heavy.

Tyler knew the moment her hands touched the cool gold that this cup was many centuries old. She didn't recognize the style of the figures, although her instincts said they were Persian; she could barely discern at least two chariot-borne warriors, and the methods used to form those figures held a curious mixture of Greek and Egyptian styles.

She drew a deep breath and handed the chalice to Kane, saying steadily, "I'm not sure. What do you think?"

Kane turned the cup in his big hands for a moment, then upended it and studied the base of the pedestal. "Hell," he muttered.

Tyler was quick to catch the note of disappointment in his voice. "It isn't—" she began, then glanced aside at Drew a bit uncertainly.

"Don't mind me," he said without looking up from his scrutiny of the ruby necklace.

Kane said to the other man, "You know what we were hoping." And it wasn't a question.

"That it's Alexander's chalice?"

"Yes."

"I recognized it," Drew said simply.

Tyler exchanged a quick glance with Kane, then said, "What do you mean?"

Drew wrapped the necklace and put it in his backpack with the other bundles, then held out a hand. "May I?" He accepted the cup from Kane and turned it in his hands slowly, his eyes narrowed as he examined it. "The figures could be Egyptian, but there's clearly a Greek influence, as well . . . common with Persian art. And this small figure here"—he indicated one of the chariot warriors on the bowl—"is bearing a royal standard. The size and design match the descriptions I've found."

"You've searched for it before?" Tyler asked quickly.

"Paper search. The two chalices weren't always together, so it was difficult." As Kane had done, he upended the cup and studied the bottom. "It doesn't have Alexander's seal, but then, only one of the pair did."

"His seal?" Tyler was puzzled.

Kane accepted the chalice again as Drew handed it over, frowning slightly. "According to legend," he told Tyler slowly, "Alexander himself suspected poison. He wanted to mark the cup that he'd drunk from, so he had his manservant heat the base of the pedestal in the fire until the gold softened and then pressed his signet ring into it."

"You didn't tell me that," Tyler accused.

Kane shrugged. "It doesn't matter. This cup doesn't have a sign of any tampering with the base. It could still be one of the pair, of course, but I was hoping for indisputable proof."

Casually Drew suggested, "Then find the other one."

Tyler felt a surge of excitement greater than any she'd felt today. "If we could do that—"

"Where do we look?" Kane said dryly. "Considering how far this one's come from Babylon—assuming it's Alexander's—the other one could have ended up anywhere in the world, even if it still exists."

"Venice," Drew said, still casual. "Or thereabouts." He was stared at, and returned the stares with a flicker of amusement. "That paper search I mentioned. I started with the last known whereabouts of at least one of the cups, in Florence, and since records after that were destroyed I backtracked. About two hundred years ago, one chalice was in the possession of a wealthy Venetian family by the name of Montegro. Maybe theirs was the chalice that ended up in Florence. Or maybe not. I was . . . distracted by other matters at that point, so I'm not even sure if the family survives today. But if they do, it wouldn't be a bad idea to check them out. You never know, after all."

"What's your interest?" Tyler asked him slowly.

He smiled at her. "The same as always. I'd love to own both chalices. If you two do go after the other one, and do by chance find it and are able to acquire it, keep me in mind. I could probably match what your respective employers are paying, and it would be a shame to split the chalices up again."

Kane was slowly wrapping the chalice in its burlap, frowning. Tyler glanced at him, then looked at Drew as the other man got to his feet and shrugged into the backpack. "Montegro, you said?"

He nodded at her. "Worth a try." He glanced off toward the end of the valley they had entered, and said musingly, "We've probably got about six hours on the bandits. If you two head north, you should run into a road within a few miles to take you into Bogotá. I think I'll head west for a few hours; with any luck, the bandits will have to decide which of us to follow. It might delay them. But I wouldn't waste any time in leaving Colombia."

Tyler gazed at him a moment, then said bemusedly, "Why do I feel an absurd impulse to thank you after you shot at us?"

"I have no idea. But I'm sure we'll meet again." Drew grinned faintly, saluted them both casually and struck out across the valley heading west. Within minutes he was out of hearing, and was soon lost to sight.

"We should move out, as well," Kane said almost absently. "Drew was right about that road being a few miles north. If we find some transport, a truck or jeep—hell, even a couple of burros—we could reach Bogotá by tomorrow afternoon."

Tyler took a deep breath. "And then?"

Kane looked at her a moment in silence. "You want to carry this, or you want me to?" He lifted the burlap-wrapped chalice slightly.

"And then?" Tyler repeated steadily.

He half shrugged, then said somewhat tersely, "We could go to Venice."

She hadn't wanted to be the one to suggest it herself, but Tyler felt relief sweep over her. "Do you think we have a chance of finding the other chalice?"

"Probably not. But I'm willing to try."

Tyler got to her feet and shrugged into her backpack, tacitly agreeing that he should carry the chalice and watching as he put it into his own pack. She felt a return of her earlier weariness but squashed it determinedly; they had a long way to go yet, and she'd be lucky if she rested at all during the next twenty-four hours or so, much less slept.

She told herself it was that dull weariness that made her suddenly more conscious of his every movement as he stood and slung his pack onto his back, and an anguished little voice in her mind asked her what on earth she was doing even considering spending as much as a week more in Kane's company.

She was out of her mind. . . .

Kane took two steps to reach her, and lifted one hand

to push her chin up slightly. "Nobody loses if we find the other chalice, right, Ty?"

She gazed into his vivid green eyes and felt her heart lurch painfully. "Right," she managed.

His almost caressing tone became suddenly sardonic. "But we still don't trust each other. Because even if we do find the other chalice, the two of them together are worth more than anything we've ever gone after before, right, sweetheart? Think of the bonus if one of us returns to an employer with both of Alexander's legendary chalices."

Tyler felt sudden tears sting her eyes, and blinked them away. It was just rage, she told herself, rage because he took endearments like sweetheart and honey and made them sardonic or flippant, and she *hated* that.

"Right," she agreed flatly. She meant to jerk free of his grasp in a gesture of scorn and anger, but before she could move Kane lowered his head abruptly and covered her lips with his.

Shock held Tyler still beneath the onslaught, but it wasn't caused by his action. She was shocked because the first touch of his warm, hard mouth sent every last vestige of her anger spinning away like something shattered beyond repair. She was vaguely aware of a soft whimper of stark pleasure in the back of her throat as her lips parted beneath the insistent pressure of his, and when his tongue explored her mouth with hot need she swayed toward him with another mindless sound of delight.

Kane's hands dropped to her waist, sliding beneath the bottom of her backpack to hold her firmly as he pulled her hard against him. Her arms crept upward, her hands tangling in his thick hair, and she felt her body come alive wildly as it pressed against his. Her breasts ached heavily as the hardness of his chest flattened them, and she could feel the pounding of her heart and his. Instinctively her lower body molded itself to his, and even through the thick bulk of their jeans she was starkly aware of his throbbing response.

He lifted his head at last with a reluctant slowness more eloquent than words could ever be. His eyes were darkened and hot, his face taut, and when he spoke it was in a rough, harsh tone hardly louder than a whisper.

"But trust doesn't come into it, does it, sweetheart?"

For a full minute Tyler didn't know what he was talking about. She was still pressed against him, her fingers moving helplessly in his hair, her entire body aching and weak and heated, and she could only stare up at him in bewilderment. Her breath came rapidly between her parted lips, and she couldn't have spoken in those first few seconds even if she had been able to string words together coherently.

Want. It was in her mind, a seductive whisper, and in her body it was an incessant demand, like a fire burning her. But then his flat words sank into her dazed brain, and shock ran cold through her again—because he was right. Trust didn't come into it, because she still didn't trust him and . . . it didn't matter.

"Damn you," she whispered raggedly.

Kane gave an odd, low laugh and released her as her hands fell away from him. "Sure you want to go to Venice?" he mocked.

Tyler turned away from him to get her rifle where it leaned near the cave entrance, and held it firmly pointed downward despite her impulses. She couldn't control what he made her feel and that terrified her, and yet, as always, faced with a choice between running and fighting, she fiercely, even unreasonably, chose to fight. She wouldn't run from this, couldn't, even though every primitive instinct she could lay claim to told her that Kane and the emotions he evoked would always be beyond her control.

"Lead on, Macduff," she mocked in return.

A gleam showed itself briefly in his eyes, but whether it was annoyance or admiration she couldn't tell. He got his own rifle and started off across the valley, heading north.

As he pushed his way through the tangle of shrubs, highly conscious of her behind him, Kane silently cursed the bandits on their trail. He would have given much to have been able to remain in the valley with Tyler for another day or so. Or, hell, even a few hours. Her instant response had both surprised and delighted him, and even though he knew the mental and emotional battles remained to be thrashed out, he also knew that physically Tyler had more or less surrendered.

Strangely enough—and Kane found his own obstinacy baffling—it wasn't enough. Tyler was a beautiful, desirable woman, but he wanted more than just a female body responding to his in passion. He wanted that stubborn, aloof part of her to respond to him, as well, wanted her totally involved mentally and emotionally as well as physically. And he wanted her trust.

Stupid. A snowball had better chances in hell.

But at least there was more time now. He had thrown down the gauntlet and Tyler had picked it up with a flash of stubborn fire in her eyes. And he felt more than a glimmer of admiration for her when he remembered that fire. She had courage and spirit and strength—and too much of all three to run from him or from anyone else.

Anyone else . . . For the first time he wondered about the men in Tyler's past. There had to be at least a few; with her fiery beauty, she drew men effortlessly. He knew that from their past encounters. The sheik in North Africa, so fascinated by Tyler that he'd even tried to literally steal her one night—he had been philosophical about the broken nose Kane had given him, saying only that he would have fought for her, and that it was perfectly understandable that Kane had done just that.

And others, all over the world, men who had tried wooing, threats, bribery, and outright kidnapping. Tyler always seemed surprised, and always disinterested. But there had to be men in her private life, Kane thought.

Had some other man discovered the same fire and courage in Tyler? Was her wariness now based purely on her mistrust of him, or had some other man hurt her? Walls came from hurt, Kane knew that, and she quite definitely had walls.

He felt something inside him tighten, and recognized

the sensation for the first time even though he had felt it before without understanding it. He had felt it in Hong Kong when Tyler had been held captive, and he had felt it in North Africa when she had been in danger. And in all the places in between, whenever she had been in peril. He had felt like this, his chest tight and a hot rage coiling inside him, and had acted instantly and instinctively to help her.

He didn't want Tyler to be hurt, not in any way. He didn't even like to think about some man in her past hurting her, yet the question was in his mind now and eating at him. And he knew he'd get the answer eventually.

THEY STOPPED ONLY briefly through the remainder of the day, and since they had found the road as predicted the going was much easier and faster than it had been until then. It was dark by the time they neared a small town. Kane found a shelter in the tumbled remains of a deserted barn.

Shrugging out of his backpack, he said, "You wait here with the packs. Keep your rifle ready."

"Where are you going?" Tyler asked, trying to keep the weariness out of her voice.

"I'm going to look for a truck or something. We could make Bogotá by noon with some wheels."

Tyler dropped her pack to the hard dirt floor and glanced upward at the stars shining through what was left of the roof. Flexing her shoulders, she said dryly, "Try and find us a hot meal, will you?"

"I'll do my best."

They were both wearing jackets now, and Tyler drew hers tighter around her as she sat down and leaned back against one of the barn's two remaining walls. She was bone-tired, chilled and hungry, and as she looked up at the tall shadowy figure that was Kane she felt a flash of longing for the hard warmth of his arms holding her and his body against hers.

"Don't go to sleep," Kane warned.

She found a flare of spirit from somewhere. "Have I *ever* gone to sleep when I shouldn't have?" she demanded.

He chuckled. "No. I'll be back as soon as I can, Ty."

"I'll be here," she said with a sigh.

TWO HOURS LATER he returned to the barn. He had found—and bought—a rickety truck with a missing muffler and four bald tires. And, with his peculiar talent for acquiring the little luxuries of life, he had also purchased, from a bewildered family on a nearby farm, a pot of stew.

chapter six

WHEN TYLER CLIMBED out of the truck just after noon the following day in the sprawling city of Bogotá, she had only one thing to say to Kane.

"Shoot it. Put it out of its misery."

Kane grinned at her, and managed somehow to look sexy despite a heavy growth of beard and eyes reddened with weariness as he patted the rusting hood of the truck. "Don't say mean things about Trigger," he told her solemnly.

She paused a moment before dragging her backpack out to rub her abused posterior. The truck had no shocks whatsoever, and the seat's springs had a habit of poking whatever sat upon it. "I refuse to ride Trigger to the coast," she said flatly. "We can get a train or a plane out of here."

"Shouldn't be a problem," Kane agreed, abandoning Trigger without a backward glance as they moved by tacit consent down the street toward a hotel that looked as if it might be able to accommodate two weary travelers with the pesos to pay for a couple of rooms. "In fact, I have a friend here with a plane. And he owes me a favor."

In a reasonable tone Tyler said, "Even if the bandits *do* trail us to Bogotá, they aren't likely to catch up with us anytime soon, not in a city of this size. So I vote we spend the night here and head for the coast in the morning. I want a bath, and then I want to sleep for about twelve hours."

Amiably Kane said, "Fine with me. But I'd like to go ahead and make arrangements for the trip. Why don't you get us a couple of rooms, and I'll see you back here in a few hours." Before she could speak, he handed her his backpack and added, "You keep the chalice."

Tyler hadn't even been thinking about that, which surprised her more than a little. But she was exhausted, and she chalked up her unusual trust to that. Because she had to say something, she said, "We're just going to leave the rifles in the truck?"

"Better that way. We don't want to attract unusual notice by carrying guns here."

"Okay."

"Got enough money for the rooms?" He grinned a little. "No offense meant, but the way you look, any desk clerk's bound to demand the money up front."

Tyler eyed him, but decided a retort wasn't worth the effort. "I have enough."

He nodded. "Try to get connecting rooms, and leave your side open, will you? I'll need to get my stuff later, and you'll probably be asleep."

She hesitated on the point of turning away from him and toward the hotel. Connecting rooms . . . and the doors left open.

A bit roughly Kane said, "Take the damned chalice out of my pack and put it under your pillow."

Again Tyler coped silently with her own lack of mistrust where Kane and the chalice were concerned. She had been thinking along entirely different lines. I'm very tired, she reminded herself reassuringly. "Fine," she said mildly.

He stared at her for a moment, his mouth a little tight, then muttered an oath under his breath and strode away.

AN HOUR LATER Tyler stood under the lukewarm spray of a shower and mused happily about how living rough made one appreciate the simple things in life. Like showers. She washed her hair thoroughly with an herbal-scented shampoo she'd bought in the gift shop off the lobby, then soaped her body luxuriously with a soap bearing the same scent.

She remained in the shower until her skin started to wrinkle, then got out and dried off, dressing in the thick terry robe which the gift shop had also provided. She had sent every stitch of clothing she had with her to the laundry, stripping naked in the bedroom and reaching around the partly opened door to hand the stuffed laundry bag and a handful of pesos to a bemused bellman waiting patiently in the hallway.

Now she wandered back out into the bedroom, towel-drying her hair, and eyed the connecting door warily. As instructed, she'd opened her side a few inches, and Kane's pack reposed on a chair near the door. The chalice was still inside. She had idly considered taking it out, but common sense told her that Kane could find it easily if he was so inclined, no matter where she hid it. Besides, she was just too tired and sleepy to worry about it.

Still drying her hair, she went over to the window and pulled back the curtains, gazing out from the tenth-floor room at the sprawling city of Bogotá. In this basin high in the Andes, the temperature maintained an average of just under sixty degrees, so Tyler wasn't tempted to open the window. She looked out for a few moments, picking out, in the distance, the cable cars that carried tourists higher into the mountains for a bird's-eye view of the city.

Finally, too tired to think, she tossed her towel toward the bathroom, brushed her damp, tangled hair off her face with her fingers and climbed into the double bed. She had already hung out her DO NOT DISTURB sign, bolted her door and put on the night latch.

The last thing she remembered was pulling the covers up to her chin and sinking down into a too soft bed that felt wonderful.

* * *

KANE MANAGED TO make arrangements for their transport to the coast and get back to the hotel within two hours. He thought Tyler's plans for the remainder of the day had sounded dandy, and he meant to get cleaned up and fall into bed himself. He got his key from the desk clerk and went up to the tenth floor after requesting that a bellman come up to get his laundry. Like Tyler, Kane had learned to take advantage of the amenities offered by hotels, especially when there was still a great deal of hard traveling ahead of him with accommodations of the find-a-corner-and-roll-out-your-sleeping-bag variety.

The room was the usual sort, with practical furniture and uninspiring prints framed neatly on the walls and everything small enough to carry off bolted down, and he barely took notice of it. He went immediately to the connecting door and opened his side. She had left her side open, with his backpack in plain view of the door. He stepped into her room silently.

She was no more than a slender mound under the covers, and from this angle all he could see was a shimmering curtain of red-gold hair spread out on the pillow. He lifted his pack from the chair, and knew instantly by the weight that the chalice was still inside. Not, he acknowledged to himself, that it meant anything, because she had been tired, and being tired made her sweet, and vague, and vulnerable.

He stood there for a moment longer, tired and dirty and beard-stubbled, gazing at her and wishing he could crawl into bed with her. Memories of her soft, slender body against his made his loins tighten and begin throbbing, but he shook his head and retreated silently back into his own room.

The spirit was certainly willing, but the body badly needed the rest more than the recreation.

He stripped and stuffed his clothes into a laundry bag, leaving out only a clean pair of sweatpants—actually the pair Tyler had briefly worn. The same bemused bellman again accepted a laundry bag and a handful of pesos held out to him by a disembodied arm, and went away muttering to himself.

Kane found the energy to shower, but decided to shave when he woke up, and barely took the time to dry off before crawling into his own bed naked and falling asleep instantly.

When he woke to a dark room, his internal clock told him at least six hours had passed, and he felt rested and hungry. Tyler would no doubt be hungry, as well, and they could always go back to bed in a few hours; it wasn't much past ten o'clock. He turned on the lamp by his bed and then reached for the phone, calling room service and ordering enough food for a small army, along with milk and coffee.

Tyler liked milk with her coffee. Not cream. Milk.

Room service informed him it would be at least half an hour, and Kane accepted that amiably. He got out of bed and took another shower, then shaved and dressed in the sweatpants. Then he went into Tyler's room, moving silently in the darkness until he could turn on her bedside lamp.

She had moved only to push one arm out from under the covers, which had fallen down below her shoulders. She was lying on her back, dressed in a white terry robe, and the lapels had slipped open to reveal the creamy inner curves of her breasts.

He felt a rush of desire so sudden and fierce it was as if he shuddered under some unexpected blow. He could almost feel her full, firm breasts filling his hands, her slender thighs cradling him between them, her silky warmth surrounding him. His body hardened in an instantaneous arousal that made sweat break out on his brow, and he could hardly breathe.

God, how much longer could he wait for her?

Kane sat down slowly on the edge of the bed, his eyes moving from the beckoning curves of her body to the vulnerable curve of her lips and the satiny skin of her delicate face. Her long lashes made dark crescents against the softly flushed cheeks, and beneath her eyelids were faint flickers of movement as she dreamed. Around her small face, fiery hair tumbled in unruly curls, like sunshine trapped in the dimness of the room.

She drew a sudden, shuddering breath, her breasts lifting jerkily, and her mouth quivered as a soft sound escaped. It was a strange sound, like a jolt of pain so deep and dreadful it could only be voiced in a whimper. Like a shriek muffled behind locked teeth. A primitive sound, as if it came from a wounded animal.

Kane frowned, holding an iron rein on his desire as he leaned over her so that his shadow fell on her face. "Ty?" he murmured softly. "Wake up, baby."

Her reaction as his quiet, husky voice shattered the silence was instant, unexpected—and violent. The dark lashes lifted to reveal wide eyes that were blank for an instant and, focusing on the big silhouette above her blocking out the lamplight, those amber eyes dilated with sheer terror. Her face went deathly white, and her lips drew back in a soundless scream as her shaking hands jerked up, palms out, in a mindless, pathetic attempt to shield her face. She seemed to sink into the bed, as if her very terror lent her slender body weight, as if that could provide some escape for her.

"Tyler!" Kane spoke with unconscious harshness, so shaken by her response that for a moment he could hardly think. This was no nightmare, no phantom conjured by the dark, this was something all too dreadfully real . . . And then, in that flashing instant, he remembered the lightly spoken words that had seemed to mean very little—then.

"*. . . I felt helpless and vulnerable. It's—it's almost a phobia with me, feeling like that. I can't take it. . . .*"

Quickly Kane straightened so that he was no longer blocking the light, so that she could see his face. And even as the answer to his earlier mental question jarred through him, he was speaking softly again, reassuringly. "It's just me, baby. Kane. You were having a nightmare."

For another endless moment the anguished, stricken eyes stared at him between her fingers, before her hands turned to cover her face and a shudder racked her. Hesitating only an instant, Kane drew her up into his arms, holding her gently but firmly against him. She was stiff at first, and he could almost literally feel her withdrawing mentally and emotionally, but gradually her body relaxed.

She didn't cry, didn't make a sound or shed a tear, and for some reason that hurt Kane more than anything else.

Pushing back away from him finally, she lifted one shaking hand to push the tumbled hair off her face and the other to draw the robe together over her breasts. Her eyes wouldn't meet his. "Some nightmare," she said shakily.

Kane opened his mouth, but a soft knock from the door in his room stopped him from saying what he wanted to. Instead he said, "I've ordered some food. It's only a little after ten, so we can go back to bed later. Hungry?"

"Starved," she answered, her voice more steady now.

"I'll have the cart left in my room. Come on in when you're ready." He rose from her bed and went into his own room to let the room service waiter in.

Tyler threw back the covers and got up, making her way into the bathroom on trembling legs. The last dark claws of terror and pain lingered in her mind, pricking now instead of raking, and the face that gazed back at her from the mirror was white and taut. She tried to control her breathing as she struggled for composure, and the sick, helpless fear gradually faded.

Dear God, it had been so long since that nightmare had tormented her sleep. Years. And its return reminded her of what the counselor had warned her when she had said that it would probably always be with her, that it would be likely to resurface with stress or other kinds of fear.

Stress. She'd been exhausted, and the changing relationship between her and Kane had unnerved her. The latter, of course, was bound to trigger the fears that her rational mind could deal with but that her subconscious shied violently from confronting. Then she had awakened abruptly, and the starkly male silhouette above her had made the nightmare seem all too terribly real.

Tyler splashed cold water on her face and dried it. The face in the mirror was still pale, made more so by the riotous flame of her hair and her darkened eyes, but it was less tense. She finger-combed her hair and tightened the belt of her robe, then took a deep breath and went to join Kane in his room.

"Coffee?" he asked as she entered. "Or would milk be a better idea?"

Tyler managed a smile, her gaze fixed on the meal awaiting them. He had brought the chair from her room so they could both sit at the table, and she did so. "Milk, I think," she agreed. She had long passed the stage of being afraid to go back to sleep after the nightmare, having learned that it seldom occurred more than once in a single night.

Kane sat down across from her. "I tried to avoid the more spicy dishes. The *ajiaco* should be good." He indicated the bowls of thick soup with potatoes, chicken and corn. "Eat, Ty."

He said nothing else while they began eating, and

Tyler made no attempt to break the silence. Conscious that he was merely waiting, that he intended to ask questions, she was engaged in a silent battle with herself.

It did no good for her rational mind to be certain she should feel neither shame nor guilt; the emotions lingered even after all these years and despite all reason. It was always the response, she knew, but knowing did nothing to lessen the feelings. There were still remnants of helpless rage and disbelief inside her. And, if that weren't enough, she had never talked about it to a man since it happened, not once. The doctors and counselors had all been women, even the police had provided a gentle female officer to take her statement, and the grinding shame she had felt had prevented her from talking to her father, despite all his loving attempts.

And now . . . to talk about it to Kane . . .

"Who did it, Ty?"

She started slightly, but kept her eyes fixed on her plate. "I don't want to talk about it, Kane. Not to you."

That hurt him. "Tyler . . ."

Don't cross the line, she wanted to plead, but it was too late for that, they had already crossed the line between professional and personal. And if she told Kane about this, if she exposed her pain to him, nothing would ever be the same between them. If she trusted him with her pain, the only thing left to her was honesty, and that left her terribly vulnerable.

"Goddamn it, tell me."

She looked up jerkily from her almost untouched

food, and once she met his eyes she couldn't look away. His voice had been very quiet, but there was something in his eyes she'd never seen before, something hard and fierce and implacable.

"Who raped you?"

Tyler put her spoon down with infinite care and sat back in her chair. In an automatic, instinctive gesture, she crossed her arms over her breasts, almost hugging herself as his stark question evoked burning waves of shame and guilt and anger. And she didn't want to tell him, not Kane, but . . .

"I don't know his name." She heard the words emerge jerkily in a low, rapid tone. "They never caught him."

A rough sigh escaped Kane. "Tell me, honey."

Some part of her mind noted and wondered at the change in that endearment—because it *was* an endearment. Not sardonic or flippant. She vaguely remembered that he'd called her baby before, in a soft voice so unfamiliar that she had hardly recognized it.

"There isn't much to tell." The words were pulled from her by the determination in his eyes, by the taut waiting in his big body, like something primitive tugging at her. "I was on my way home from school, crossing a park. It was raining, that's why there was no one except . . . except him in the park."

"How old were you?"

"Sixteen."

Kane almost jerked, feeling that stark answer like a blow. Sixteen, just a girl who had blossomed during the previous year, probably still bewildered by the changes in her body and shy at the male glances that had grown more intent. He felt a hard, hot rage tighten around something in his chest, wishing savagely that he could get his hands on that soulless bastard for just five minutes, that's all it would take, just five minutes to break every bone in his miserable carcass.

Then he heard Tyler's low, toneless voice going on, and another nameless bastard joined the list.

"I had a boyfriend, we were going steady. When I—when I went back to school, he asked to give his class ring back. He said his friends were saying I must have asked for it . . . and that I was . . . damaged goods."

"You know that isn't true," Kane said, his voice rasping over the words.

"My mind knows. Maybe it even knew then. But the feelings . . . wouldn't go away. There were doctors and counselors to talk to me and try to help. They kept telling me rape was an act of violence, not of . . . of passion. That I'd done nothing to provoke him and I shouldn't feel guilty or ashamed." Her brows drew together in a childlike frown of distaste. "But it was a long time before I felt clean again."

Kane sat very still, watching her pale face, the distant, unfocused eyes. She looked almost frail, like something ethereal, and the wild mass of her bright hair, freed from its usual severe style, made her white face seem very small and very young. But her eyes weren't young. Her eyes were far too old. She had been cruelly wrenched out of childhood, hurt in a way no woman should ever be hurt, and the scars would be with her for the rest of her life. Even now . . .

"No wonder you can't stand feeling helpless," he said roughly.

She looked at him, focused on him. "It's been ten years. The nightmare is—rare now. There were years of therapy before I learned to deal with what happened. The fear of being helpless, that one lingered. I learned to defend myself because I never wanted to feel helpless again." Then her mouth twisted with a touch of bitter humor. "But nature didn't balance the scales, and muscle and size *do* make a difference; so I learned to carry a knife, and to handle guns."

"And to build walls. Since then, you've never let a man get close, have you, Ty?"

Just one man. But the words remained unsaid; he knew he had gotten close, he had to know, so she ignored that question. She felt driven to make him understand something else, perhaps because so much of their past had involved deception. "There was a sense of grief for a long time. Something was . . . stolen from me, in violence and pain and fear. Not just virginity, but my dominion over my own body. I was pinned in the mud and brutalized—and I couldn't stop it. *He* stopped it when he—when he was through. And left me in the mud."

"Honey . . ."

She glared across the table at his white face. "You asked, Kane. You wanted to know." Her voice was fierce.

He half nodded, an odd spasm of pain tightening his features briefly.

Tyler drew a short breath. "They say the physical healing is quickest and easiest. For me, it could have been worse. The doctors told me that. I had three broken ribs, a fractured arm, assorted bruises and cuts and— tears. I healed. As good as new. Almost. But he took something I can never get back. *My choice.* It should have been my choice. In the backseat of a boy's car, or in a bed, or behind the bushes at some party—it should have been my choice." She heard her voice thicken with grief and rage, staring across the table at Kane's face through a shimmering veil of tears she couldn't shed.

Before he could speak she drew another breath, this one longer and deeper, and her voice steadied. "I had no control over what happened to me. For months after- ward I couldn't bear to be alone, not even for a moment, and I felt helpless about everything in my life. I hated that, hated what he'd done to me. It was like putting my- self back together one piece at a time. It took me years to feel like a whole person again."

After a long moment Kane said slowly, "And now you—court danger. Try to control it."

Tyler shrugged a little, a weary gesture. "I don't know. Maybe. Maybe I need to face all the fears he left me with. I've learned to fight."

"And now you're fighting me." Kane leaned forward a little, his very posture insisting on an answer. "But *what* are you fighting in me, Ty? When I hold you and touch you, you aren't afraid. You want me as much as I want you. So it isn't sex. What? What are you fighting in me?"

She felt painfully vulnerable in that moment, and if she had not taught herself to be a fighter she would have run from his question because sure safety lay only in that response. But she was a fighter. And these last days had given her the truth of her violent response to Kane, a truth she could no longer avoid. Honesty was all she had left, and how ironic that honesty was her last defense against Kane.

"Tyler . . ."

With a twisted smile, she said, "He stole something I can never get back, Kane."

Kane's face hardened and his mouth went grim. "And you believe I'll do the same?"

"You have before." She held up a hand when he would have responded, and said, "Oh, I know those things we went after weren't really important. It was a game, and we both played by the rules. Rivals, enemies. But it's different this time, and we both know why. This . . . between us, it's personal, not business. Somewhere along the way, we crossed over the line, and the rules have been shot all to hell."

"Trust," Kane said flatly. "That's what it comes down to. We can be enemies without it, partners. We can even have sex without it, because we sure as hell have the desire. But we can't be lovers."

Tyler hesitated, then met his eyes with all the steadiness she could muster. "Maybe you don't want a lover, just the sex. No emotions, no . . . connections. But I can't risk that, Kane. Not for myself. I can't risk seeing myself in pieces again because the choice was stolen

144

from me. It has to be an emotional choice, not a physical one."

Kane found it ironic that Tyler was just now confronting the knowledge he had faced days ago. Physically he could arouse her past the point of no return, and they both knew that. But he had also known, days ago, that the choice had to be Tyler's, that he couldn't steal what she wasn't willing to give.

A little harshly he said, "I want more than sex, Ty. I can buy sex on a street corner. I want you."

She felt her body respond to his grating voice and the demand of his desire, and a tremor shook her. Very softly she said, "I don't want an enemy in my bed, Kane. Or a rival. I'm not even sure I—I want a lover. But we both know I can't control what you make me feel. If I give in to those feelings without making a conscious choice to do that, it'll be as destructive to me as it was to give in to that man because I wasn't strong enough to fight him."

"No," Kane said. "It's different."

"Not to me. It's the truth, and what I feel."

Kane felt as if he hadn't drawn a deep breath in hours, but he did now because his chest was hurting. He leaned back in his chair and let the breath out slowly, but the dull ache wouldn't go away. There was something wrong with this, something that didn't fit, but he couldn't make it come clear in his mind. He believed that *she* believed what she was saying, but his instincts told him it was wrong somehow.

After a moment he stirred and said with deliberate

dryness, "So you need to make a clear, rational, logical decision to take a lover."

Tyler felt heat flood her cheeks, although she couldn't have said why. "It isn't as cold-blooded as you make it sound," she objected.

"That's just what it is. Tyler, by its very definition, physical desire is something we don't control—it controls us. It's a drive, an instinct millions of years old, it isn't a logical thing." Keeping his voice deliberate, he went on, "So what happens if you coolly decide at some future date that you're ready to take a lover—and the desire isn't there? Will you just find some likely candidate because you'd rather betray your body than your mind?"

The flush drained from Tyler's face, and she stared at him. "No! I'd never . . ."

Kane went on as if she hadn't spoken. "We've got—what?—a few weeks ahead of us at best? Then we go our separate ways, with or without the second chalice. You back to London, me back to the States. And maybe we'll run into each other six months or a year from now. Or maybe not."

"So it's now or never, is that what you're saying?" Her amber eyes had begun to glitter with anger. "Lust today, for tomorrow we may die?"

He didn't have to force his grin. As always, he had found the quickest and surest way of angering her. This was the Tyler who would fight him on a level where he stood a chance, and he felt no remorse at needling her. Her guarded posture had altered to become stiff annoyance; rage had chased the shadows from her eyes and she looked like a cat about to hiss and claw at him.

In a mild voice he said, "You're the one who has to make a choice, Ty. It's up to you. I was just pointing out one of your options."

Her glare narrowed. "Well, you made the point."

"Good." He nodded briskly. "Then why don't we finish eating and get some more sleep. Tonio wants to leave before nine in the morning."

Tyler blinked, then picked her spoon back up and began eating the cool soup. He had shaken her off balance again, damn him. Determined to keep that knowledge to herself, she managed to hold her voice calm and steady. "Tonio? Your friend with the plane, I assume."

"Right. He's going to fly us to Santa Marta. Where, you'll be interested to hear, there's a cargo ship now loading. Her destination is Greece."

She stared at him as an uneasy suspicion prickled in her mind. "Don't tell me."

"Afraid so. Dimitri's ship." Kane smiled a little, but said, "Sorry, Ty, but it's the only ship heading in the right direction, and it *will* take us all the way to Italy."

Tyler lost her appetite. She put down her spoon again and took a drink of her milk. "Great. That's just great. I'll have to spend days on a ship that should have sunk from sheer age a decade ago, being leered at by a crew of pirates, and listen to Dimitri try and entice me away from you—because of course I'll be pretending to be your woman again."

They—actually, Kane—had created that particular

fiction on their previous trip aboard Dimitri's infamous ship, after Kane had caught one of the crew trying to creep into Tyler's sleeping bag in the middle of the night. Kane had thrown the sailor overboard, which might have been a little drastic except that he could swim and Dimitri stopped long enough to fish him out of the Mediterranean. After which, Kane made a brief trip from bow to stern, telling every man on board with a chillingly mild smile that the next one who dared to touch his woman would be dead before he hit the water. And he made the promise in fluent Greek, to avoid future misunderstandings.

"It worked the last time," Kane murmured.

Tyler admitted that silently. The leers had continued—out of Kane's sight—and Captain Dimitri had tried his hand at verbal persuasion, but she hadn't been forced to defend herself. She had been somewhat amused at the time, and realistic enough to have shrugged an acceptance of Kane's protection; she disliked having to depend on any man for anything, but the cloak of Kane's fictional possession had allowed her to sleep nights, and at that point the rest had more than made up for the blow to her pride.

Besides that, Kane had an odd habit of defending her honor, something that had at first enraged her and, later, bemused her somewhat. And no matter how many times she'd told him to let her get herself out of sticky situations prompted by unwanted male attentions, he had never listened to her. After a while she had resignedly accepted his actions, attributing them to his occasionally primitive instincts; she had never stopped to wonder why he was so protective of her, and she didn't want to wonder about it now.

"Unless you have a better idea?" Kane added.

"No." She sighed. "This will be a much longer trip than before, and I don't fancy sleeping with a loaded gun and one eye open." She drank the last of her milk and pushed her chair back. Getting up, she said, "What time are we leaving here?"

"I'll order breakfast for seven. That okay?"

"Fine." She went toward her room, but paused in the doorway as Kane asked a quiet question.

"Will you be all right?"

He meant the nightmare, she realized, and nodded. "I'll be fine. Good night, Kane."

"Good night, Ty."

She went into her room, leaving the connecting door open a few inches, and crawled back into bed. She turned off the lamp on her nightstand and lay in the dark room listening as Kane pushed the room service cart out into the hallway and then returned to bed himself.

Tyler couldn't fall asleep immediately, even though the nightmare had disturbed her sleep before and left her feeling something less than rested. She was still tired, but couldn't seem to close her eyes. Thoughts met and tangled in her mind, snatched at by emotions so that nothing made sense.

She didn't regret her honesty with Kane, because he seemed to have understood. But he had also, quite mildly, made it plain that if he were going to be the lover she "chose" she'd better be making up her mind about it. And even though she had known she was raising a last defense against the desire between them, his mild acceptance had disturbed, and even hurt her. Not because she didn't trust him not to push her—she did, oddly enough. But because . . .

Because he didn't seem to care terribly about the matter. He wanted her, yes. That was obvious, and he certainly made no secret of it. Or at least he had made no secret of it up to now. But then he had spoken of the distinct possibility of not seeing her again for six months, a year—ever—without so much as a flicker of emotion in his voice or on his face. Nor had he even implied that if they were to become lovers they wouldn't, afterward, go their separate ways.

That seeming indifference and total lack of a commitment of any kind should have shored up her resistance to him, but instead, angrily conscious of an echo of shame, she couldn't help but wonder if Kane was another man with no taste for . . . damaged goods. He wouldn't have expected her to be a virgin, but a sexual history that consisted entirely of a single brutal memory might well present a hurdle he wasn't eager to attempt.

Tyler felt a throb of pain, and even as it ebbed dully she refused to examine the cause. She told herself fiercely that it would be best if Kane lost interest, best for them both. They could cross back over that stupid line and be rivals again, and know the rules. The safe rules.

It was almost dawn when she crept from her bed and went into the bathroom. She closed the door and turned on the light, then shed her robe and turned on the shower. The water was hot, and she stood under it for a long time, soaping and rinsing her tense body over and over again.

IT WAS JUST over an hour later when Kane pushed open the connecting door to find Tyler fully dressed in jeans and a flannel shirt and sitting on the bed as she braided her hair into its accustomed neat style.

"Breakfast is on its way," he offered, then noticed the plastic-wrapped clothing lying over the dresser by the door.

"They brought your clothes up as well when I called down for mine," Tyler explained.

Kane looked at her for a moment, then picked up the clothing and said, "Let room service in if they come before I'm out of the shower, will you?"

"Sure." She wasn't looking at him.

He retreated, frowning a little. She was aloof this morning, and he didn't like it. Was she regretting, now, a painful confession sparked by a nightmare? He had forced himself to be deliberately low-keyed, even though he had ached to hold her in his arms and comfort her, to wipe away the remembered anguish. But she had been on the thin edge of control, and he hadn't dared take advantage of that. So he had needled her instead, and her own temper had steadied her.

He had lain awake long into the night thinking, studying the germ of a realization. But he didn't know quite how to handle the conclusion he was left with. It *was* Tyler's choice, whether they became lovers, it had to be after what she'd gone through. And yet the terrible experience that made that choice so vital was blinding her, he thought, to the reasons for her own reluctance to take that step.

He had to make her see—and he couldn't afford a mistake in doing that. She had stubbornly and courageously taught herself to face all her fears except one. But that one was the most devastating, and it sickened him to think of an act of violence so terrible that it remained an open wound on her spirit even after ten years.

Kane saw the irony of it. If he hadn't begun as Tyler's enemy, there would never have been a question of a personal relationship between them. On the personal level, she was far too guarded, too aware of attempts to get close to her. If he had met her simply as a man attracted to her, she would have run—and rationalized her reasons. But they had met in a dangerous situation, immediately rivals and even enemies, and having neatly assigned him that place in her life Tyler had felt safe.

Until this encounter. Until awareness as heated as the steamy jungle had surrounded them. And, too late, she had realized that her enemy was a man, and that he had gotten too close. She couldn't run; she wouldn't let herself fight, not the way she needed to fight.

"Hey, breakfast." The announcement was accompanied by a rap on the bathroom door.

"Coming." Kane finished shaving, then got an iron grip on his patience and went out to join her.

chapter seven

THREE DAYS LATER Tyler leaned somewhat gingerly against a rusted railing and gazed off across a dull gray expanse of ocean, her loose hair blown back from her face by the steady breeze. The sun was hidden somewhere behind the clouds, not yet below the horizon. It was just a lull in the storm, she knew, but she had taken the opportunity to go up on deck and get some fresh air.

The cabin she and Kane occupied was hardly worthy of the name, having been stripped of all its fixtures years before, but it was the only empty cabin, and held the added advantage of being on the opposite end of the ship from the crew's quarters.

With an eye to the main chance, Dimitri had long ago converted the cabins to storage space and carried, in addition to his legitimate cargo, a number of crates and boxes that would never pass through customs. In any case, since Dimitri never smuggled drugs or guns, officials tended to more or less ignore him. And he rarely carried passengers. When allowed on board at all, they were expected to make the best of scanty accommodations.

Kane had done his best, and with his scrounging talents his best wasn't bad at all. He had firmly taken possession of the small cabin before Dimitri could stuff it full of cargo, and had managed to bring aboard a thick mattress to provide extra cushioning against the steel-plated deck. With their sleeping bags laid atop the mattress, the bed was reasonably comfortable.

They actually had a small bathroom with a tiny shower to themselves, and if the mattress took up most of the floor space in the cabin and there was no porthole, at least they had privacy and a door with a working lock.

The crew remembered them, but Kane nonetheless repeated his announcement of so long ago. He had also been extremely possessive of Tyler, remaining close to her almost all the time and offering the crew few opportunities to leer. And Captain Dimitri wore a disgruntled expression on his florid face after Kane had several times frustrated his attempts to entice Tyler.

As for the only woman on the ship, she was all too aware of ragged nerves and a pain she didn't want to explore. Kane had returned to his old mocking self when they were alone, and that coupled with his public possessiveness—blatantly for show—had served to steadily reinforce her belief that there was no longer a choice for her to make. Kane had made it himself.

Tyler might have salvaged something, self-respect or pride, but their enforced intimacy left her trapped with him. They slept in separate sleeping bags, but shoulder to shoulder on the mattress, and the body he had awakened ached long into the night.

She wasn't looking forward to the coming night, because they had hit rough seas for the first time and, though it was calm now, the forecast promised more rough weather within hours. Tyler was a good sailor, but the thought of her being tossed into Kane's reluctant arms while the ship heaved beneath them was one that made her feel sick.

"Where's the watchdog, missy?" Dimitri's voice was jovial, but there was a touch of wariness, as well.

Tyler straightened from the rail and turned to him, thinking for the tenth time that the captain of this heavily laden vessel looked more like a young Santa Claus than a smuggler. His tightly curling hair and beard were black, his dark eyes gleamed merrily, and his cheeks were like polished apples. He was portly, though surprisingly light on his feet, and his accentless voice was caressing when he spoke to her, bland when he addressed Kane, and a bullhorn bellow when he was ordering his crew.

Replying to his question, Tyler said dryly, "Where you should be, Captain. On your bridge. He went to check on the weather up ahead."

Dimitri gestured expansively. "We won't be into the

rough until after midnight, missy. It's just a low-pressure system, nothing to worry your pretty head about."

Tyler didn't bother to point out that hurricanes originated in low-pressure systems, and she ignored the caressing tone. He was far more dangerous than he looked or sounded, but she wasn't afraid of him. Then she saw Dimitri's eyes widen fractionally as he gazed past her toward his bridge, and wasn't surprised to hear Kane's mild tones.

"Hello, Captain. Taking in the scenery?"

Dimitri smiled widely at him, murmured something about a course change coming up, and sidled around the much larger man as he made his escape.

"I can handle him, Kane," Tyler said, turning to face him. "I'm not afraid of him."

Kane's face, so impassive these last days, tightened suddenly. "Yeah, I know. You aren't afraid of any of them, are you, Ty? Just me."

She automatically grasped the rail for balance as the ship wallowed heavily between one trough and another, staring up at Kane. "I'm not afraid of you!" she flared.

"No?" He laughed harshly. "Every time I get within two feet of you I can see you stiffen. What's that if it isn't fear?"

The ship rolled again, and Tyler used the movement as an excuse to turn away from him. "I'm going below. I feel queasy."

"You don't get seasick," Kane retorted, following as she made her way through the jumble of crates Dimitri had chosen to lash to his decks.

"I might this time," she muttered, moving through an open hatch that would be bolted shut if the weather worsened. The hallway was narrow, and worn iron steps led down into the dimness of the cabin area. Tyler found her way more by memory than sight, since Dimitri had removed most of the lights along the hallway.

The light was on in their cabin; it was a large hurricane lamp that Kane had brought on board, and not subject to Dimitri's habit of turning off electrical lights to save power. Tyler took a step toward the mattress, and the door thudded shut behind her as hard hands grasped her shoulders and turned her around abruptly.

"I can't take any more of this, Ty. We have to talk. I'm not going to let you bury your nose in one of those books you bought before we left port, not this time."

Tyler was holding on to her control with every last ragged shred of her pride, and the strain was obvious in her thin voice. "There's nothing to talk about, Kane." She lifted her chin and managed a bright smile. "You've made your choice, and that's fine. Sorry you have to be penned up here with me, but—"

"What?" He stared down at her, frowning. For an instant he had no idea what she was talking about, but then it hit him. Struggling with his own worry about how to handle her fear, he hadn't stopped to consider that she might view his careful distance as a rejection. But she obviously had, and he realized now that he couldn't have picked a worse time to draw back no matter what his reasons were.

She had told him about being raped, about a boyfriend

who had considered her "damaged goods," and Kane
had withdrawn from her physically. God, he should have
held her then, comforted her the way he'd wanted to.

"I don't blame you," she said in a light tone that
didn't hide the stark control. "Really. I—"

"Hell," Kane growled, and abruptly slid his hands
down her back to her hips. He yanked her against him,
widening his legs and holding her against him so she
could feel the hard ridge of desire. "Does that feel like I
don't want you anymore?" he demanded roughly, ignoring the hands that were braced against his chest. "You've
been driving me crazy since the day we met, and nothing's changed that."

Tyler caught her breath as he moved against her and
heat bloomed deep inside her. She was staring up at
him, at the vibrant green fire in his eyes, and the fierce
need she saw there made her body tremble with desire
and relief. But even then, she was fighting the feelings,
holding her upper body away from him and struggling
to control the wild sensations inside her.

She opened her mouth to voice a desperate protest,
but Kane's head bent and his lips covered hers. And this
time he took her mouth, possessed it with deliberation,
his tongue invading with an utter certainty of her response. She couldn't smother the moan as pleasure
jolted through her, or prevent her hands from sliding up
to grip his shoulders convulsively.

The protest was still there, in her mind, but the response of her body to him was overwhelming and she
was helpless against it. When he finally lifted his head,

she was trembling, shaken, her breath coming swiftly.

Kane drew a deep breath, and for an instant held her even more tightly against him. Then he drew away and guided her to sink down on the mattress. He saw her eyes widen, but he made no effort to press her back onto the sleeping bag, to continue what he'd started. Instead he sat down and leaned back against the bulkhead, saying nothing until his own breathing steadied and he could speak in a careful, even voice.

"You have to face it, Tyler."

She drew her knees up and wrapped her arms around them, staring at him. She felt baffled and uneasy. "Face what?"

"Your fear."

Her chin lifted. "I told you before—I'm not afraid of you! I hate that, I hate being afraid—"

"I know." His voice remained steady. "That's why you can't admit it to yourself. It's the one fear you've never been able to fight. Even to face."

Only vaguely conscious of a flicker of panic, she snapped, "It isn't fear. I just don't trust you, that's all."

"You do trust me, Ty, when it counts. When it matters. You've slept in my arms, trusting as a child, and unconscious certainty is the deepest kind. All the tricks in the past, they were part of a game we both played, and that *didn't* matter."

"Kane—"

He went on inexorably. "Then we crossed that line you were talking about, and the games were over. I'd gotten too close, and it was too late for you to run. You found out you couldn't control your need for me, and it scared the hell out of you. So you decided that you didn't trust me, and didn't want an enemy in your bed. A defense, Ty. A mental defense against something you couldn't physically control."

"I was telling the truth!" she cried.

"You tricked yourself," he said flatly. "Don't you see? It isn't mistrust. It's what happened to you ten years ago. Your body's forgotten the pain, but your mind hasn't. And you can't make the choice you *need* to make—until you face the reality that you're terrified of sex."

Tyler felt as if he'd hit her. She drew in a breath sharply, staring at him. "No. No, you said that wasn't it. You said the way I—the way I responded to you meant that wasn't it."

"I was wrong." His voice had softened. "The body heals and forgets pain, but the mind never does, Ty. It never forgets pain or fear unless it's taught to." He sighed roughly. "Honey, you've taught your mind to fight everything else that bastard left you with. You've learned to defend yourself, to face danger coolly, to overcome all the fears—except one."

"It was an act of violence." She was very cold, and her voice shook. "Not sex. I know the difference."

"How can you?"

The soft question was stark in the quiet of the cabin, and the motion of the ship was slight. There was no excuse she could grasp now, no distraction to avoid facing this—truth. She sat stiffly, her eyes burning with the tears that had never been shed, and his low voice was shattering the last, deepest defense, the one she hadn't even been consciously aware of.

"Ten years, Tyler. You're a beautiful, desirable woman, and in ten years you've never let a man close enough to touch you."

"You," she whispered.

"I was an enemy, not a man." His lips quirked in an odd smile. "I was . . . safe."

To label Kane "safe" was the most absurd thing she'd ever heard, but Tyler understood what he meant. All the violently negative emotions he'd stirred in her had blinded her to the reality that he stirred positive ones inside her, as well. Until it was too late. Until the needs of her body and her emotional confusion had made escape impossible.

And now . . .

Kane hesitated, hurt by the frozen whiteness of her face, the blank desolation in her eyes. Primitive terrors were the most deeply buried, corroding fears of all, and after ten years Tyler was confronting the worst, most primal fear a woman could ever face. She had been so young, so vulnerable in her shyly awakening womanhood, and an act of violence had changed her life forever.

She stirred suddenly, her face still frozen, and began very methodically removing the rubber-soled shoes she'd bought in Santa Marta. In a queerly conversational tone, she said, "I think I'll go to bed." She tossed the shoes aside, her eyes flickering around the tiny cabin as if she were looking at it for the first time. "It's going to storm again anyway. Get off my sleeping bag, will you, please? I want to—"

Kane reached out and grasped her shoulders, making her look at him. "Tyler . . ." he said gently.

She stared at him, and her shoulders moved under his hands as her steady breathing became ragged. The blind look in her eyes became something else as they filled with tears, and when the tears spilled, her frozen mask shattered.

"He hurt me." Her voice was little more than a whisper, but it held both the uncomprehending anguish of a child and the dreadful agony of a woman. "He hurt me . . ."

Kane pulled her into his arms and held her cradled across his lap. He stroked her soft hair and murmured a wordless comfort, even though she couldn't have heard him over the raw sobs jerking her body. The sounds seemed to claw their way out of her like something alive and vicious, muffled against his chest, and she clutched his shirt as if that were her only lifeline.

When she was finally drained and limp, he found his handkerchief and gently raised her chin. She was silent as he dried the last of her tears, her eyes fixed on his face with some emotion he couldn't read lurking in the amber depths.

"Why did you do that?" she whispered huskily. He had dried her tears, she thought vaguely. She had sworn no one else would ever do that for her, but he had.

"What?" He smiled a little.

She drew a shaky breath. "Make me . . . face that."

He was silent for a moment, still holding her across his lap and fighting a growing consciousness of her soft weight. Then, a bit roughly, he said, "You were cheating both of us, Ty. Running instead of fighting." One big, warm hand surrounded her face, and he held her eyes intently with his own. "And it's my fight, too. I earned the right."

Something inside her acknowledged that, accepted it. They had fought so often and in so many ways, sparring, snapping, mocking, competing with each other; together they had fought outside threats, back-to-back and side-by-side. They had fought fairly and with trickery, loudly and in silence. They had fought, finally, to this point. All the years of therapy and counsel had failed to uncover her deepest fear, yet Kane had fought his way past all the barriers she had desperately flung up, and had found it.

She swallowed hard. "I—I don't know if I can."

He stroked her cheek gently. "You can. The only question is if you trust me enough. I won't hurt you, Tyler. But you have to trust me not to."

She managed a shaky laugh. "I think this is where I came in."

He smiled, but his eyes remained intent. "No. This is different."

She knew that, and if she hadn't the look on his face would have told her. He wanted her, but he was waiting, leaving the choice up to her. Very deliberately, he was putting control of the situation in her hands, asking for her trust but not demanding it. And it was the basic kind of trust between a man and a woman, the kind that was all that really counted in the end.

Her enemy . . . Suddenly, as if it had always been there, she made the distinction. She had never trusted Kane as a rival, and possibly never would, but she trusted him as a man. Trusted him enough to put her life in his hands on more than one occasion, enough to sleep in his arms without a qualm. She trusted him enough to tell him what she had never told a man before, to share her pain and shed tears no one else had ever seen. But she didn't know if that trust was strong enough or deep enough to conquer a primitive fear.

"Tyler?"

She wondered, vaguely, if there had ever been a choice to make. It wasn't logical or rational or reasonable. It probably wasn't even sane. But for the first time in her life she wanted a man, and that desire was the only possible means of fighting her fear.

"I want you," she whispered.

His eyes darkened in an instant response, and the hard arm under her shoulders raised her until he could kiss her. His mouth was warm, the small possession of his tongue slow and gentle. He seemed totally absorbed in kissing her, taking his time, exploring her mouth while his fingers stroked her cheek lightly.

Tyler felt her body heat and begin to tremble, and there was no fear in her mind, just a vague uneasiness. There was no threat, not now, just slow waves of pleasure. Tentatively her tongue touched his, her mouth opening wider for him, and the heat built inside her. She felt him lift her, still kissing her, and her arms went around his neck as he eased her back onto their bed.

She drew a shuddering breath when he finally lifted his head, her eyes flickering open dazedly as she looked at him. He was lying beside her, raised on an elbow, flaming eyes fixed on her face. His other arm lay heavily across her middle for a moment and then shifted as he slowly began unbuttoning her shirt.

A flare of panic made her gasp. "Kane—"

"Shh." He kissed her again, deeply, and again until pleasure drowned the panic. Her shirt was opened, and when he raised her gently she helped him by automatically pulling her arms out of the sleeves. He unfastened her bra as he eased her back down, slipping it off and tossing it aside before she could react.

He had been concentrating fiercely on moving slowly, but when the scrap of lace covering her breasts was gone it was all he could do to hang on to his resolve. She was beautiful, just as he'd known she would be, and the sight of her round, firm breasts, the coral nipples tight and hard sent a shaft of pure flame through him. He bent his head and drew one hard bud into his mouth while his hand moved to surround the other breast, his thumb rasping gently over the nipple beneath it.

Tyler gasped again, this time wordlessly, as her body arched in a helpless response. The burning pleasure was instant, spreading outward in ripples of sensation that stole her breath and clouded her mind. All her consciousness seemed focused only on what he was doing to her. The erotic suction of his mouth was a caress like nothing she'd ever known before, and her body responded to it with a wildness she couldn't begin to control. She was on fire and couldn't be still, her head moving restlessly, her legs shifting, pressing together in a mindless attempt to ease the throbbing ache that kept getting worse, stronger, until she thought she'd go mad with the awful tension.

She was so wrapped up in the sensations, so totally involved in her awakened body, that it seemed perfectly natural to lift her hips when he unfastened her jeans and pulled them and her panties off. But her eyes opened wide suddenly, and an inarticulate cry of alarm escaped her when his warm, heavy hand began to ease her legs apart.

"Easy, baby," Kane murmured huskily. He shifted his hand to her quivering stomach and rubbed gently while his mouth caressed her breasts, and gradually he felt the stiffness ebb. His hand slid lower, settling over the soft red-gold curls, then remained there, unmoving, waiting.

Tyler's frightened memories of cruel hands and brutal force faded, even as the burning need of her body intensified wildly. He was so close . . . so close . . . Instinct demanded that she open herself to him, and with a shudder her body obeyed as her legs parted. She felt a burst of raw pleasure as he stroked her gently, and a moan jerked from her throat. The inferno inside her burned out of control and she couldn't be still, couldn't think, couldn't do anything except give in to the blind, primitive drive toward release.

It seemed to last an eternity, tension spiraling until she could hardly bear it, and then her senses shattered, her body shaking and throbbing violently in a powerful wave of ecstasy.

Tyler was hardly aware of the gasping sobs that escaped her as she lay trembling in the stunned aftermath of that explosion. Her eyes opened slowly, finding Kane as he rapidly stripped off his clothes and tossed them aside, and her breath caught when he returned to her. She hadn't expected—somehow she hadn't known he would be so beautiful. But not all the beauty of rippling muscles and easy grace could hide the raw power of his big body, the male strength she could never match.

"I won't hurt you, Ty." His voice was low and a little rough, but the hands stroking her body were gentle, and despite the burning hunger in his eyes he was clearly in control.

"I know." She heard herself whisper that, and didn't question the truth of it. Still, she struggled to overcome the panic when he widened her legs gently and eased between them, when his big body rose above her. Helpless . . . God, there was no other position that left a woman so utterly vulnerable, pinned in place by a strength she couldn't fight.

Kane braced himself away from her, responding to the fear in her eyes even though his need for her was tearing him apart. His entire body ached, rigid with the effort of control, and her body was ready for him, moist and warm, waiting to accept what her mind feared. She was unconsciously holding him off, her hands trembling against his chest while her breasts rose and fell with the jerky gasps of panic.

He lowered his head and kissed her deeply again and again, murmuring, "It's all right, baby . . . it's all right." Carefully, he eased into her, giving her time to accept him, watching her face as her body's willingness and his own care fought against her fear. Her eyes were wide, but the fixed look slowly disappeared as her body accepted him without pain. Desire was stirring again in the amber depths, and her hands stopped holding him away as they slid up to his neck.

"Kane," she murmured, as if assuring herself that it was him, that she had nothing to be afraid of.

He murmured her name in return, assuring her that she was no nameless victim but a woman desired. Slowly he let her feel more of his weight, but braced himself on his elbows. She responded by lifting her hips slightly, tentatively, her eyes drifting half shut as the mat of hair on his chest rasped her sensitive breasts and her body accepted him completely. Her breathing was steadier now, deep and slow.

The silky heat of her was tight around him, and Kane gritted his teeth as a hoarse groan rumbled in his throat. His control was threadbare, and only the fierce need to make certain of her pleasure allowed him to move slowly and cautiously. He fixed all his will on arousing her to the peak she had reached only once before, kissing her, stroking her body as he thrust gently.

And the intense satisfaction he felt as she came alive beneath him made the strain worthwhile. Her soft little cries and throaty moans deepened his own taut pleasure, holding him on the ragged edge of exploding until purely sensual shivers like nothing he'd ever felt before feathered along his spine.

He was deep inside her when the hot inner contractions of her pleasure caught him wildly, and he heard her wordless whimper even as a rasping groan tore free of him and his own tension snapped with a fury that shuddered through him.

When he could think again, Kane didn't want to leave her, but he knew he was heavy and wasn't about to risk a return of her instinctive panic. He raised himself slightly to look down at her, then gently kissed the lips that were curved in a wondering, bemused smile. Her eyes were closed, her face softly flushed. Her eyes opened slowly to gaze up at him, and glowing in the amber like something trapped in resin for eons was the sensual exhaustion of female satisfaction.

"You're beautiful," he murmured, his own eyes gleaming with the dual pleasure of an equally satisfied male body and a somewhat arrogant male mind.

Sleepy humor widened her smile as she saw and recognized that look for what it was, and a ghost of a laugh escaped her. "If you start crowing," she murmured in a warning tone, "I'm going to start carrying my knife again."

He couldn't help but grin down at her. "A gentleman never crows," he told her, wounded.

A mock frown drew her brows together. "What's that got to do with you?"

"Cat." Kane kissed her again, then gently withdrew from her. She didn't try to hold him, but willingly returned to his arms when he got them both into his sleeping bag. He reached out with a long arm to turn down the lamp still burning a foot or so from the mattress, and the tiny cabin was lit only by a dim glow.

He hadn't noticed the motion of the ship until then, but realized that it had grown a bit rougher; the storm was building outside. It didn't disturb him, since he and Tyler were both good sailors. They'd probably sleep through the worst of it, he thought, unless the ship sank. And it wasn't likely to sink, not with cargo aboard; Dimitri wouldn't allow that.

He felt a little sigh escape Tyler, and his arms tightened around her; she was already asleep, he knew, her slender body boneless in that way that never failed to make something inside him turn over with a lurch. He thought back to the first days of this trip, when he had wondered if taking her would be enough, if he could afterward forget her. He had thought it unlikely even then; now he knew that he would never be able to forget Tyler.

And he was uneasily aware that after this there was just no predicting her attitude toward him. She was staunchly independent, and the rueful conversation of minutes before had told him only that she intended to be matter-of-fact about this new turn in their relationship.

He knew only too well the risk he had run in forcing her to confront her fear, and the question lingered in his mind now. Tyler had chosen this, but had she done so out of desire and deeper feelings for him—or simply because she was a fighter and it had been the only means to conquer her fear?

He didn't know. But as sleep tugged at him, his arms remained firmly around her and his last conscious thought was a grim resolve he didn't examine very closely because it simply *was*.

The fiction had become fact. She was his woman now. Partner, rival, enemy . . . lover. And he meant to make certain she recognized that as well as he did.

TYLER HADN'T SLEPT well the last few nights, but that night she slept deeply and dreamlessly until past dawn. She didn't know another day had begun when she woke in the cabin that boasted only artificial light, but she thought she'd slept for a long time. The cabin was stuffy enough so that Kane had left the sleeping bag unzipped, and she slipped away from him cautiously.

How on earth had she ended up on top of him? Bemused, not quite certain what she was feeling about all this, she concentrated on not waking him, and a glimpse at the luminous dial of his watch told her it was nearly seven. In the morning. He didn't stir when she left him, which surprised her since he usually slept with the lightness of a cat. Still, he was no doubt tired. . . .

Tyler felt herself flushing. Swearing silently, she

KAY HOOPER

collected the clothes that had been flung all over the floor. She put yesterday's shirt and underwear aside, then dug into her pack for a clean shirt and panties, and the small zippered pouch that contained her toothbrush and a few other items. The bathroom was tiny; her elbow was brushing the musty shower curtain when she closed the door behind her. An experimental flick of the light switch caused a dim bulb to flicker awake.

She didn't look at herself in the cracked mirror over the tiny basin, but quickly put her hair up with the big barrette she kept in the pouch, and then took a hasty shower. She tried not to think about the difference in her body this morning, but it wasn't really something she could ignore. There was a faint soreness in her muscles and deep in her body, and her very flesh felt sensitized, as if all the nerve endings were closer to the surface.

When she finally faced her reflection in the mirror, she saw that her lips were fuller, redder, even now, hours after his hungry kisses. She saw her eyes go distant at the memory, and muttered to herself as she got her toothbrush from the pouch. She brushed her teeth, and put the brush away, then pulled a small plastic case from the pouch and stared at it.

Kane had been right in his belief that she had never let a man get close in ten years, but both Tyler and her doctor had been practical in considering her unusual lifestyle, and she had been on the Pill for the last few years. Since Kane was always careful to give her as much privacy as possible, she'd been able to keep to her schedule without his noticing. But there had been a couple of days without her pack. . . .

Well, there was nothing she could do now but wait. Her periods were irregular, not even the Pill had changed that, but she thought another couple of weeks would provide the answer.

The carefully matter-of-fact thought shattered suddenly, and Tyler realized dismally that it wasn't going to work. She couldn't be bland about this, couldn't accept with casual ease the fact that she had a lover. She could pretend with Kane, but not with herself. It wasn't casual, not to her.

Kane was her lover. And the single inescapable reason he was her lover was that she loved him.

Automatically Tyler finished in the bathroom and then crept out into the cabin. He was still asleep. She put her things away, then eased out into the hallway and headed for the ship's galley, more to be moving than because she was hungry. On deck she paused, drawn to the rail by the clear sparkle of an ocean washed clean by the storm she had slept through.

When had it happened? she wondered vaguely as she stared out over the water. She knew things about him that only dangerous situations could reveal, things the average person could learn about a lover only after a lifetime, if then. Yet she didn't know the simplest facts of his life, his background. He could make her angrier than any man she'd ever met, yet he had been the one who had put the last broken piece of herself back into place and healed what another man had done to her.

Tyler drew a deep breath and turned away from the rail, heading once more for the galley. It didn't matter when it had happened. Or where, or how. It didn't even matter why, because it was nothing she could change. She was in love with Kane.

WHEN SHE ENTERED their cabin an hour later, Kane was just coming out of the bathroom. He was wearing jeans but was barechested, and had obviously just shaved.

"You're supposed to leave a note on the pillow," he growled.

Tyler set a thick mug on the upended crate wedged into a corner; they'd been using the crate as an occasional table. "I'll remember next time," she responded calmly. "I brought you some coffee, but I thought you'd rather go to the galley for breakfast. Nikos is a surprisingly good cook, but he doesn't deliver and I hate carrying trays."

Kane took a step and pulled her into his arms, kissing her hungrily. Her hands slid over his chest and up around his neck as she melted against him, and when he raised his head at last to stare down at her she was heavy-eyed and a little breathless. He moved his hands down to her hips, curved them around her firm buttocks as he held her hard against him, letting her feel his desire for something other than breakfast.

She cleared her throat in an uncertain little sound, and said with a stab at lightness, "This is going to sound like a ridiculous question, but you're not married, are you? I mean, I draw the line at getting involved with married men."

His lips quirked slightly even as his hands shifted to begin unbuttoning her blouse. "No, I'm not married."

"A girl in every port, I suppose?" She was trying to keep her voice steady and having little luck. He opened her blouse to bare her naked breasts, and when his hands closed over them gently all the strength drained out of her legs.

"Only the ports where I found you, baby," he murmured.

Tyler lost interest in the conversation for the time being. The response of her body to him no longer shocked her, but the swiftness of it, the instant need for him, disturbed her on a deep level, and she knew why. Because it was casual for him, an appetite to be satisfied, and if he displayed the control and skill to make certain she was with him all the way, well, that was only the mark of an experienced, unselfish lover.

But right now she didn't care about that, she didn't care about anything but the touch of his big hands, his mouth on her, his body hard against hers. She was dimly aware of clothing falling away from them, her desire escalating so rapidly that she was whimpering when he lowered her to their bed. And when he gently spread her legs and settled between them, her panic was only an echo shunted aside instantly by need.

She wanted him now, wanted him with a burning hunger that was a starving thing because she loved him and this was all she could have of him. Her arms wreathed around his neck and she moaned when she felt the slow, throbbing push inside her. Wildfire was burning her nerves, her senses, he was filling her with himself and it was more than she could bear. Her legs lifted to wrap around his hips and she writhed suddenly with a strangled cry as her pleasure peaked in a stunning explosion of sensation.

Kane held her tightly while she shuddered, astonished and delighted by her capacity to enjoy what she had feared for so long, her wild response driving his own desire higher. The tight, hot clasp of her body shattered his control, and he slid his hands beneath her, lifting her to meet each deep thrust. He barely heard himself groaning hoarsely as she held him with her slender legs, her arms. He could feel the ebbing tension inside her begin to build again as she instinctively matched his rhythm, so attuned to him that she was rushing toward the peak again. And this time they reached it together, hurling over the rim of something that was almost insanity.

IT WAS A long time later when Kane raised himself on an elbow beside her and gazed down at her. Her eyes were closed and one of her hands rested on the arm lying heavily beneath her breasts, her body totally relaxed. God, she was incredible. He had considered it something of a miracle that she had trusted him enough to accept him as a lover, both because of her fears and their stormy past relationship; her total response to him, abandoned and uninhibited, was nothing short of staggering.

The satisfaction he found himself was unlike anything he'd ever known before, yet the moment he caught his breath and looked at her, he wanted her again. And it was more each time, deeper and stronger, something that edged into savagery.

"What are you thinking?" she murmured without opening her eyes.

He drew a deep breath and somehow managed to make his voice light. "I'm wondering how much Nikos would charge to deliver," he said. "Otherwise, we're going to starve."

Her mouth curved, but before she could laugh Kane covered her lips with his.

chapter eight

A CITY FOR lovers. From the balcony of their hotel room, Kane could see the bell tower in St. Mark's Square and, beyond, the mouth of the Grand Canal. Venice was lovely, the weather clear and cool, and for two days he and Tyler had enjoyed a rare taste of first-class accommodations while they performed the necessary research to chase down Drew Haviland's paper search to the second chalice.

Kane went back into their room and settled into a comfortable chair by the bed, watching Tyler. She was lying on her stomach, maps and notes and papers spread out across the wide bed, propped on her elbows as she frowned down at the open book between them. Her hair flowed around her shoulders like wildfire, glowing in the late morning sunlight that came in through the open balcony doors.

"Interesting family," she commented absently. "And the name dies with the present contessa. It's a pity."

They had indeed found a surviving member of the Montegro family, but only by marriage; the contessa, in her sixties, had been American-born and had married Stefano Montegro thirty years before. She had been a widow raising a young stepson, but had never borne a child of her own. To all intents and purposes, the Montegro name had died with Stefano ten years ago.

"There's the villa," Kane reminded her. "According to our information, it's been in the family hundreds of years, and she inherited it."

Tyler looked across at him suddenly, her amber eyes bright with interest and speculation. "It says here that when Hitler's goons looted the area, they were mad as hell to find just a few trinkets in the villa. Think the family hid their valuables?"

"I would have."

"A secret room?" she suggested.

"Maybe. But the chance of it still being stuffed with the family silver are slight. It's been more than forty years, and the family hasn't been what you'd call rich for the last twenty. Stefano may have been a hell of a guy, but he was a rotten businessman. If the contessa wasn't a stubborn woman, she would have sold the villa years ago."

Tyler returned her gaze to the book. "I don't know; how many people could afford to buy Palladian villas these days? A hotel chain, maybe, or a crazy billion-aire."

Kane didn't offer a response, but merely watched her absorbed face. He had found himself doing that often since they'd become lovers a week ago. He had seen the slow change in her, the gradual blooming of a woman accepting and finding pleasure in her own womanhood. And it had been a slow thing, despite, or perhaps be-cause of, her instant response to him physically. In his arms she was a deeply sensual woman, but she was only now accepting his presence as a lover; she was no longer self-conscious while dressing or undressing around him, no longer tentative about touching him, or elusive after waking in bed with him.

He was delighted with the changes in her, but he was also aware that she was still matter-of-fact about their relationship, and clearly considered it one without ties or promises. When he had belatedly brought up the sub-ject of birth control, she had assured him calmly that there was no problem, she was on the Pill. And when he had casually asked if she'd thought about moving back to the States, she had merely replied that she enjoyed London and felt no inclination to move.

He thought of his ranch, thought of returning there alone, without Tyler, and he didn't like the hollow feeling it left him with. Maybe it was unfair to want her to give up her life in London and live with him, but, hell, there were museums in the States where she could work as a consultant if she wanted to work, and it would be easier to move her out of a flat than it would be to abandon a ranch he'd worked ten years to build. She was *his,* damn it, he felt that certainty in his bones, and he had no intention of letting her get away from him.

"It says here," she said in that absent tone, "that the contessa's involved in historical preservation. I wonder . . ."

Kane wasn't thinking of the chalice, or of the contessa or her villa, or anything but Tyler. She was lying there on her belly, wearing one of his shirts that just barely covered the seductive rise of her bottom, kicking her bare feet in the air slowly, and he was coming apart just looking at her. God, he was worse than a horny teenager with sweaty hands, always wanting to touch her, to grab and hold on tight.

He rose from the chair before he was even aware of it, taking two steps to the bed. He used one arm to sweep the clutter of notes and books and maps carelessly to the floor, then turned her onto her back in a single motion. Tyler looked up at him with eyes that were briefly startled, but they held no panic now, there had been no panic for days. The surprise vanishing, her arms slipped up around his neck, and her legs moved to cradle him as his weight settled on her.

"I thought we were going to have lunch in St. Mark's Square," she murmured.

"Later," he growled.

THEY MISSED LUNCH, but Kane promised her dinner in the Square instead, which was fine with Tyler. They shared a shower, and then she left him shaving in the bathroom while she sat on the tumbled bed wrapped in one towel and drying her hair with another one. She listened to the sound of water running, her absent gaze moving to the phone, settling there.

Think of the chalice. It was something she reminded herself of often, using that businesslike focus to keep her balance and avoid any suggestion of clinging to Kane. It had become a virtual litany by now, a toneless exhortation aimed at the part of herself that ached to cry out her love and hold on to him with all her might. Because she couldn't do that, couldn't cling to him. Couldn't tell him she loved him.

He'd said nothing to indicate she was anything more than an enjoyable bedmate, and if there was a new look of satisfied masculine possessiveness in his green eyes, it was doubtless only because this conquest hadn't been easy and the male animal was always triumphant after such a chase. His passion would burn itself out, probably soon, because a fire so hot had to be refueled eventually by emotions deeper than desire.

And then he'd say good-bye or, as in their past encounters, simply vanish out of her life.

Dear God . . .

How many women had loved him? She could imagine, but tried not to because the images evoked feelings so primitive she could barely hide them from him. He was a consummate lover, virile and skillful, arousing her to a degree she'd never believed possible, satisfying her utterly. She didn't want to believe it was a normal thing to him, an average thing. That other nameless women had seen his vivid eyes blaze with hunger, felt his hands tremble, his body shudder in pleasure, heard that electrifying raspy sound of stark need in his low voice.

Think of the chalice.

She lost herself in him, and it was growing harder and harder to make herself separate from him afterward. The feeling of oneness was so overwhelming it was as if her flesh, her very bones, became a part of him. No longer only a brief but intense sensation during his lovemaking, that affinity caught her unawares at odd moments, stealing her breath as she looked at him or felt him moving out of her sight.

Think of—

The water was turned off in the bathroom, and Kane came into the bedroom buttoning his shirt. "A gondola ride," he said.

"What?" She was proud of her tone, a little blank, slightly amused.

"You've been here before. Ever taken a gondola ride along the Grand Canal?"

"No," she admitted, tossing her second towel aside and finger-combing her damp hair.

"Good. After dinner, we'll take one." He eyed her with a slight lift of one brow, which managed to convey a world of exaggerated masculine patience. "And since you're not ready yet, I'll go arrange everything and come back for you."

Tyler returned his gaze for a moment, then took the

bait mildly. "You men have been using words to that effect for far too long; it's high time you stopped getting away with it. I would have been ready ages ago, but *you* got my hair wet."

He grinned. "So I did." He bent and kissed her with slow thoroughness, then said, "I'll be back in a few minutes, baby," and left their room, whistling softly.

She stared at the closed door almost blindly until her breathing steadied. Baby. Caressing, not sardonic or flippant. But he probably called all his women baby, and—

Damn it, think of the chalice!

Tyler fixed her gaze on the phone and made herself think safe, painless professional thoughts. The only way to visit a private villa, she mused, was to be a guest. An invited guest. Which was a bit difficult when you were a stranger. Unless, of course, you were able to produce impeccable references and had a good reason for wanting to visit the villa, a reason of which a contessa interested in historical preservation might approve.

She didn't hesitate, but immediately picked up the phone.

"I WANT YOU."

The words were low, barely above a whisper, but the sound of them went through Tyler like an electrical current. Her head tipped back against his arm as she looked at him, and the current was pulsing, beating with hot blood, roaring inside her. Not here, she wanted to say, because the gondolier was so close and they were in an old gondola floating quietly along an older canal, and even though it was dark, they weren't alone.

She couldn't say it, couldn't make a single protest. It didn't matter where they were, because the searing force of the current was lashing her. She stared into his eyes, helpless, burning, mindless, his. She wanted to plead with him not to do this to her, not to leave her with nothing, and in the same breath beg him to take her until she was drained, empty, until there was nothing left.

Kane's glittering eyes dropped briefly to her trembling lips, then lifted again, trapped her, mesmerized her.

"Say it," he whispered.

She knew what he wanted, knew he wanted her to admit that he could take her here and now, that she wouldn't be able to stop him. That she couldn't control this need he had created in her, it was like a drug she couldn't do without. She was lost and they both knew it, rudderless, adrift. She held on to him, trembling, because there was nothing else.

"Say it." The demand again, whispered, raw.

"Yes." It was almost a sob, a sound of defeat and triumph, an admission she had to make. And if that admission sent pain piercing through her, it was only because it meant so much more to her than it did to him. To him it was simply an affirmation of his power over her, the sexual prowess that left her totally helpless in his arms; to her it was an acceptance of a truth that freed her from ten years in an emotional prison.

She had battled fiercely to control her life after what had happened to her, swearing that she would never again be powerless because she wasn't strong enough or fast enough or brave enough to fight when she had to. She had fought Kane with all she had, layer after layer of herself, with every ounce of strength and will she could command—and she had lost. But in her defeat, she gained something she hadn't expected. One man had taught her the bitter anguish of defeat, and with that had changed her life; Kane had taught her the proud glory of surrender, and with that had freed her spirit.

"Yes," she whispered again, her shaking body pliant against the hardness of his.

Kane's lips touched hers with the lightness of a sigh, and then he silently drew her head to his shoulder and just held her. But she could feel the heat of his big body, the faint tremors of something held so tightly it shook with strain. Beneath her hand on his chest, she felt the hammering of his heart, as if he'd run some endless, dreadful race.

Had it meant that much to him? Could simple desire so powerfully affect an experienced man like Kane? Tyler was blind to the old buildings rearing on either side of the canal, and she didn't notice the dark, musty scent of a city like no other in the world, a city built on water. She was nourishing a tiny spark of hope, a longing so deep in her heart it was wordless.

Neither of them said anything, and Kane didn't let go of her in the gondola or in the motor launch that returned them to their hotel. And as soon as they were in their lamplit room, still without a word, he stripped her clothes off with the single-minded determination of a male animal intent on possession. Tyler was so shaken with desire that she couldn't help him rid them of the clothing, couldn't move at all except when he moved her.

For the first time he was a little rough with her, hasty, almost wild, as if waiting even seconds was more than he could stand. She didn't care. As always, she was instantly ready for him, desperate for him, clinging to his shoulders as he kneed her legs apart and entered her with a powerful thrust. Tyler arched beneath him with a moan, wrapping her legs around his hard hips, her nails digging into the muscles cording his shoulders.

Kane dug his fingers into her hair, holding her head still as he kissed her hungrily, taking her mouth with the same primitive urgency with which he took her body. It was a mating, quick, primal, their bodies relentless in the blind drive for satisfaction.

AN UNEASINESS PRODDED Kane, and he responded to it by raising himself on his elbows and beginning to ease away from Tyler. He was heavy, pinning her, and he was still reluctant to risk any return of her panic in that. Always before, she had made no protest when he left her, but this time her legs tightened around him.

"No." Her voice was husky. "Stay with me."

He could feel the ebbing tremors of her body, faint aftershocks in her flesh. He lowered his head to kiss her swollen lips, the flushed curve of her cheek. God, she was so beautiful, her face glowing, the eyes that opened slowly holding a luminous amber fire. And secrets. He could rouse her to passion, even to surrender, hurl her into the same frenzy that gripped him, but her thoughts were still a mystery to him.

"What are you thinking?" he muttered, because he was going crazy trying to find a way across the distance between them.

"Nothing. I'm not thinking at all." Her hands moved over his back slowly, her nails scratching lightly in a tickling caress.

"Think about me," he ordered, conscious of a wry smile tugging at his lips.

Her long lashes veiled the amber eyes even more. "I'm feeling you," she murmured. "Isn't that enough?"

No. But he didn't say it. Instead he began kissing her again, wanting her again with a hunger that grew and grew until it was a living thing inside him, clawing, desperate. It was a long time later when he finally got them both under the covers and reached to turn out the lamp.

TYLER WAS AWARE of two things when a buzzing disturbed her sleep; that they'd left the balcony doors open last night, and that Kane's shoulder was wonderfully comfortable. She murmured a complaint when her pillow moved, then worked an elbow beneath her and levered herself up slightly as his voice woke her fully and she realized he had answered the telephone.

"Just a minute." He took the receiver away from his ear and looked at her, his mussed, shaggy hair and morning beard making him look unbelievably sexy. "For you. Keith Dutton?"

Tyler stared at him blankly for a moment, then remembered. "Oh. Right." She sat up, shivering as the chill of the room struck her naked flesh, and snatched the sheet up to cover her breasts as she took the phone from him. "Keith?"

"I gather," he said politely, "that I just woke up Kane Pendleton."

She felt herself flushing, which was ridiculous. "I told you he was with me," she muttered.

"You didn't tell me he was in your bed." Before she could respond, Keith's tone became plaintive. "And after North Africa—to say nothing of your other encounters these last years—you swore you'd kill the man if he ever crossed your path again. Over and over, you kept swearing that. I distinctly remember you mentioning slow torture or, failing that, both barrels of a shotgun."

"Yes, well. Things change," she offered lamely.

"Obviously. I guess it was bound to happen, though. When you rub two flints together, you've got to expect a fire sooner or later. You picked the right city for it; it can only burn down to the waterline."

"Very funny."

His voice lost part of the mockery and became at least halfway serious. "Watch out that you don't get your fingers burned, Tyler. The scars last a long time."

"I will." That warning, she thought, had come far too late. She didn't look at Kane, but was very conscious of him lying beside her.

"Sorry, but I feel a certain responsibility, kiddo. After all, I dandled you on my knee."

"You did not," she said indignantly. "Cut it out, will you? Do you have any news for me?"

"As a matter of fact, I do—"

Kane watched Tyler's face as the quick flush faded and her expression became absorbed. She was just listening now, giving away no clue to the conversation. Who was Keith Dutton, and how the hell had he known how to contact Tyler? Was he here in Venice, or back in England? How long had he known Tyler?

Kane knew there had been no other man in her bed, but that certainly did nothing to ease the sudden, fierce stab of pain he felt. That note of easy familiarity in her voice when she had spoken to Dutton told him this man was close to her, perhaps in a way that he himself could never be, a mental or emotional closeness. Did Dutton know the enigmatic part of Tyler, the secrets in her eyes? Had he fought with her? Had he loved her helplessly for years just like—

Kane looked at her, at the morning light bathing her in gold as she sat in the bed with the sheet held to her breasts, the smooth flesh of her back bare to his gaze. Her glorious hair tumbled around her shoulders in silky curls, a gleaming mass of living fire. He saw the clean, delicate bone structure of her profile, the graceful line of throat, the stubborn chin, the slender, seemingly fragile body. And suddenly he couldn't breathe, suddenly she was so beautiful it broke his heart.

He reached out a hand slowly, touching her warm back with just the tips of his fingers because he needed to touch her, tracing the straight, deceptively fragile line of her spine upward. She moved under his touch, a sensuous ripple like a cat being stroked, unthinking, instinctive pleasure.

He loved her. He had always loved her. Under the stifling sun of Cairo, he had met—no, clashed—with a woman of caged fire. In that ancient, dusty city, she had glared at him, her bright eyes spitting fury, her magnificent body stiff, and he had been lost from that moment.

Had he sensed then that she was wounded, that she would have clawed and bitten like a cornered animal if he had tried to step closer? He wasn't sure. Maybe. Or maybe it had been his own unconscious resistance to the emotions she'd roused in him that had made him willingly accept the role of enemy and not look beyond that for so long.

She was talking, now, to that man on the phone, her voice quick and eager, but Kane didn't take in the words. She was his physically, a passionate bond of the flesh that she willingly accepted, yet her heart and her thoughts, those secret thoughts, she wouldn't allow him. He didn't know how to reach her there, in her solitary places. But he had to find a way, somehow, because if he lost her now it would kill him.

"Kane—we're in!" She leaned across him to cradle the receiver, and his arms kept her there. She squirmed a bit, yanking the covers up over her shoulders. "I didn't know Venice was so cold in October," she muttered. "Kane—"

"Who's Keith Dutton?" he asked, feeling his pulse quicken with instant desire as her hard nipples, chilled and tight, rubbed against his chest.

She snuggled into his warmth, but her voice was rapid and businesslike. "He's worked for museums all over the world—the Palazzo Ducale this year—and I thought—"

"Who is he?" Kane repeated.

Tyler pursed her lips at him, not quite a pout, clearly impatient. "I've known him for years; he worked with my father on several digs. The point is that I thought he might know the contessa, so I called him—"

"When?"

"While you were arranging for the gondola ride." Her voice quavered just a bit when she remembered that electrifying trip along the canal, then steadied. "He *does* know her, and he's fixed it up so we've been invited to spend a few days at the villa. Isn't that great?"

Whatever reaction she'd expected from Kane, it certainly wasn't the one she got. She could feel his body stiffen, and watched in bewilderment as his eyes narrowed.

In a grim tone, he said, "In a hurry, Ty?"

"We've learned all we can here," she pointed out, wondering what in the world was wrong with him. "We have to get inside the villa, and it isn't open to the public."

"What's the plan?" His voice was still hard.

Tyler was completely off balance by then, and getting mad about it. "Keith and I decided that the best way"—she broke off as he sort of growled, then went on defiantly—"to get invited by the contessa was to use our own credentials. I can have references telexed from half a dozen museums, and since you have two separate degrees in archaeology—" She interrupted herself this time to say sweetly, "So *nice* to hear that from Keith, by the way."

"You never asked," Kane muttered.

She glared at him. "The contessa thinks we're researching some of the old Venetian families, and the Montegro library is stuffed with family books and papers. Keith says she's wanted to get somebody in there to catalog everything for years, but her stepson always talked her out of it. Anyway, he's out of town for a few days, so the timing couldn't be better."

"We aren't going to catalog her library," Kane said flatly.

"Of course we aren't." Tyler jerked away from him and sat up. "We'll try to find some mention of the chalice and we'll snoop around the villa. What the hell's wrong with you, Kane?"

"Nothing." He flung the covers back and got out of bed. Their clothing was scattered across the room, and he muttered to himself as he found his briefs and jeans, and stepped into them.

"I get it," she snapped angrily. "It was *my* idea, that's why you're rumbling like a thundercloud."

"You know better than that," he growled, zipping his jeans.

"Then, what?" Tyler had forgotten the chill of the room in the heat of her baffled fury. She was kneeling in the middle of the tumbled bed, gloriously naked, and held her hands wide in a gesture of bewilderment. "If you want to fight, that's great. Glad to oblige. Just tell me what we're fighting *about* so I can gather my ammunition!"

Kane turned to stare at her, and a sudden rueful grin pulled at his lips. "Baby, your ammunition would stop an army in its tracks."

Tyler glanced down at herself, then jerked her furious gaze back to his. "Damn you, Kane—"

"Here." He tossed her his shirt. "Put that on."

She shrugged into the shirt, fastened a couple of the buttons, then looked at him. In a tone of absolute astonishment, she said, "Are you mad about Keith?"

Kane wondered which would be the safest admission: that the other man's very name made him grind his teeth together, or that it hurt him to see her so eager to complete the "business" ostensibly keeping them in Venice—and together. After a moment he went to the bed and sat down, eyeing her. "Tell me he's sixty-five and doddering."

Her anger gone, still gazing at him in surprise, Tyler cleared her throat and murmured, "No. Thirty-five or so. Plays tennis."

"Damn," Kane said.

"You weren't jealous?" she ventured.

He looked reflective. "Well, I could be wrong, but I think that's what it was. Is."

"Why?"

"He knew you before I did," Kane said simply.

Tyler didn't quite know what to make of that. Jealousy didn't necessarily indicate caring, not in a man as innately possessive as Kane seemed to be. But she could hope, even though she wasn't willing to let him see that wistfulness.

"Oh." She cleared her throat again and made her voice cool and dry. "Dog in a manger, Kane? Well, never mind, it isn't important."

"Isn't it?" His voice was silky. He watched a baffled frown draw her brows together, but it was a fleeting expression and she shrugged.

"No reason it should be. Look, don't you agree that we have to get inside the villa? We have to check out the family history and see if there's mention of the chalice. Because even if we don't find the second one . . ."

"We may discover that our chalice legally belongs to the Montegro family," Kane finished. He would have been wishing both chalices in hell by now except that the first one had brought Tyler and him together, and the possible existence of the second one, he was beginning to believe, was the only thing keeping her with him now. How much time did he have before she left him?

"We have to make sure," she said. "The chalices have been split up so many times, only one of them may have been in the family. But which one? Keith says that the Montegro library has family journals at least two or three hundred years old; if we can't find the answer there, we won't find it."

Kane leaned back on the bed, resting on his elbow. "Agreed. And you got us invited to the villa."

"Keith did."

If Kane hadn't known his jealousy had made no impression on her, he would have suspected her of deliberately needling him. But there was no guile in her clear amber eyes, and her tone had been absent.

"And," she went on briskly, "we're expected sometime this afternoon. We have to go shopping, both of us."

He knew what she meant, but he wasn't in the mood to be reasonable about this. "Why? We're supposed to be researchers; the contessa won't expect us to show up in designer clothes."

Tyler raised her eyebrows at him. "She won't expect us to show up with backpacks, either. And I don't know about you, but I'm ready for something other than boots and denim."

"Your vanity's showing, Ty."

She stared at him for a moment, her face completely expressionless, and then slid off the bed gracefully. With the total calm that generally heralded a storm, and a very sweet smile, she said, "Either you badly need a cup of coffee, or else you're determined to pick a fight. As I said before, glad to oblige if you want to fight, but you'll have to tell me what we're fighting about. In the meantime, I'm going to take a shower and go shopping."

Kane remained where he was until he heard the shower, then pushed himself up off the bed. What he felt for Tyler, the helpless love and fiery desire as well as the grinding uncertainty, was making him as edgy as a bear fresh out of hibernation; all his senses were quivering, and he was hungry, impatient. He *wanted*. He wanted Tyler, all of her, and the only hold he had on her was so damnably unsure it was driving him crazy.

He shed his pants and briefs, then joined her in the shower. She turned to him, her eyes glittering, and as he pulled her wet body into his arms she might have whispered, "Bastard." Kane didn't care what she called him, because her arms were around him, her hard-tipped breasts rubbing against his chest, her soft belly and loins yielding. He didn't care what she called him because his mind was fixed on the compulsion to make her his so utterly that she could never leave him.

TYLER WAS STILL feeling a bit shaken by the interlude in the shower late that afternoon as their rented car left Venice behind. Shaken and confused, and fighting not to hope too much. If Kane's desire for her was going to burn itself out, she thought, it would have to do so with the fury of a nova, because it certainly hadn't diminished. In fact, with every day that passed he seemed to want her more, his hunger urgent and unhidden.

But he was . . . different. Always before, Kane's temper had been fierce but, like a storm, soon over and forgotten. He'd never been a man to brood, and if he was mad she always knew why. Yet for the last few days, he had been moody, unusually terse. And unusually volatile, cheerful one moment, inexplicably angry or darkly passionate the next.

She wanted to hope that his brittle temper meant something, but she was afraid that what it meant was that he was growing restless or uneasy. That despite all her efforts not to cling, he was beginning to feel trapped by her—and his own desire.

"You're very quiet," he said suddenly.

They were heading north where, about twenty miles away, lay the small town of Treviso and the Palladian villa belonging to the Montegro family.

"Just thinking," she responded. Tyler hadn't had much time to think since the morning. Shopping for clothes and the like had taken time, even though she and Kane had separated and met back at their hotel with their purchases.

"The contessa dresses for dinner," she'd warned him as they were about to split up.

"Black tie?" he'd muttered with all the reluctance of a man who viewed formal dress as the social equivalent of a straitjacket.

"There's no time to be fitted—and you'd have to be," she had said, eyeing his broad, powerful shoulders. Kane had given her a look she couldn't interpret to save her life, but had merely said that he'd meet her back at the hotel in two hours.

Now, watching his profile as he handled the car expertly, Tyler had the feeling that he'd managed to acquire a dinner jacket despite the scant time, just as she had expected. He had looked mildly satisfied with himself, and had been carrying a garment bag in addition to a large suitcase. Like Tyler, he had found and bought used bags, and like her he had packed everything as it had been purchased.

Remembering the shopkeepers that had bemusedly watched her filling her own garment bag and suitcase, Tyler found herself acknowledging, for the first time, that she and Kane were really somewhat unorthodox. They had wandered around Venice wearing denim and khaki, even in the best restaurants and their fine hotel, and neither of them had thought about it. Nor had they been denied entry anywhere at all, no matter what the dress code.

Tyler looked at Kane's big, powerful body, relaxed behind the wheel of the car, and wasn't terribly surprised that no snooty head waiter had challenged them. Even now, wearing dark slacks and a white shirt instead of the rougher attire she was accustomed to, Kane possessed an aura of primitive strength that didn't invite careless confrontations, especially over unimportant things like dress codes.

"How did the contessa strike you?" he asked suddenly, sounding restless. Tyler had called her just after lunch.

"Very American," she replied dryly.

Kane sent her a glance. "How do you mean?"

Tyler reflected for a moment. "Well, I know she's lived here in Italy for thirty years, but I'd swear she just left Alabama. Pure Southern drawl. Very gracious and welcoming. She said she was sure we'd find plenty of interesting information in her library, and that she hoped we could stay at least several days, longer if possible."

He glanced at her again, his eyes probing hers, intent. "Did you happen to mention to her that we wouldn't need separate bedrooms?"

"I didn't have to bring up the matter." Tyler couldn't help but laugh a little, even though all her senses were straining to read each nuance of his deep voice, searching for the meaning in every glance. "She was very brisk about it. 'Two bedrooms, my dear, or one?' I said one, and she said fine."

"Good," Kane said.

Tyler hesitated, and her own uncertainty made her blurt, "I wasn't really sure that's what you wanted, but—"

"What?" This time, his glance was very readable because it was utterly incredulous.

She shrugged defensively, controlling a leap of hope. "For all I know, you've got some stuffy job as a professor back in the States."

"What the hell does that have to do with anything?"

"Well, a hotel is one thing and a private home something else. The academic world tends to be fussy about the reputations of its professors. Maybe you wouldn't want it known that you were shacking up—"

Kane whipped the car violently onto the shoulder of the road and stopped, then turned in the seat to stare at her. His eyes were glittering dangerously, but his voice emerged very quietly. "I have a ranch, Ty. In Montana. I don't teach. And I don't give a sweet damn if the whole bloody world knows we're lovers. Understand?"

She nodded, a bit wary. She would have felt on safer ground if he'd yelled or snapped; that deadly quiet was unnerving. Holding her own voice steady and calm, she said, "I just didn't want you to feel . . . obligated. I didn't automatically assume you'd want to share a room, and I wanted you to know that."

"Assume it from now on."

Tyler couldn't discern any emotion in his voice, and so the command did nothing to ease her uncertainty. She managed another shrug. "Everything ends, Kane." She was trying to tell him she wouldn't cling, wouldn't hold on if he wanted to leave her. When. When he wanted to leave her. She tore her eyes away from his hard, compelling face and stared through the windshield. "Shouldn't we be going? I said we'd be there by four, and—"

His fingers bit into her jaw as he turned her face back to him, and he caught her gasp as his lips covered hers. He kissed her with a slow, dark hunger, a stark possessiveness, sliding his tongue deeply into her mouth, his big hand moving down to hold her throat caressingly. His free hand grasped one of hers and carried it to his thigh, guiding her fingers until she felt the hard ridge straining beneath the fabric of his pants.

A stab of pure heat jolted through Tyler, her entire body reacting wildly to his desire, and she trembled under the force of it.

Kane lifted his head, staring down at her with glittering eyes while his hand held hers firmly against him. "God, you make me crazy," he muttered thickly, a savage bite in his voice. "Not everything ends, Ty. Some things last forever."

When he released her hand, she drew it slowly away from him, feeling feverish, fighting the driving urge to go on touching him. She watched dazedly as he pulled back onto the road, and when he hauled her to his side she didn't even try to resist.

For the first time she realized that Kane was caught as surely as she was; the anger in his voice had told her that. And she'd been right in thinking that his desire would burn itself out only with the fiery explosion of a nova.

The flame between them could very easily end in destruction.

chapter nine

THE VILLA ROSA had, astonishingly, survived the
World War II air raids that had badly damaged the town
of Treviso. It perched on a hill outside the town, with
the Alps rising behind it, and the classical Roman temple design of its massive single porch made it look like
a place of rest for the gods at the foot of Olympus. It
had a low dome at the center of the roof, Roman statu-
ary adorning the porch and the corners of the house, and
extensive grounds that were lovely even in their un-
kempt state.

It was a ruin of a place, worn by its four centuries of
existence and yet still standing despite wars and pollu-
tion and the constant erosion of nature.

Getting out of their car at the foot of the steps leading to the templelike porch, Tyler studied the place,

comparing the dignity of this decaying grandeur with the bland modern glass-and-steel highrises now sinking their impersonal roots into the earth and their snouts into the clouds. If any of those monotonous buildings stood in four centuries, she thought, who would care?

"It's a shame, isn't it?" Kane murmured, joining her as he shrugged into a dark jacket.

Tyler nodded, reaching up absently to straighten his collar. "I was just thinking how little original style is left in the world. It all seems to be old and falling into ruin."

"Not all of it," Kane said.

Tyler was about to ask him what buildings he was thinking of when the heavy front door opened and a somberly dressed old man peered out at them. Kane took her hand in his and they went up the steps to the door. The old man nodded at them, his blue eyes bird-like with interest but his lined face impassive, and when he spoke it was in the clear, precise tones of an English butler. The kind of butler, Tyler reflected, that, like the villa, was a product of a lost way of life.

"Miss St. James, Mr. Pendleton. Welcome to Villa Rosa. The contessa and Mrs. Grayson are waiting in the drawing room. This way, please." He stepped back and opened the door wider.

They entered the villa, and both Tyler and Kane felt as if they were stepping back in history. Marble floors worn by countless feet, Veronese frescoes cracked with age, the cool, musty smell of centuries and inexorable decay. Tyler felt Kane's hand tighten around hers, and again she was conscious of that deep sensation of affinity as they followed the butler past an impressive staircase and across the entrance hall to a set of double doors.

He opened the doors for them, and in the instant before he announced their names they heard a somewhat shrill voice raised in nervous complaint.

"But, *strangers,* Elizabeth! How you could have invited them here—"

"Miss St. James and Mr. Pendleton," the butler announced crisply.

A tiny, white-haired lady rose from a brocade chair and came toward them, her smile as welcoming as that other voice had been annoyed. Elizabeth Montegro wore a plain silk dress with such innate dignity and style that Tyler realized only later that it was ten years out of fashion. Her delicate face was almost unlined, her green eyes still beautiful, and her voice was the slow, rich sound of the American South.

"I'm so glad you both could come," she said, shaking hands briskly with each of them. "I'm Elizabeth Montegro." Her accent lent the surname a curious cadence that was pleasing.

"Thank you for inviting us, Contessa," Kane replied, his deep voice holding all the easy charm he could command when he chose to exert himself.

"My pleasure, believe me. Fraser, see that their bags are taken up, please."

"Immediately, Contessa," the butler replied before backing out of the room and closing the doors softly.

She smiled at them, then half turned to nod toward the other woman in the room. "My stepson's wife, Erica Grayson."

While they murmured polite noises at each other and sat down on old brocade chairs, Tyler studied the other woman and remembered Keith's swift summation.

The stepson is Simon Grayson; he's some kind of consultant, Tyler. His wife is a cold fish by the name of Erica. And for "fish" you can read piranha; the woman could devour a man boots, bones and all. They live with the contessa because—according to rumor—Erica enjoys living in style and Simon spends too much on her pretty baubles to be able to afford a mansion for her. Rumor also has it that she'd dump him in a heartbeat if she could find someone as easy to manage with money.

Tyler could believe it, even without seeing Simon Grayson. Erica was a dark woman somewhere in her thirties. She had a predatory gleam in her black eyes, rings encrusting almost every finger, and her ethereal slenderness was burdened with a heavy rope of pearls and at least three gold chains. Her silk dress, unlike the contessa's, was very much in style, her black hair worn in an elaborate and queenly coronet, and she was quite beautiful in a sulky way.

She had held out a languid hand to Kane, her eyes both speculative and openly hungry; after a single glance at Tyler's casual skirt, sweater and neat single braid, she had offered a dismissive hello and thereafter focused her sultry attention on Kane.

"Keith Dutton was quite enthusiastic about you two,"

the contessa told Tyler as they all sat down. "He said you were researching some of the old Venetian families?"

"Preliminary research, at the moment," Tyler replied, smiling at the older woman. "There aren't many private journals and family papers that haven't been published or at least cataloged, so we haven't decided what to focus on yet."

"What's your own area of interest?" the contessa asked curiously.

"Heirlooms," Tyler replied promptly. "You can visualize so much of daily family life, even centuries ago, when you study the valued possessions handed down from each generation to the next. They're often mentioned in journals, particularly if there's an interesting story or set of circumstances connected with the object."

Erica laughed softly, one thin hand playing with her pearls—brushing them and her fingers gently against her breasts—as she eyed Kane. "And your . . . interest, Mr. Pendleton? Do you enjoy dusty journals and interesting stories?" Her tone gave the seemingly innocent question several layers of a very different meaning.

"Certainly." His tone was lazy, his vivid eyes veiled as he looked at her. "Although Tyler and I tend to be more active in our research than at present—climbing around ancient ruins rather than sitting in private libraries."

"All over the world, I imagine?" the contessa's voice was wistful.

"Most of it," Kane confessed, smiling at her.

"It sounds so exciting," she said.

Tyler said, "That's one word for it." She carefully avoided looking at Kane. "Vilely uncomfortable more often than not, but I wouldn't trade any of our adventures for tour guides and five-star hotels."

Erica stirred slightly, and her discontented mouth tightened. "Have you been together long?" she asked throatily, looking only at Kane from under her lashes.

"Years," he replied, returning her stare with nothing but polite attention.

The contessa sent her stepson's wife a quick look, then smiled almost apologetically at Tyler and said smoothly, "I'm sure you'd like time to unpack and settle in before dinner. We dine at six, and please don't feel you have to dress formally. I keep to the old ways, though Simon and Erica tell me I should be more casual and modern. . . ."

Tyler, who was developing an acute dislike for Erica, smiled back at the contessa. "We don't get many chances to dress up, and I'm looking forward to it." She and Kane rose as the contessa got up to pull an old tasseled bellrope by the marble fireplace.

"Fraser will show you to your room," the contessa said as the doors opened almost instantly and the butler stood waiting. "Please make yourselves at home."

"Thank you," both Tyler and Kane said, and then followed the butler out.

Five minutes later, alone with Kane in their room, Tyler stood gazing around slowly. The villa had been modernized a few decades back to provide adequate

plumbing and other necessities, but it was relatively un-
changed by modern conveniences. This room was huge
and bright, and if the silk hangings of the four-poster
bore the fine slits of age and the velvet draperies at the
two big windows were faded from sunlight, it was still a
splendid room.

The furniture was a blending of heavy bulk and or-
nate detailing, the woods holding the dull patina of age
and care, and the rugs, though threadbare, were still
beautiful in their muted colors and artistry. Paneled
walls provided some insulation from the cold stone of
the exterior, and a brisk fire burned in the grate.

Tyler opened one of the two big wardrobes and began to methodically unpack. "What do you think?" she
asked Kane.

"I like the contessa."

"So do I. And I hate lying to her."

Kane glanced at her as he hung several shirts in the
second wardrobe. "We aren't lying. We *are* researching
an old Venetian family—the Montegros."

"We're looking for the chalice. Don't split hairs,
Kane." She picked up the airline flight bag that he had
found to carry the chalice in and set it in the bottom of
the wardrobe. She was frowning.

Kane watched her for a moment in silence. He felt as
if there were suddenly a wall between them, as if she
were deliberately distancing herself from him—already.
As if she saw the end of this "adventure" looming just
ahead, and wasn't prepared to wait to begin saying good-
bye to him. Even after the interlude in the car . . .

Was that it? he wondered suddenly. Was it less a matter-of-factness about their relationship than a determination on Tyler's part to remain fiercely independent? Had his passionate, almost desperate possessiveness in the car served only to make her feel smothered and trapped? She had been very silent afterward.

For one of the very few times in his life, Kane felt helpless and uncertain. He wanted to tell her that he loved her, that he needed her, that he wanted no more partings between them, but he was afraid of pushing her even further away from him. Afraid . . . God, he was scared to death of losing her.

"Kane?" She was staring at him, still frowning. "Are you all right?"

He took two steps to stand before her, one hand lifting to cup her cheek. He bent his head and kissed her lightly, then said, "We aren't hurting anyone, Ty. If anything, we have a chance of helping the contessa. If our chalice ends up belonging to her, she could sell the thing for enough to keep her in comfort for the rest of her life. We aren't planning to steal from her. Maybe the second chalice is here, but we aren't going to take it; we just want to find out if it still exists."

She was staring up at him, her amber eyes shadowed by some emotion he couldn't read. Her emotions had always been transparent to him, yet now she was hiding even in that way.

"Something else is bothering you. What is it?" he demanded, an unconscious tension in his voice.

Tyler couldn't tell him the truth; that Erica Grayson's

blatant advances to him had awakened a demon of jealousy inside her and that it had made her all the more aware of the uncertainty of their relationship. She couldn't tell him that. So she fell back on another fear, one that had been virtually absent from her thoughts since they had become lovers.

"If we—if we end up with only one chalice . . ."

His eyes narrowed. "I thought we'd gotten past that, Ty," he said roughly. "Do you still believe I'd steal the thing from you, or trick you in some way? Even now?"

"I don't know." It was almost a whisper. "I don't know what I believe."

"You trust me, you have to." His voice was still harsh.

Tyler fumbled for an explanation that wouldn't sound as if she was being demanding or possessive. "I trust you to be honest with me—there," she managed, nodding toward the bed. "I trust you not to pretend, not to offer—bedroom lies. But that's only part of what we are, Kane."

"Rivals."

"Has that changed?" She looked at him, a wordless hope drowning inside her.

Kane hesitated, then grasped her shoulders gently. "Yes." His voice was quiet now, slow and almost tentative. "We crossed the line, Ty. You said it yourself, the rules are different now. And we can't use what we are now to play the games on the other side of that line."

"What are we now?" She needed to hear his answer.

"Lovers." It was instant, certain.

"And when we're not lovers anymore?" The question

was impossible to contain. "Do we step back over the line? Do we go back to being enemies and rivals, and fight for the chalice then?"

Again, Kane hesitated, afraid of pushing too hard, of holding on to her too tightly. But she seemed to be asking for some kind of reassurance, and he had to risk it. He tried to make his voice calm, but he knew the strain showed through, knew that he sounded too intense. "Tyler, we won't stop being lovers just because we find—or don't find—the chalice. We won't stop being lovers because we leave Italy." His hands tightened gently on her shoulders.

She looked up at him and said in a small voice, "There's an ocean between us."

He hoped she was talking about the Atlantic. "We'll work it out. I want you in my life."

Tyler managed a shaky smile, the hope inside her alive again. "Sure about that?"

Kane followed her lead and deliberately lightened the conversation. "Definitely." He kissed her, adding in the same intentionally light tone, "I haven't spent all this time chasing you just to settle for a few weeks in your bed, you know."

She gave him a startled look, but quick amusement flashed in her eyes. "I seem to recall chasing you in a number of places, including North Africa—literally chasing you," she said in a dry voice.

"All right, so I'm a bit unorthodox." Kane disappeared briefly as he carried his shaving kit into the bathroom, then returned to the bedroom and grinned at her. "I knew you'd come after me then, and seeing you on a camel was worth the wait."

Tyler couldn't help but laugh, though her most vivid memory of that "chase" was the soreness she had felt for days afterward. Her earlier uncertainty had lessened; just knowing that Kane saw some future for them beyond their return to London was more than she had expected, and she was determined not to ask for more than he offered.

They worked in companionable silence for a few minutes to complete the unpacking, but she had to comment when she saw him hanging a black dinner jacket in his wardrobe.

"So you did get one after all," she murmured.

"It wasn't easy," he admitted with an obvious air of satisfaction. "The shop charged the earth for fitting—" He broke off suddenly and stared at her. Slowly, a gleam of rueful amusement showed in his eyes. "You little witch."

Tyler allowed a wicked smile to curve her own lips. "Well, you wouldn't have gotten one if I hadn't made it a challenge."

"How long have you been managing me?" he demanded.

Clearly he was more pleased than angry at the realization; that surprised Tyler somewhat, but she kept it light. "Only on occasion, and always for your own good," she said virtuously.

217

"Uh-huh." His eyes narrowed in a look of mock danger. "I'm going to have to pay more attention to your needling."

She kept her face innocent. "Worried, Kane?"

"Only for my immortal soul," he said dryly.

Almost an hour later, as he watched Tyler moving around the room getting dressed, Kane reflected that he wouldn't mind not calling his soul his own if Tyler claimed it. He was still feeling a bit sheepish over the realization that she had quite easily gotten him into a dinner jacket without in any way saying that she wanted him to wear one, and he couldn't help but wonder how many of his past actions owed their existence to her deft guidance.

Not that he cared.

In all the time he'd known her, Kane had never before seen Tyler in formal dress; he had never seen her wear jewelry other than a somewhat masculine watch and plain gold studs in her earlobes; he had never seen her wear makeup or arrange her glorious hair in anything but a neat, simple style.

Now, fascinated, he watched her. She was so accustomed to his presence by this time that she didn't seem to notice his attention; she wore the intent yet curiously detached expression of a woman performing the little feminine rituals so alien to most men, and Kane couldn't take his eyes off her. There was grace in every movement, from the tilt of her head as she replaced her simple earrings with heavy gold hoops to the way she lifted her arms to arrange her fiery hair in a sophisticated chignon.

Light, deft makeup had given her lovely face an exotic air that was intensified by her clear amber eyes and the faintly Oriental design of her earrings. She was wearing a sleeveless black gown that was high-necked in front and backless. A wide, softly glittering black belt accentuated her tiny waist and made the rich curves above and below it all the more eye-catching.

Kane could attest to the fact that she wore only a pair of brief black panties under the dress, and his own secret knowledge of the bare, creamy flesh demurely hidden by thin dark silk was driving him crazy.

She stepped into a pair of black pumps and slipped a heavy gold bangle over one delicate wrist, then surveyed herself briefly with a critical gaze in the dressing mirror in one corner of the bedroom before turning away with a faint, unaware shrug.

She didn't know, Kane realized dimly. She had no idea of how beautiful she was. It was incredible.

"We're going to be late," she said briskly. "Yes, I know it's my fault, so you don't have to say it."

"I wasn't," he protested as she picked up his dinner jacket from the bed and held it for him. He felt her fingers absently smooth the material over his shoulders as he shrugged into it, and that unconsciously familiar touch affected him like nothing he'd ever felt before. He turned and pulled her into his arms. "God, you're beautiful."

Tyler was a little startled, and a soft flush rose in her cheeks. "Thank you. You look pretty good yourself." *Pretty good?* she thought a bit wildly. The starkly formal black dinner jacket made him so sexy she could hardly keep her hands off him. He was so big and obviously powerful that no clothing could hide it and, if anything, the formality only increased her awareness of the hard, muscled body cloaked by civilization.

His hands moved slowly down her bare back and curved over her bottom, holding her against him. "I don't suppose we could skip dinner," he murmured.

She managed to keep her voice steady despite her weakening legs and the curl of heat his touch always evoked. "What would the contessa think? Um, we're going to be late."

Kane bent his head to kiss her, not lightly this time, and then released her. And when they rejoined the contessa and Erica Grayson downstairs moments later, he held Tyler's hand firmly tucked into the crook of his arm.

It was a strange evening. Tyler, who had looked forward to talking with the contessa, found herself with ample opportunity since Erica attached herself to Kane with a blatant disregard for her marriage vows or his relationship with Tyler. It wasn't quite so apparent at dinner, but once they returned to the sitting room for coffee afterward, the dark woman made her designs on Kane flagrantly obvious.

The contessa was clearly upset by Erica's behavior, but it was distress rather than surprise; evidently it was Erica's habit to go after handsome men whenever her husband wasn't present—and possibly when he was. She had smoothly claimed a place beside Kane on a low sofa and talked to him in a husky voice, occasionally stroking his arm or lapel with her nervous fingers.

Tyler didn't hear what was said, since she kept her own attention fixed on the contessa, but the quiet murmur of the dark woman's voice quickly began grating on her nerves. She had the satisfaction of knowing that the attempted seduction was apparently having the opposite effect on Kane, since his mild smiles and veiled eyes were signs of temper rather than enjoyment, but Tyler could easily have slapped Erica for the distress she was causing the contessa.

It didn't really surprise her when the contessa commented on the situation; strong emotions tended to push aside the normal formality of virtual strangers, Tyler had found.

"I'm sorry about Erica, my dear," the contessa murmured with a somewhat strained smile. "Simon usually keeps her in line, but when he isn't here . . ."

Tyler smiled with genuine warmth at the fragile old lady. "Please don't let her upset you, Contessa." She suddenly remembered a female bandit intent on a more colorful seduction, and her smile turned wry. "Kane has a strong effect on most women, so I'm not really surprised." But she was, because Erica's determination was so obvious it was almost as if she were playing a role in which she had no clear idea of the limits. And to act the vamp, much less with such exaggerated intensity, under the eyes of her husband's stepmother was both ludicrous and insane, Tyler would have thought.

The contessa's smile became more natural. "I shouldn't think you'd have to worry about other women; he rarely takes his eyes off you."

Before Tyler could react to that surprising statement, the contessa continued.

"I'll try to keep Erica out of your way while the two of you work in the library, but if she does disturb you, please don't hesitate to tell her so. She usually sleeps late and spends much of her time in her room."

"Contessa—"

"Please, my dear, call me Elizabeth."

"If you'll return the favor."

The contessa chuckled. "Gladly, Tyler. Does anyone shorten that, by the way?"

"Only Kane. How about you?"

"My husband did." Her eyes turned misty. "My second husband, I should say. Stefano. He called me Beth. An odd diminutive for an Italian to use, isn't it?"

"I would have expected Liza or Lisa, something like that," Tyler agreed.

"Stefano was an unusual man. He loved America even before we met there, though he afterward said that was the reason for his affection for the States. But he was very proud to be Italian. He fought during the war—" She broke off and gave Tyler an apologetic smile. "I don't know why I'm boring you with these old facts."

"Please, I'm very interested." It wasn't a lie; Tyler was interested, both for the sake of the contessa, whom she liked very much, and for the sake of the reason they were here.

Still, as Elizabeth continued to gently and fondly tell Stefano Montegro's story, Tyler allowed it to sink into her mind without examining what she was being told. From the corner of her eye, she saw Erica's painted talons resting possessively on Kane's thigh, and it required all her self-control to avoid giving the dark woman a glare that would have skewered her.

She felt primitive, and the strength of those emotions shocked her somewhat. Jealousy and possessiveness were alien to her, or at least had been until now, and even though she was reasonably sure Kane wasn't susceptible to Erica's wiles, she couldn't master her own feelings. Despite his earlier words, the lack of a commitment between her and Kane made her uncertainty linger painfully, and those other alien emotions . . .

Get your claws off him! He's mine!

God, was that really her thinking like that? With all her independence, all her certainty in the belief that no one had the right to own another human being, she still couldn't bear the sight of that woman's predatory hands on her man.

And wasn't that, really, how she had always thought of him? With that small, possessive pronoun? My enemy. My rival. My lover. My man. Mine.

". . . his father had hidden away the valuables," Elizabeth was saying. "And, after the war, when Stefano came home, the town was all but destroyed; he was surprised to see Villa Rosa still standing and unharmed."

"He must have been pleased," Tyler said automatically.

"Oh, yes. But his father was on his deathbed, and

the war had changed so much. There was little money then, for anyone, and so much rebuilding to be done. Stefano did what he could, but it was very difficult for him. . . ."

What would Kane say if she told him she loved him? How would he feel about that? Trapped or smothered? Would his desire for her die? Would he, God forbid, pity her? One-sided love was a thing to be pitied, after all, a thing fit for compassion. . . . And her love was that. It made her so rawly vulnerable that she wanted to scream with the anguish of it.

Tyler had felt strong emotions before, had flinched under the brutal force of them. She had known pain, bitterness, grief, rage, hatred. But all of those primitive feelings paled in comparison to what she felt now, what Kane had awakened in her. For the first time she understood what the poets had tried to say about love, about the madness of it.

Everything else in her life shrank to a dim insignificance and became terrifyingly unimportant.

"If you'd like, Tyler, I can show you the library now. Stefano made an effort to organize some kind of reference system, but I'm afraid it's very haphazard." Elizabeth sounded a bit distressed again.

Tyler glanced aside to find that Kane and Erica had left the room while she had been totally involved with her own miserable thoughts. She managed a smile for the contessa. "Thank you, I'd like that very much."

As they rose, Elizabeth said unhappily, "Erica

probably offered to show him around the villa. I don't know what's gotten into her; she's never been like this before."

Tyler heard the ghost of a laugh escape her lips. "Don't worry about it, Elizabeth, please. Kane can take care of himself." And she never doubted that, of course. Kane Pendleton was the least helpless man she had ever known, and perfectly capable of remaining on his own feet.

Particularly since Erica had no henchmen to knock him out and tie him to a bed.

WHEN HE CAME into their room a couple of hours later, Kane was feeling puzzled, disgusted and definitely on edge. The first two emotions were due to Erica Grayson, who had hung all over him until he was certain his dinner jacket had been stamped with her musky scent. She had played the vamp with an almost shrill, desperate determination, and Kane couldn't believe it was because she'd been bowled over by him. He was neither that vain, nor that gullible. So what was the woman after?

He was on edge partly because of Erica and her murky motives, and partly because of Tyler. She had seemed completely fascinated by her conversation with the contessa, not looking at him even when he'd gotten up and left with Erica, and her lack of interest had hurt him more than he cared to admit.

Coming into their room now, he looked around swiftly and felt a surge of relief mixed with wryness when he saw her standing by one of the windows; obviously no pang of temper or jealousy had prompted her to pack her bags and move into another room.

Only the dim glow of a lamp on the nightstand lit the room, leaving the corners in shadow, and he couldn't read her expression. She had changed into something white and flowing, and taken her hair down, but she didn't move to meet him or speak.

So it was up to him. "Damn that woman," he muttered, jerking his tie off and flinging it toward a wardrobe. "She must have taken a bath in that perfume of hers. I probably smell like a cathouse."

"You do," she said dryly. "At least, I assume so. I can smell it from here." She sounded faintly amused and nothing more.

His jacket joined the tie on the floor. "I'm not wearing this again, Ty, not unless I can get it cleaned first." He crossed the room to the bathroom door and reached in to flick on the light. "And I'm definitely going to take a shower."

Tyler reached up to draw back the curtains, turning her head away from him and gazing out on the moonlit countryside with an abstracted air. "You should," she murmured. "That lipstick's the wrong shade for you."

It wasn't the words, but the faint quiver in her voice that caught Kane's eager attention. He wanted to go to her and yank her into his arms, because that slight tremor had sounded like unhappiness; he didn't want her to be unhappy, but the realization that she felt anything at all over Erica's pursuit delighted him.

"She wouldn't take no for an answer," he said somewhat gruffly, wanting to hold her but unwilling to do so while he smelled of another woman.

"Some women are like that," Tyler said quietly. "Go take your shower, Kane. It's late."

He hesitated, then went into the bathroom.

Tyler didn't move until she heard the shower running. She released her grip on the velvet drapes and looked at the crushed material bearing the imprint of her hand. Then, very deliberately and with utter calm, she left the bedroom.

Elizabeth had shown her briefly around the villa before they had parted to retire for the night, so Tyler knew where she was going. Her slippers made no sound on the smooth marble floors, and she didn't pause until she faced a closed door in a silent corridor of the west wing of the house. She knocked softly, and a sultry voice immediately invited her in.

Tyler felt her eyebrow lift with a kind of dry amusement. So Erica had expected Kane to seek her out here? She made a mental bet with herself as to the dark woman's probable position on the bed, then opened the door and went into the bedroom.

She lost her bet; not even her imagination could have conjured the theatrically seductive pose Erica had assumed. The woman was lying on her side on an artfully tumbled bed, her dark hair trailing over her shoulders and glistening in the light of a number of candles placed around the bed. She was wearing a black lace teddy, the wide, plunging V-neckline of which bared her breasts almost to the nipples and ended at the base of her belly. She was on her side, one leg drawn up and her head propped on a hand, and the smile on her face was pure feline.

The smile died quickly when she saw Tyler, and a tide of red swept up over her surprised face.

"Hello," Tyler said with gentle courtesy. "I thought we should talk a bit." Her soft voice, like Kane's mild smiles, didn't hide the pure steel underneath.

Erica flounced up on the bed, apparently undisturbed by the fact that one breast was in imminent danger of escaping from the teddy. Her voice was sulky when she said, "I don't believe we have anything to talk about."

Tyler shrugged. "Then I'll do the talking." She was beginning to feel puzzlement over Erica, an unwilling curiosity. "It's really very simple. Stay away from Kane. If your own marriage vows haven't the power to stop you—I have."

Erica's lips curled and her dark eyes flashed. "Power? You know nothing of power. And you have no hold on him. He needs a woman who will burn in his arms—" She broke off abruptly, obviously realizing how absurd that sounded in the face of Tyler's flaming red hair and brilliant amber eyes, both attributes denoting quite a bit of fire. Her flush deepened to an ugly, mottled scarlet.

Tyler stared at her in growing astonishment and not a little confusion. What on earth, she wondered, was *with* this woman? She acted like the prototypical vamp in bad B movies and sounded even worse. Tyler's simmering anger cooled as she tried to figure out what was going on. Because of her tumbled thoughts, her voice was almost absent when she spoke.

"Look, if you want to fight over him, I'm willing. But I'd better warn you that I get mean when I fight. And I know how to fight dirty."

Erica made a sound probably meant to indicate regal disgust; it was actually a snort, and not a very ladylike one at that. "I would never demean myself—"

"Demean yourself? Erica, you've already done that." Tyler hardly knew what to say to this absurd woman. It was the strangest encounter she'd ever had, and considering the past three years that was really saying something.

"I can take him away from you!" Erica flared.

"Why? I mean, what are you planning?" Tyler was honestly curious, and it was apparent in her voice. "Do you mean to divorce Simon? Kane wouldn't stomach being a gigolo, you can bet on that. And if you're just after a little slap and tickle while hubby's away, that won't work, either; Kane's too honorable to sleep with both of us under one roof." Tyler reflected for a moment, then added thoughtfully, "And even if he wasn't, he knows I'd start carrying my knife again."

Erica sputtered for a moment.

Tyler watched her curiously. She had come here with the angry intention of stopping Erica, but now she was intent mainly on discovering the motives of this woman. There *had* to be a motive somewhere.

"I enslave men!" Erica announced finally.

Feeling her eyebrow rise again, Tyler fought back a laugh. "You won't enslave Kane," she said, and then added consolingly, "Venus herself couldn't do that; he's too independent and too damned stubborn."

Erica would have stamped her foot in frustration if she'd been standing; since she was sitting on the bed, her foot made a stamping motion in midair.

Tyler laughed out loud that time, unable to help herself. "Erica, this is ridiculous. Kane's in my bed, and you're married to another man. What do you think you're going to gain by all this?"

"I'll get him." Erica was breathing in jerky little pants, her black eyes almost wild. "I can turn a man to jelly in my arms, take him to heaven. I can . . ."

She went on in that vein for a few minutes, while Tyler watched her in fascination. The thought that she might be literally insane skittered through Tyler's mind, but she dismissed it; there was something else here, something . . . desperate. Erica was right on the edge, but the edge of what?

What the hell's going on here? she wondered.

"All right, I get the point," Tyler interrupted finally, seeing that the dark woman was working herself into a frenzy. "But you'd better get mine. Stay away from Kane."

Erica smiled a brittle smile. "I'll get him into my bed. Unless you take him away from here, I'll get him."

Tyler felt the hairs on the back of her neck stirring, and suddenly understood what Erica's motive was; she knew now what the other woman was trying to do, even if she didn't yet know why.

She kept her voice calm and even. "Oh, I never run from a fight, Erica. Ask Kane. He knows. And I learned to fight in places you couldn't imagine. Think about that." She turned and left the bedroom, closing the door softly behind her.

chapter ten

AS SHE ENTERED their bedroom, Kane swung around to face her with a scowl. "Where the hell have you been?" he demanded harshly.

It wasn't normal for her to meekly accept that sort of question, far less in that tone of voice and from Kane, but Tyler was so distracted by her encounter with Erica—and by the towel that was all Kane wore at the moment—that she hardly noticed. She had intended to be evasive if Kane finished his shower before she returned and discovered her missing but, again, she was so rattled that she answered with the truth.

"I went to see Erica," she murmured, wondering if she'd ever be able to look at him without feeling a shock of desire. No. Never. Especially when he was like this, half naked and beautiful. Had he been about to dress and hunt for her? One of the drawers in his wardrobe was open with clothes spilling out.

Kane went still, some of the anger draining visibly from his big frame. "Why?" he asked in a different voice.

She wanted to be evasive about *that,* but Tyler just couldn't lie to him. Even more, the various tensions and puzzlements of the day boiled up in her suddenly and escaped with a force she had no way of fighting. Her hands lifted to rest on her hips as she assumed an unconsciously challenging stance, and she faced him defiantly with no more than two feet separating them.

"You told me to assume you wanted to be in my bed, so that's what I assumed. I went to tell Erica to stay away from you unless she wanted to tangle with me. Satisfied?"

"No," he said somewhat thickly.

Tyler glared at him. "Great. I'll go tell her she can have you. I'll be *damned* if I'll fight for a man as stubborn and contrary as a Missouri mule!"

Kane laughed and took a quick step so he could pull her stiff body into his arms. "No," he repeated huskily, "I'm not satisfied. You make me hungry, and I can never get full."

She blinked, then caught her breath as her lower body instinctively molded itself to his and she felt the hardness of his arousal. Her flash of rage vanished as swiftly as it had come. Somewhat uncertainly, she said, "That wasn't what I meant."

Kane pushed the filmy white negligee off her shoulders and let it drop to the floor, his darkened eyes drawn to the creamy golden curves of her breasts. The white gown she wore was demurely high-necked, but since the bodice was fashioned of eyelet lace there was nothing chaste about it. He could feel her tightening nipples against his chest, feel her stiff anger vanish as her arms went up around his neck.

"Damn you," she murmured helplessly. "I was mad. What happened to my mad?" She could feel his warm lips against her throat, feel his chuckle.

"I don't know, but on you even mad looks great."

His words reminded Tyler of Erica—on whom mad looked really awful—and she tried to focus her thoughts. It wasn't easy with his lips on her and his hands sliding down over her bottom, but she tried. "Kane . . . about Erica—"

"I don't give a damn about Erica. Do you realize this is the first time I've ever seen you in a sexy nightgown?"

"I hadn't really thought about it."

"Hadn't you?"

Tyler felt heat rise in her cheeks, and hoped to heaven a blush looked better on her than it did on Erica. "All right," she muttered as he lifted his head to look down at her. "I had thought about it. And *don't* tell me my vanity's showing!"

"Did you buy this for me?" He was smiling, a peculiarly masculine smile of enjoyment.

She was somewhat beyond evasion; the effect this man had on her was a little frightening. Eyeing him with a certain amount of bitter resentment, she said, "You really want your pound of flesh, don't you?"

His hands moved gently over her bottom, slow, intimate, holding her against him. "I want everything I can get from you, Ty, haven't you figured that out yet?" Before she could answer, he repeated, "Did you buy this sexy gown for me?"

He didn't sound like a man wary of feeling trapped or smothered by a woman, Tyler realized. She frowned a little as she gazed up at him, trying to ignore the sensations he was rousing in her body at least long enough to understand this. Stalling for time, she said, "You should have seen what Erica was wearing."

Kane's eyes narrowed. In a deliberate voice, he said, "I don't care if she was stark naked and built like Helen of Troy. Answer the question."

"Yes. All right? Yes, I bought it for you."

He kissed her angry mouth until it softened, until her lips parted for him and a murmur of pleasure purred in the back of her throat. When he lifted his head at last, her lips were faintly swollen, her eyes dazed with desire.

"Damn it," she whispered, dizzy with desire and the seesawing of her emotions.

Kane couldn't help but grin. She was still mad at him, or at least wanted to be; that fighting spirit of hers was something he'd never be able to conquer even if he wanted to, which he didn't. He had fallen in love with her when she first raged at him, her heartbreaking eyes blazing with fury, her magnificent breasts heaving angrily, and her fiery temper could still get to him faster than any other of her moods.

Still smiling, he said, "Getting any kind of admission out of you is like pulling teeth. You really love making me work for it, don't you, Ty?"

"Work for what?"

He kept his tone light. "I know you're crazy about me, but will you admit it? No."

Tyler smiled up at him very sweetly. "Crazy being the operative word." This kind of sparring, she thought, was safe. Light, humorous, ultimately without meaning. A kind of verbal sexual teasing in a lamplit room.

"You're a stubborn woman," he murmured. "A maddening woman." His fingers were moving against her bottom again, slowly gathering the silky material of her gown as he drew the hem up. "But I can make you want me. Even when you're furious."

She gasped as she felt his big, warm hands on her naked flesh, the heat inside her spreading wildly. A distant part of her wondered why she even bothered to deny her feelings to him; he was too experienced not to know that her desire was so swift and powerful only because deeper emotions fed the flames. He had to know. He had to.

"Can't I?" he demanded.

"Yes," she murmured unsteadily. She found the knot holding the towel around his lean waist and fumbled with it until the terry cloth slid to the floor. He had pulled her gown up to her waist, holding the material bunched in one hand at the small of her back, and she bit back a moan as his hardness pushed at her. Her forehead rested on his shoulder for a moment and her hands stroked compulsively over the solid muscles of his back, feeling them move under her touch.

God, she wanted him. It was like an addiction, a craving in her soul. Her mouth slid over his bronze skin, and she tasted his clean flesh, breathed in the tangy scent of soap. All her senses expanded with a rush that was almost painful, until she was so acutely aware of him it was as if there was nothing else in the world. His breath was coming roughly, like hers; his skin was heating from the fire inside it, like hers; and she could feel his heart hammering, his body shivering as she touched him.

Kane uttered a rough sound and abruptly stepped back, quickly pulling the gown up over her head. "Have I told you how exciting you are?" he asked in a rasping voice, lifting her naked body easily into his arms.

Tyler nudged her slippers off automatically, clinging to him as he lowered her onto the bed and joined her. "No," she breathed, staring up at his taut face, feeling a sense of wonder that she could make him want her like this.

"You are." His mouth trailed down between her breasts, brushing fire across her flushed, swollen curves. His hands were stroking her body slowly. "Wildly exciting. You looked like a queen tonight, so damned beautiful and sexy I could hardly keep my eyes off you. And my hands."

Tyler could feel her body begin to move against him, restless and wanting, her hands trembling as she held on to him with a rising desperation. "Kane . . ." He was torturing her with his slow caresses, his own body tensed and shaking, his expression fixed in a look of utter absorption, and she was on fire with needing him. "Kane, please . . ."

A chuckle that was more like a growl rumbled in his throat as he held her twisting body firmly and continued the maddening caresses. "Why do you think I left the sitting room when I did?" he demanded gutturally against her breast, his thumb rasping over one tight nipple while he tasted the other. "I couldn't be still, just like a turned-on kid with raging hormones and no control. I wanted to pull up that silky skirt and take you right there, no matter who was watching."

She moaned deeply and pulled at his shoulders, seduced by his words and his touch, wild to feel him inside her. He resisted her silent plea, teasing her aching breasts with tiny licks and hot nibbles, letting her feel his teeth and his tongue.

"Damn you," she whispered, and slid one hand down his hard stomach, closing her fingers around him. She felt him jerk, heard his breath catch with a hoarse sound, and her own excitement spiraled violently as she explored the throbbing power of him, hot and rigid in her hand. She stroked him slowly, watching his vivid eyes flicker, his face tighten with a pleasure that was almost agony.

"God, baby . . ." His control shattered. With a groan, he rose above her, spreading her legs and pulling them high around him, entering her with a strong thrust of urgent need. He thought he'd explode when her hot, moist flesh tightly surrounded him, and he drove deeper in a primitive craving to merge their bodies completely.

She returned his passionate force with a lithe strength of her own, her flushed, beautiful face taut, her half-closed eyes luminous with the fire he had ignited. It was like before, like always, desperate and uncontrolled, almost a battle, like two wild things mating to sate a need they hardly understood.

"YOU WERE JEALOUS," he murmured.

Tyler pushed herself up on an elbow and gazed down at his relaxed face. She started, absurdly, to deny it, but then remembered his own wry admission of jealousy. Keeping her tone dry, she said, "Well, I *knew* Erica wasn't sixty-five and doddering."

His mouth curved, and sleepy eyes opened to look up at her. "Good."

She made a face at him, but didn't resist when he hauled her closer. Absently fingering the pelt of black hair covering his chest, she said, "Kane . . . about Erica."

He yawned. "What about her?"

"She really went after you."

"Can I help it if I'm adorable?"

Tyler pulled at several hairs until he winced.

"Ouch." He eyed her somewhat ruefully.

In a reasonable tone, she said, "Look, I'll admit that you're sexy—"

"How sexy?"

She narrowed her eyes and glared at him. "Very sexy. But—"

"No buts. I don't want to hear buts."

"But," she continued firmly, "Erica was just trying too damned hard. You're a stranger, she's married—and she didn't even try to spare Elizabeth's feelings. Or mine. She's hell-bent to get you into her bed, and it's just—" She broke off abruptly and added, "What's more, she expected it to be you knocking on her door tonight instead of me."

"She got the wrong idea," Kane murmured.

"Oh, yes?" Tyler's voice was very polite.

He grinned a little. "Well, I told you the state I was in when we left the sitting room. Since she was rubbing up against me like a cat in heat, I imagine she noticed."

"And thought she was turning you on?" It made Erica's confidence in ensnaring him more understandable, Tyler reflected.

"Could be. She acted like it. But then, she acted like that all evening."

Tyler stared at his neck, even though no trace of the lipstick remained. She forced herself not to think about that. Except that her voice didn't obey her mind. "Did she miss your mouth, or was she *trying* to get lipstick all over you?" Damn! She sounded like a shrew.

"Shrew." But Kane was smiling. Then the smile faded and he said seriously, "You know, I think that's just what she was doing. It's hard to believe, but even as . . . as frantic as she seemed to be, it was sort of . . . bravado. Something she almost had to do."

"She was branding you. For me to see."

Kane frowned a little. "I don't get it."

"Neither did I, until I talked to her. What she more or less said was that as long as you were here, you wouldn't be safe from her, um, seductive wiles. I think she fully expected me to panic, grab you by the collar and hustle you out of here."

He gazed up at her, still frowning, one hand toying gently with her tumbled hair. "Are you saying that whole vamp bit was designed to make us leave the villa? Baby, that doesn't make sense."

"No, because we don't know why. But I think I'm right, Kane, I really do. Nothing about her was natural tonight; it was like she was playing a part—being *forced* to play it—and scared to death of not doing it right."

"Surely she could have found an easier way of getting rid of us," he objected.

Tyler chewed on her bottom lip as she thought about it, until Kane lifted a hand to cup her cheek and used his thumb to gently ease her lip free.

"Don't do that," he murmured. "It makes me crazy."

She had to laugh, but said, "I'm trying to think; stop distracting me."

"I can't think of anything but you right now," he retorted, and pulled her head down firmly.

The conversation ended for the time being, and both of them were too pleasantly exhausted to resume it. The lamp was turned off, and they fell asleep still entwined.

It was hours later when Tyler woke up, and she couldn't figure out why; dawn was no more than a faint gray light in their silent bedroom, the house quiet and peaceful. Then she heard a sound from outside, faint and muffled. She eased away from Kane and slipped from the bed, crossing to the window and shivering unconsciously at the cold floor beneath her feet.

The window was open just an inch or so, which explained how she'd managed to hear anything at all from outside. She pulled the drapes aside and gazed out. Nothing moved, and in the gray light she could see nothing unusual, nothing out of place.

But she felt tense, jumpy.

"Ty?" Kane's voice was sleepy, puzzled. "Baby, come back to bed."

With a shrug, Tyler abandoned the window and returned to him, sliding under the covers and cuddling up to his warm body as he pulled her close.

"Why'd you get up?" he murmured.

"I thought I heard something."

"What?"

"Just a noise; it woke me up, I guess. But I didn't see anything."

He murmured something wordless and pressed a kiss to her forehead, recapturing sleep with no effort. But Tyler lay awake for a long time, bothered. She felt uneasy, the way she had from time to time in the past when there had been puzzling undercurrents in a situation.

After experiencing stark, primitive fear herself, it was almost as if some barrier of civilization, some protective veil, had been ripped away from her. People who had known the physical and emotional trauma of violence, her father had said, were changed forever by it, left wary on the deepest levels of themselves. Instincts that most people never needed in their lives were born—or released—in violence.

Now, in the gray light of a silent dawn, Tyler felt those instincts stirring. Like an animal bristling at the stench of fear, she felt tense and anxious, her unconsciously straining ears listening for . . . something.

But the house was silent. Gradually Tyler forced herself to relax. The steady rise and fall of Kane's broad chest and the thud of his heart beneath her cheek lulled her senses, until finally she drifted back to sleep. She had strange dreams, remembering in the morning only that they had disturbed her, that she had been searching for someone whimpering in pain.

ALL THE NEXT morning Tyler and Kane worked in the big library. Despite their active adventures in the past, both were competent researchers, and it took them very little time to become familiar with the haphazard system Stefano Montegro had tried to impose on nearly four hundred years of chaos. They briskly decided that Kane would wade through the stack of household ledgers and inventories they had unearthed, while Tyler studied the available journals and diaries.

They had already agreed to explore the villa later in the afternoon; the contessa told them at breakfast that she always rested after lunch, and it seemed to be Erica's habit to do the same. The dark woman's pursuit of

Kane was apparently reserved for evening hours, since she put in no appearance at breakfast and they saw no sign of her during the day.

They were working companionably in a silence broken from time to time as one or the other of them made a comment. Since he was dealing with the big, heavy ledgers, Kane sat at the mahogany desk while Tyler was curled up nearby in one of the reading chairs.

"Here's something," he said when they had been at work no more than an hour or so.

Tyler looked up from frowning over the faded ink and spidery writing in the journal on her lap. "What?"

"It's dated 1894. Household inventory." Steadily he read, "Item: one heavy cup, no handles, on a pedestal base; figures of Greek design, warriors and chariots, et cetera. Gift." He looked up at her with a wry frown. "It doesn't even say who the gift was from. Or when it was given. This entry could have been carried over from an earlier inventory that doesn't even exist anymore."

She stared at him. "No mention of its being made of gold?"

"No. But none of these entries bother to mention if any item is made of precious metals. Two lines above the cup, there's a terse entry concerning a dagger. From the description, you'd think it was just another knife, but I happen to know *it* was made of gold, the handle at least, and studded with rubies. It's in a museum now, and has been for the past fifty years. It's called the Rose Dagger."

Tyler accepted his certainty about that. "Then the cup could well be our chalice."

"Could be. And it doesn't help that there's no mention of a mark on the base of the pedestal. It could have been missed or ignored, or there might not have been one."

She sighed. "So we still don't know which chalice belonged to the church in Florence, and which one the Montegros owned."

Kane straightened in his chair and flexed his shoulders slightly. "Any luck at your end?"

"No. This is one of the oldest journals—a diary, really—dated from 1860. Unfortunately it belonged to a very silly girl named Melina."

Kane grinned at her. "Why's she silly?"

"I just read three pages describing her newest ball gown. It'd be bad enough in English, but in Italian it's hell. Stop laughing, or I'll make *you* read it!"

They paid no attention to the passing hours as they worked, and were disturbed only once as Fraser crept in with a tray of coffee and sandwiches sometime after noon. Tyler, immersed in the second of Melina's three diaries, thanked him absently in Italian. She hardly noticed when he left again.

"Come up for air," Kane requested, leaving the desk to pour coffee for both of them. "Are you still on Melina? I thought she was silly."

"She is. But it's a fascinating kind of silliness. She writes about *everything*. Fashion, what people talk about over dinner, the servants, her parents . . . a sexy stable-boy."

"She didn't write that he was sexy, I imagine?" Kane set a cup of coffee on the table beside Tyler's chair, then leaned over her shoulder to gaze at the diary.

Tyler tilted her head back and looked up at him. "No, but she described their tryst in an empty stable for five pages. I think it's safe to assume he was sexy."

"Maybe I should read it, after all." He kissed her lightly before she could respond, then added, "Take a break. We'll have lunch and then go exploring. I don't know about you, but my eyes are beginning to cross."

Tyler had no fault to find with the suggestion, and after finishing the sandwiches and coffee they set out to explore the villa. They had both dressed casually for the day, choosing to wear jeans, and neither was disturbed by the dust they stirred up as they wandered among the closed rooms on the third floor. The contessa had told them that this floor was unused and had been for some time, but she had also invited them to look around and they took her at her word.

It was a lonely place in its disuse, a part of the house cut off from life. Heavy furniture under Holland covers, rugs rolled up along walls, some windows bare and some shuttered. An occasional dark painting hung on a stained wall, so covered with layers of varnish that there was no hope of guessing what subjects the unknown artists had depicted.

"It's so sad!" Tyler burst out as they headed back down the hall to the stairs. "A slow death. This place should go out in style, with laughter instead of this awful silence."

Kane took her hand and squeezed it slightly. "I know. But this house was built for a way of life that's gone, Ty. It can never be the kind of private home it was once."

Tyler sighed an agreement and tried to make her voice brisk. "Well, we can't do much poking around on the second floor; it's mostly taken up with suites for the family and servants and a few guest bedrooms like ours. Elizabeth has a suite in our wing; Erica and Simon have one in the other along with Fraser and his wife. She's a good cook, isn't she?"

"Mrs. Fraser? Very good."

They were moving down the stairs by then, and a glance at the cracked frescoes on the curving wall depressed Tyler all over again. Before she could say anything, however, they reached the second floor and found themselves facing a stranger.

"Good afternoon," he said cheerfully. "I'm Simon Grayson."

HE WAS A medium man. Medium height and weight, medium coloring, a voice in midrange. His smile was easy, his handshake firm and cool. He seemed polite and mild. And smooth.

"Are you finding everything you need in the library?" he asked as they continued down to the ground floor. "Mother told me about your research. It sounds fascinating."

Tyler responded almost at random. "The Montegro family is fascinating. Between the journals and the ledgers, there's a lot of information about them."

Simon smiled at her. "I'm afraid that I'd be defeated at the outset by all that spiky writing. You read Italian, then?"

She glanced at Kane, who was unaccountably silent, then nodded at Simon. "Yes, we do. I can claim only French and Italian; Kane probably has half a dozen languages." She knew, in fact, that he had at least that many.

Kane neither confirmed nor denied it; he had stopped at the closed library door and stood with one hand on the handle, and was looking at Simon with a kind of detached, vaguely polite attention. Despite his powerful size and rugged handsomeness, the abstracted air gave him the look of a scholar with his mind fixed on some weighty problem.

Tyler was baffled, since she'd never seen him look like that before, but some instinct alerted her to say nothing about it in the presence of Simon Grayson. Instead she said casually, "We'll probably work the rest of the afternoon. Will we see you and Erica at dinner?"

Simon took the polite dismissal with good grace. "Of course. Until this evening, then." He smiled and strolled off toward the stairs.

Kane opened the door for her, then followed her into the library. She leaned back against the door and watched as he began pacing restlessly.

"He didn't waste any time, did he?" Kane muttered.

She frowned a little. "You think he came back early from his trip because we're here?" She didn't bother to keep her voice low, since the thick stone walls and massive wooden door made the room virtually soundproof.

"I'll bet Erica called him as soon as the contessa told her about us. Elizabeth said he was in Brazil, didn't she? Last night at dinner?"

"Yes."

Kane grunted. "The hell he was. He came tearing back here to cover his ass, and it wasn't from Brazil; he couldn't have made it back so quickly."

Tyler pushed away from the door and moved across the room to sit on the arm of a chair. "Kane, what're you talking about?"

He stopped pacing and faced her. "Damn it, you were right. Erica was trying to get rid of us. I don't know if the method was her idea or his, but you can bet he told her to do it."

"He wouldn't have told his own wife to—" She broke off suddenly. "Simon wants us out of here? But, why? He doesn't even know us."

"He knows we're researching in here, reading the family journals and ledgers. Which means we could well stumble across information he'd much rather keep for himself. He must have nearly had a heart attack when Erica told him we were coming here and why. You said he'd always talked Elizabeth out of having this stuff cataloged; the last thing he wants is someone picking around in here, especially a couple of adventuring archaeologists. Who both speak and read Italian." Scowling, he added, "Damn it, we always start out with a simple goal, and end up tangling with crooks!"

Tyler had to laugh, but she was still bewildered. "Kane, will you start at the beginning, please? What do you know about Simon Grayson that I don't?"

Kane eyed her for a moment, then said, "Why don't we just leave, now? I know you, Ty, you'll get fierce about the contessa and we'll both end up in trouble."

She didn't take the bait. "Tell me."

He swore softly but with exquisite creativity. "All right. Simon Grayson deals in the black market for art objects. He supplies them."

Her mouth fell open. "What?"

"Cute, isn't it? Interpol's had their eye on him for three or four years now, but they've never been able to nail him."

"Are you sure?"

"Positive. I never connected the name, but I recognized him. A friend with Interpol showed me a photo about a year ago. They wanted to know if I'd ever encountered Grayson. He's been driving them nuts by selling untraceable art objects into the black market. They believe he has a stash somewhere; they even got an agent in the villa once, but he couldn't find a thing."

Tyler felt limp. "Why haven't they arrested him?"

"You know how it is. They *know,* but they can't prove it in court. The middlemen he deals with are pros and not likely to even admit knowing him. It was just an unlucky chance that they got onto him at all; he made the mistake of using a ruby necklace to pay off a gambling debt— Erica's, I imagine. The necklace, appraised and cataloged around the turn of the century, was listed as having disappeared sometime during World War II; at that time, it belonged to another old Venetian family in this area. I forget the name. Anyway, the guy Simon bought off with the necklace tried to sell it, and Interpol was alerted."

"Couldn't he testify against Simon?"

"He could. Except for one thing. A few hours after he'd made an informal statement to the police, he ended up in the morgue. Hit and run."

"They think Simon did it."

"Thinking isn't proving. Simon was supposedly a hundred miles away at the time. With Erica."

Tyler chewed her bottom lip. "Damn."

"I told you not to do that," Kane growled.

It took her a moment to realize what he meant, and she was a little surprised by her ability to distract him. She stopped chewing her lip. "Sorry. Kane, we have to do something."

"I knew you were going to say that." He half closed his eyes.

She was surprised again. "When have you ever run from a fight?"

Kane started pacing again, reluctant to tell her that he wanted to run from this one because of her. The thought of Tyler in danger made him sick with fear—and she courted danger, she'd taught herself to face it. She'd rush in with that fiery spirit of hers, just the way she had in North Africa and Mexico and Budapest and the Sudan and Hamburg and Hong Kong, and all the other places their jobs had taken them. Matching her strength and her wits against crooks with nothing to lose and a taste for violence. Damn, damn, *damn*.

"Kane?"

He loved her courage, even the maddening independence revealed in every defiant lift of her chin, but he wanted her safe and that instinct was too primitive to be denied. He'd wrap her in cotton wool if she'd let him, but she wouldn't let him, he knew that only too well.

"He's dangerous, Ty," he said finally, evenly.

"All the more reason." She sounded puzzled. "Those art objects have to be the Montegros'; he has no right to them, no right at all. He's robbing Elizabeth."

"The ruby necklace wasn't the Montegros'." He was reaching for objections, and he knew it.

"I can't explain that," she admitted. "But the answer's here in the library, it must be. In the journals and diaries or the ledgers. Whatever it is, he probably didn't dare take the chance of destroying anything in here for fear of Elizabeth finding out."

Kane knew he had lost. He should have kept his big mouth shut about Simon Grayson's little scam, but it was so natural to discuss it with Tyler that he hadn't stopped to think. All he could do now was work with her, be alert to those reckless actions of hers, and guard her back. He didn't intend to let her out of his sight as long as they remained at the villa.

"Kane?"

"All right," he said briskly, heading for the desk. "So now we're looking for two things. The chalice, and some indication of what was hidden, when it was hidden, and where."

Tyler gave a gasp suddenly and began searching through the pile of diaries and journals beside her chair. "Stefano's father," she muttered. "I know I saw a couple of his journals, and Elizabeth said he hid the valuables during the war."

Kane had seated himself at the desk, and now looked across at her with a frown. "Wouldn't Stefano have known about that?"

"I'm not sure. Damn, I wish I'd listened more closely." Tyler found the two leather-bound volumes and sat down in her chair with them. She looked at Kane. "Stefano's father, Vincente, was on his deathbed when his son returned at the end of the war; I don't know if he was even capable of talking. And this area had been damaged so heavily that Stefano could have assumed the valuables had been destroyed or looted."

"Elizabeth knew they'd been hidden," Kane observed.

"Yes. But I don't think she knew *where*. And if she didn't know, neither did Stefano. From what she said, I got the impression Stefano had assumed the stuff was hidden away from the villa . . . somewhere nearby, maybe. And he didn't spend a lot of time here as a child, he was away at school; he might not have known there was a hiding place in the villa."

"We don't know, either."

"No, but we can find out." Tyler opened the first of Vincente Montegro's journals, flipped through a few pages, and then sighed. "He didn't date the entries by year, only the day and month. I'll have to read every page."

Kane smiled a little. "Is it ever easy for us?"

"No." She looked up at him. "Do you really think Simon's dangerous?"

"I think we'd better assume he is. And since we won't know—until we find it—exactly what he's afraid of us finding, we'll have to be very cautious about talking to him." Kane looked at the stack of ledgers on the desk. "I'll go on looking through this stuff, but our best hope is probably the journals."

Tyler nodded in agreement, then bent her head over Vincente Montegro's first journal. His handwriting was clear, at least, and she was secure enough in her knowledge of Italian to be able to read it with fair ease. Vincente, however, had an annoying habit of sprinkling his entries with phrases in other languages. After asking, and receiving, translations from Kane of bits of entries in German and Latin, she finally looked up at him with a curious frown.

"How many languages *do* you have?"

He looked a bit sheepish. "Both my parents taught languages at the college level . . . and they were linguists. My brothers and I were multilingual almost from the time we could talk."

Distracted, she said, "How many brothers?"

"Two, both younger. Matt's a professor at Cal Tech, and Craig runs a computer business."

Tyler stared at him for a moment. "How many languages?"

"French, Spanish, Greek, Italian, German, some Latin, Arabic, a smattering of Japanese, Cantonese—"

"I'm sorry I asked," she said somewhat blankly.

Kane grinned at her. "Read your journal."

She returned to her study of the journal, thinking that Kane was the most surprising man she'd ever known. Two separate degrees in archaeology, a linguist, a mountain climber and a pilot—she hadn't known *that* until he'd taken the controls for a while during their flight from Bogotá to the coast. He was an expert with guns, a competent sailor, was adept with mechanical things like engines and possessed an infallible sense of direction.

He was a Renaissance man.

chapter eleven

BY THE TIME the afternoon waned, Kane and Tyler were no closer to finding their answers. He had continued to wade through the ledgers and household accounts while she read Vincente Montegro's first journal. But neither of them found what they were looking for. When they went upstairs to dress for dinner, Tyler took with her Vincente's second journal and, with a shrug, Melina's final diary, as well.

"You never know," she told Kane. "And I'd rather not leave them down here tonight. Simon will probably want to find out exactly what we've been reading."

To Tyler's amusement and Kane's disgust, they found upon reaching their room that his dinner jacket had been cleaned and neatly rehung in his wardrobe.

"Fraser, I suppose," Kane said irritably. "You never

see the man unless he's serving something, but he always makes his presence felt. Is there a maid? I haven't seen one."

"A girl from the town comes in daily, according to Elizabeth. But the jacket was probably Fraser's doing. I'll bet he's used to cleaning up after Erica."

"Cat," Kane said, and ducked into the bathroom to take his shower before she could throw something at him.

Sometime later, as she was dressing, Tyler said absently, "I wonder when Simon got here."

"Does it matter?" Kane asked, watching her.

"I don't know. He just appeared so suddenly." She was arranging her hair in a thick braid to hang down over one shoulder, a style that exactly suited her evening gown with its square-cut neckline, full sleeves, and snug bodice. The gown was a soft gold color, and the full skirt fell in graceful folds to her delicate ankles. Tyler was, as always, detached and critical of her appearance. "I look like a peasant girl," she muttered to herself, turning from the mirror.

"You look beautiful," Kane said deeply.

She gave him a startled look. "Thanks, but I wasn't fishing."

"I know that." He smiled a little. "Forget that dig I made at your vanity, Ty. You don't have an ounce of conceit."

A little uncomfortable, she shrugged. "I always wanted to be tiny and raven-haired. Instead I ended up tall, all legs and cursed with a shade of hair that clashes with practically everything."

Kane took her hand and tucked it in the crook of his arm as they left the bedroom. "Hair like fire," he murmured. "Eyes of pure gold. A mouth that drives me crazy. Long, beautiful legs that wrap around me like warm, strong silk . . ."

Tyler couldn't believe it. They were walking down the stairs, formally dressed, outwardly sedate, and he was seducing her. Her legs felt weak and shaky, her skin flushed and hot, and an ache of desire throbbed slowly inside her. She glanced up to see that his eyes held a hot flicker of desire, and amusement.

"Kane," she protested softly, wishing that she could feel angry at his obvious enjoyment; he knew exactly the effect he could have on her simply with words that evoked sensual images. She lifted her free hand to briefly touch her hot cheek, hoping that no one else could guess the state she was in.

"After dinner," he said, "we're going to go for a moonlit walk outside."

"We are?"

"In the best romantic tradition. I'm trying to sweep you off your feet, you see," he added conversationally.

Tyler couldn't respond to that with more than a startled look, because they reached the sitting room then and Kane led her inside. And, as the evening progressed, she didn't get much of a chance to think about it.

The contessa was her usual gentle self; Erica was dressed in royal blue and diamonds, and almost utterly silent; and Simon was playing Master of the Manor to the hilt.

She didn't know if it was her heightened senses or not, but Tyler was almost painfully aware of undercurrents the entire evening. It didn't take her long to realize that Simon was at the center of them; he was the stone dropped into a quiet pool, spreading ripples of unease. At first Tyler thought that only Elizabeth was unaffected, but she soon realized that the contessa was simply showing it less; there was strain in her lovely eyes, and the firmness of control held her lips steady.

Erica was jumpy, responding to her husband's occasional bland endearments in a smothered voice and hardly looking at anyone else; Simon was cool and dry and faintly superior. Kane was laconic, and Tyler wasn't sure what she was feeling.

"How's the work progressing?" Simon asked as they gathered in the sitting room for coffee after the meal.

Tyler looked at him. "Slowly." She mentally reviewed what she and Kane had decided they could tell Simon. "At this point, we're primarily organizing the ledgers and journals into some kind of order. You know, according to date and, in the case of the journals, author. We need to see what kind of time span we have, if there are any large gaps, like that."

"I imagine there will be a number of gaps," he said indifferently. "Aren't there usually, among family papers?"

"That depends on the family." Tyler smiled at him brightly. "The Montegros seem to have been a literary lot."

"Stefano said that," Elizabeth murmured. "His own

father kept a journal, and he was encouraged to, as well. Have you found Vincente's journal, Tyler?"

They hadn't counted on the contessa's innocent questions, Tyler reflected wryly, and answered as best she could. "Yes, his is the most recent. We'll start with the oldest ones, though, and read forward."

"Read?" Erica's dark eyes looked haunted. "I didn't think—silly of me, I suppose—"

Simon interrupted the disjointed phrases coolly. "They both read Italian, darling. I thought I told you."

Erica's cup clattered unsteadily against its saucer. "Oh. Yes, of course," she murmured. The glance she sent her husband held a pathetic mixture of fear and entreaty.

Tyler, who suddenly saw and understood the reason behind Erica's heavier than usual makeup, felt herself stiffen. Beside her on the low sofa, Kane slipped an arm around her and grasped her shoulder warningly. So, she thought, he had seen, as well.

She kept her voice light and casual. "My Italian's a bit rusty, but I imagine I'll get by well enough."

"If not," Simon murmured, "you're welcome to ask me to translate. My Italian is fluent. So is Mother's, of course."

"Thank you." Tyler kept the smile on her lips, but Kane must have realized that she was on the raw edge of exploding, because he rose to his feet and pulled her gently to hers.

"I realize it's early," he told Elizabeth with his charming smile, "but I promised Ty a moonlit walk. Would you mind very much if we said good night now?"

She returned his smile, the tension around her mouth easing. "Of course not. The old gazebo is still standing, and the garden is quite lovely in the moonlight. Just please be careful of the uneven ground; we've had some flooding in the area. If you aren't back by the time we retire, I'll have Fraser leave the front door unlocked, and you can lock it when you come in."

"Thank you," Kane said, and led Tyler out before she could do more than repeat the thanks.

A few minutes later as the soft scents of the untended garden closed around them, Tyler said tensely, "Her face was swollen. He's been hitting her."

"I know."

She glanced up at him as his fingers tightened slightly around hers, and even though she couldn't see his expression clearly she recognized the flat sound of his voice. Kane was as angry as she was. "Elizabeth's afraid of him, too. You don't think . . ."

"That he's violent with his stepmother? No. Not physically, at least. She's too strong a woman to stand for that. But she may be at least partially dependent on him financially, and you can bet he uses what power he has against her."

They walked in silence for a few moments, moving farther from the villa, and then Tyler said, "No wonder Erica was trying so hard. And I think . . . God help her, I think she loves him."

"How could she?" Kane murmured.

"I don't know. I mean, I really don't understand how

love can survive that kind of violence. But the way she looked at him . . . She's terrified, but . . . suppliant. She has the reputation of going after other men, but I'll bet Simon tells her to. For whatever distorted reasons of his own."

"Probably," Kane agreed. "She certainly doesn't enjoy doing it, yet, in a way . . ."

"In a way, she does. How do people get so twisted, Kane?"

She sounded a little lost, and Kane stopped them, turned her to face him. "I don't know, baby. But we can't untwist them."

Tyler slid her arms around his waist and rested her forehead against his broad chest for a moment. "I'm ruining your romantic moonlit walk," she murmured wryly.

He kissed the top of her head, then smiled at her as she looked up at him. "No. But try to remember there isn't a lot we can do about some things. If we can find what we're looking for, maybe we can put Simon out of circulation for a while and even help Elizabeth financially. But we can't fix all the broken things in their lives. We can't, Ty."

"I know." She sighed. "I'll stop thinking about it."

"Maybe I can persuade you to do that." He pulled her a bit closer. "Could you think about me instead?"

"Well, if you ask me nicely . . ."

* * *

THEY WALKED IN the garden for a long time. The air grew chilly, but neither of them noticed. Kane made her laugh by describing her as a "pagan maid in the moonlight" when she stood inside the small, Roman-templelike gazebo, then drove laughter out of her mind when he held and kissed her passionately.

He seemed bent on courting her, as if they weren't already lovers, murmuring words of desire that heated her blood and stole the strength from her legs. Touching her with a hunger that was potent and curiously moving. He made her feel incredibly desirable. He made her feel, for the first time in her life, really beautiful.

It was late when they finally started back toward the house, walking slowly. Tyler was almost reluctant to go back into the villa, her feelings about the people who lived there confused and painful and uneasy. But Kane held those feelings at bay, and she loved him more than ever because of that. He made her want him until nothing else mattered.

They had reached the foot of the wide steps leading up to the porch when she noticed a faint light about twenty yards off to the right. It took her a few seconds to recognize the interior light of their rental car, which was parked there.

"Kane," she murmured, keeping her voice low. "Someone's been in our car. The dome light's on."

His arm tightened around her and then, as always, he moved quickly to deal with the situation. "Wait here," he breathed, and glided away from her like a shadow.

Tyler half turned to watch him, wishing her eyes

were as good as his in the dark. The area where the car was parked was in the murky shadows cast by the villa, and she could just barely see Kane as he neared the car. A moment later the car's interior light went out.

And, in that instant, Tyler felt the hairs on her nape stirring as a soft scraping sound reached her ears. She tensed like a deer alerted by the cocking of a gun, all her instincts shrieking a soundless warning inside her head.

"Tyler!"

Kane's hoarse shout galvanized her as nothing else could have done. She leaped instantly away from the steps toward him, a sudden understanding of what was happening lending her that extra measure of strength and quickness that had so often meant the difference between life and death. As it did this time. Behind her there was a thunderous crash, and she felt small shattered pieces of what had fallen pelt her legs.

And then Kane's arms were around her, holding her with a strength that was almost crushing, and she could feel his heart hammering violently.

"Ty . . . baby, are you all right?" His voice was still hoarse, shaking. And the hands that framed her face as she looked up at him were trembling.

She nodded, finally found her own voice. "I—I think so." She felt cold with the shock of what had happened, but forced herself to think. "It was one of the statues, wasn't it?" she asked, not wanting to look behind her.

"That bastard. That murderous son of a bitch—"

Tyler was shaking her head. "It could have been an

accident. The villa's four centuries old." And there was, she knew, easy access to the porch roof from at least four of the third-floor windows.

"For God's sake, Ty—"

"Think," she urged him quietly. "If it was Simon, he's already back in his room. Everyone else is in bed, and they wouldn't have heard a thing; all the bedrooms are on the other side of the house. And the villa *is* old. The statue had to be loose, or he could never have pushed it over. We don't have any proof, Kane."

"I don't need proof," he said.

Tyler could feel the rage in him, like a deadly inferno, and her awareness of that was the only thing holding her own calm shell in place. Kane was unarmed, and though she had no doubts of his ability to kill Simon with his bare hands, she also had no doubt that the other man would probably be waiting inside his bedroom with a loaded gun trained on the door.

"Please, Kane." She kept her voice soft. "If you go after him now, you'll end up in jail." *Or worse.*

After a long moment Kane drew a deep breath. His arms gradually relaxed, and he bent his head to kiss her gently. He didn't say a word, as if he didn't trust himself to speak. He kept one arm around her as he guided her around the mound of rubble at the foot of the steps. They went into the silent house. A few faint lights had been left burning for them. Kane locked the massive front door behind them, but left the lights on as they 't upstairs.

'r room awaited them as it had the night before,

with the lamp glowing softly and the covers of the wide bed turned back invitingly. Kane locked the door. Tyler had begun to shiver with a delayed reaction to the shock, and the sore places on her lower legs where pieces of the statue had hit her warned that she'd have bruises by morning; there would have been cuts if the material of her long skirt hadn't protected her somewhat.

She knew Kane wouldn't like seeing those marks on her. And he didn't, though he noticed the reddening marks, because he immediately ran a hot bath for her and put her in it, still utterly silent. His face was white and still, his vivid eyes darker than she'd ever seen them. Anger and what looked like pain tightened his firm mouth when he saw the marks on her legs, but he handled her very gently as he bathed her and then dried her warmed body with a fluffy towel.

Then he carried her to bed. Tyler said nothing as she watched him undress, but as he slid into the bed beside her, her anxiety over his silence made her say his name hesitantly.

Kane leaned over her, gazing at her face with that odd, fixed look in his eyes. He lifted a hand to touch her cheek very lightly, and then kissed her. He was gentle at first, but there was something inside him clawing to get out, and the force of it shuddered through his body and made his kisses grow rough and urgent, and his hands hard with need.

"Kane?" she whispered as his lips left hers to burn their way down her throat. She was a little tense, uncertain. She wasn't afraid of him, but this dreadful silence was scaring her.

"I almost lost you," he muttered in a jerking voice half muffled against her skin. His hands were moving over her almost frantically, as if he were reassuring himself of her warmth and life. "Let me love you, baby . . . For God's sake, just let me love you. . . ."

Tyler's anxiety vanished as his rough words emerged, and her body came alive. Her response to his touch was as powerful as always, yet he was different and she was responding to that, as well. She could hardly believe what all her instincts were telling her, yet she had to believe even though he didn't say the words she needed to hear. He had been shaken by her narrow escape, too shaken to be able, now, to hide what he was feeling.

He loved her as though afraid of never again having the chance to hold and touch her, his hands trembling as he stroked her body, his own big frame shuddering almost convulsively with desire. He kissed her again and again, catching her soft sighs and whimpers in his mouth. He muttered rasping words against her skin, words that were stark, graceless, bluntly sexual.

Tyler was burning, dizzy. His desire ignited her own with a ferocity she'd never felt before, and even as her body went wild in his arms, it seemed as if some ultimate barrier inside her shattered. She had surrendered to him long ago, but now she wasn't simply giving way to something too strong to fight, she was giving herself fully and freely.

There was a need in him that was naked, intense, the sound of it raw in his voice and the look of it dark and haunted in his eyes. He desperately wanted something from her, something more than passion, and the very strength of his need compelled her to offer him everything she had to give.

It wasn't a reasoning decision on her part, or even a conscious one. She loved him, and he needed. She offered her body, accepting his eagerly; she offered the wild fury of her desire for him, returning his urgent passion with nothing held back. But he needed more, and she gave willingly.

"I love you," she moaned, crying a little, holding on to him with all her strength because he needed that, too. He jerked at her words, a low groan bursting from his throat, burying himself deeper as if he were trying to fuse their bodies in the eternal instant when violent pleasure shuddered through them.

KANE LIFTED HIS head at last to gaze down at her softly flushed face, her shimmering eyes. She was still holding him in a mute refusal to let him leave her, and there was a stark vulnerability in the tremulous curve of her lips.

"Say it again," he murmured, needing to hear it.

Her lips quivered, but those beautiful, wet eyes met his gaze steadily. "It was the one thing I never guarded," she whispered. "The one thing I never expected you to steal from me. I love you, Kane."

He half closed his eyes. "Thank God. Ty . . . baby, I've loved you since the day we met."

"What?" She stared at him numbly.

He couldn't help but smile at her total astonishment. "I didn't know it for a long time. I just knew I couldn't get you out of my mind." His hands lifted to frame her face, his thumbs brushing gently at the silvery evidence of tears at the corners of her wide eyes. "Your big gold eyes and flaming hair, your temper and the cool way you faced trouble. Everything about you fascinated me— even the habit you had of tricking me every chance you got."

Tyler drew a shaking breath. "I never realized . . ."

He kissed her. "I was afraid you were feeling trapped after we became lovers. You're so damned independent."

"I thought *you* were feeling trapped."

"I am." He kissed her again. "Trapped in something I never want to escape. Lord, Ty . . . I love you so much it's like madness. When I . . . when I saw that statue falling tonight . . . I've never been so terrified in my life."

She threaded her fingers through his thick, silky hair and lifted her head off the pillow to kiss him. A bit ruefully, she said, "Maybe we should thank Simon for that. I was too scared of clinging to tell you I loved you. Until tonight."

"I wish you would cling a little," he said, matching her tone. "Damn it, I want to wrap you in cotton and spoil you to death."

Tyler gazed at him gravely. "I wouldn't mind being spoiled, at least some of the time. But, Kane—"

"I know." He grinned faintly. "Don't think I'm picturing a demure little hausfrau with a smudge of flour on her nose. You're a hellion, Ty, a fighter, and that's the woman I fell in love with. I have no doubt you'll scare the hell out of me at least once a week, because you just can't stay out of trouble—"

She raised her head to kiss him again. "Trouble?" Her amber eyes were innocent.

"You're a lightning rod for it," he said firmly.

"Look who's talking," she murmured. Slowly, provocatively, her even white teeth began worrying her lower lip.

Kane felt an instant jolt of desire, but eyed her somewhat warily. "You're doing that deliberately," he muttered. "To distract me. You're an evil woman." He had always suspected that if Tyler ever chose to be deliberately seductive, a man would be putty in her slender hands; he had been right.

"I love you, Kane," she said softly, her big eyes warm and shimmering.

He groaned and lowered his head to kiss her hungrily. So what if he was putty in her hands? Big deal.

SOMETIME LATER, TYLER sat up beside him. "I'm not sleepy," she announced.

He opened one eye to peer at her, then opened the other because she was glowing with happiness and

271

incredibly beautiful. "It's after midnight," he murmured.

"Are you sleepy?"

"No."

"Good." She leaned over him to open the drawer of the nightstand, producing the two diaries. "Then I think we should read these tonight. Simon's obviously made up his mind to get rid of us, and if we give him time to pull another stunt like he did tonight, you're going to kill him."

Kane sat up and banked the pillows, then settled back against them. "I'd only be doing the world a favor, to say nothing of Erica and the contessa," he pointed out.

"Yes, but the Italian police might not see it that way. We have to get evidence against him, or at least find out where the art objects are."

He nodded a reluctant agreement. "Okay, but I don't want you out of my sight as long as we stay here. Please, Ty," he added as she looked at him gravely. "I know you tend to land on your feet just like a cat, but I don't think I can take another scare like tonight—at least not right away."

Tyler smiled at the last rueful words. "All right. It's no hardship, staying with you." Then, sternly, she said, "Just don't expect me to hide behind you. I'll guard your back, but I won't hide."

"I know that." A slow smile curved his lips. "And there's no one I'd rather have guarding my back."

"I'm glad." She settled beside him, turning over onto her belly as she handed him Vincente's journal. "You read Vincente; all those languages are impossible for me. I'll stick with Melina."

"You're fascinated by her," Kane noted in amusement.

"Well, since she writes about practically everything in her life, maybe something will ring a bell."

It was over an hour later when Kane said, "Ty."

She looked up at him quickly. "You've found something?"

"Listen to this. 'I fear the worst. Even now, the countryside shudders under enemy fire, and we have heard the stories of atrocities; burning and looting. It is said that the vile Hitler means to plunder Europe of its riches. Today, several of my neighbors came to me with a plan. They are still young men, unlike myself, and mean to fight for our country. They have sent their families to safety, and have asked me to store their valuables at Villa Rosa.' "

Kane read slowly, obviously being careful of correctly translating Vincente Montegro's multilingual writing. " 'Their families know nothing of this; we feel it safer that only the six of us know. We have drawn up a list of each family's possessions, so that the valuables may be returned to their surviving members once this hateful war is over. I have sworn a blood oath to do this.

" 'I sent the servants into town on errands, and my neighbors helped me to make all safe. Even if the walls of Villa Rosa fail to stand, I have no doubt the secret room—' " Kane looked up at her. "The rest of the page is missing."

"Damn," Tyler said softly. "So Simon was at least that careful."

Kane studied the journal on his lap. "I'm only about halfway through; maybe there'll be something else further on."

She nodded, but didn't hold out much hope. After a moment she said, "Stefano couldn't have known; he would have honored his father's blood oath. The necklace, Kane, the ruby necklace that Simon used to pay the gambling debt: it was never returned to the family that owned it. Those five men must have died during the war, and Vincente died before he could tell Stefano what they'd done with the valuables."

"He knew they'd been hidden," Kane agreed, "but he had no idea where. Why didn't he read his father's journal when he got home after the war?"

"I don't know. Maybe we can ask Elizabeth about it." Tyler returned to Melina's diary, feeling depressed. She read almost without attention, a part of her mind trying to figure out where a "secret room" might be in the villa.

Absently Kane said, "So Simon had an added reason to keep this from Elizabeth. Not only because he wanted all the Montegro wealth for himself, but because he was selling items that didn't even belong to her. She wouldn't stand for that—"

"Kane!" Tyler gasped.

He looked at her. "Not Melina?"

Tyler drew a breath and began reading softly. " 'My cousins enjoy playing a game of search, and they are vilely bad tempered when they cannot find me. They beg Mama to tell them where I hide, but 'tis a Montegro secret, and she would not betray it. She scolded me for discovering it myself, saying I was too young and flighty to be trusted, but I will never reveal our secret! My cousins have searched the cellar again and again, coming so near me that I laughed to myself, knowing they would not think to press the stone hand of a pagan god.' "

"I'll be damned," Kane said blankly.

Lifting his eyes from the diary, Tyler looked bemused. "Melina. Silly Melina. The cellar . . . A *wine* cellar! Palladio designed some fancy ones, I know. There must be a statue or something of Dionysus. No, the Roman version. Bacchus. The god of wine."

"Guarding a hidden room," Kane murmured. "Clever."

"It's the middle of the night." Tyler's eyes were shining with excitement. "We could go and look now."

Kane hesitated, though he was as eager as she. "I don't know, Ty. I don't trust that bastard to be asleep in his bed."

"He's already tried—and failed—once tonight," she pointed out reasonably. "He'll have to regroup and consider his options. Think it through."

"Yes, if he's being logical about it. But is he? Maybe we should wait until morning and talk to Elizabeth."

Tyler waited silently, watching him. She had known Kane before this adventure, but her love gave her even greater insight now, and she knew what he'd decide. Despite his newfound anxiety over seeing her in danger, he was something of a lightning rod himself and could no more choose the safe path than she could. They were two of a kind, and she gloried in that certainty.

"Hell," he said finally, his lips curving, vivid green eyes alight. "Let's do it."

Half an hour later, both dressed in dark sweaters, rubber-soled shoes and jeans, and armed with their flashlights, they made their way silently downstairs and toward the rear of the villa where the kitchen was located. They found the heavy wooden door leading to the cellar and went cautiously down, Kane leading the way.

There was a switch at the top of the stairs, which they had made use of, and a number of shaded lights hanging from the ceiling of the cellar provided adequate illumination. Three walls were lined with tall racks, sadly depleted so that few bottles remained, and the rest of the floor space was taken up with stacks of odd bits of broken furniture and old trunks.

Directly across from the foot of the stairs, standing upright and apparently a part of the wall itself, was a marble slab. Carved from the stone was the muscled figure of a naked and bearded man, a cup in one hand and the other upraised as if to halt anyone who approached.

As they crossed the room and stood before the life-sized sculpture of Bacchus, Tyler giggled as a sudden thought crossed her mind. When Kane looked at her questioningly, she murmured, "I wonder how many parts of his anatomy Melina fondled before she found the right one."

Kane grinned at her. "She does seem to have been a

mite precocious." He looked at Bacchus, then said, "You do the honors, Ty. You're the one who stuck with Melina."

In spite of their light words, they were both tense, and Tyler's hand trembled just a little as she raised it and touched the cold stone of the god's hand. She pressed steadily, feeling it give beneath the pressure; there was a sharp click, and the marble slab swiveled easily on a central axis.

For an instant they both stood staring at the blackness of a doorway, then they exchanged looks. Kane flicked on his flashlight and aimed it into the opening.

The room was relatively small, no more than twelve feet square, the walls, floor and ceiling constructed of stone. And it was nearly half filled with wooden crates, iron strongboxes, and other containers. In the beam of the flashlight, the blackened gleam of tarnished silver was visible; at least three of the crates were filled with platters and cups and candelabras. Kane moved the beam of light slowly, revealing a number of very old jewel cases piled haphazardly atop one another, along with numerous paintings rolled up and propped against the walls.

"My God," Tyler said softly. "Some of the richest families in Italy lived in this area. Kane, most of this stuff has to be priceless." She was on the point of turning her own flashlight on and going into the room to explore more carefully, when some faint sound or her own instincts warned her. Kane whirled around even as she did, both of them staring at the wicked barrel of a pistol held in a steady hand.

"Quite priceless," Simon agreed coolly. "And people are always willing to pay for priceless things." He laughed a little, the sound like the dry rustling of leaves.

"You fool," Kane said flatly. "Do you really think we can disappear without questions being asked?"

"Oh, but you'll be found. Or, rather, your bodies will. Mother did warn you, after all, that the ground around the villa is treacherous. I'm afraid you're both going to lose your footing and fall. There's a certain place I know where you'll fall a very long way."

He was, Tyler thought with the clarity danger always lent her, talking too much. It was the classic blunder of villains, particularly amateurs like Simon Montegro. Her mind worked quickly. Her peripheral vision caught a slight flicker as Kane's flashlight twitched, and that motion was enough to alert her to what he had in mind. Rivals and enemies they might have been, but in three years dangerous situations such as this had welded them into an efficient—and decidedly original—team.

Tyler dropped into that accustomed role with total ease and even a surge of almost savage enjoyment. She laughed.

Simon jerked slightly, his cold eyes sending her a sharp glance as the unexpected and inappropriate sound pierced the silence. "What're you laughing at?" he demanded.

"You," she told him dryly. "Of all the melodramatic postures, yours is the worst, Simon." She had his attention now, and held it easily. "And you're so damned pathetic. Stealing from your stepmother, beating your wife. You're really a worm of a man, aren't you?" She could feel Kane tensing beside her, readying himself.

"Bitch," Simon muttered.

Tyler wanted to tell him that he really shouldn't have said that because he'd pay dearly for it later, but she didn't waste her breath warning him. She laughed again. "Do you really expect us to be herded along meekly and pushed over a cliff? Honestly, Simon, that's so—"

She never finished the sentence. In common with most polite people, Simon was waiting for her to finish it; that was a human trait she and Kane had learned to take advantage of in the past. They had also learned through experience that Tyler could throw an object and accurately hit a target within her reach.

Simon's hand was her target, and the flashlight she threw while she was still talking hit with her usual accuracy. The gun went flying, and Kane lunged with a growl.

Tyler went to get the gun, returning somewhat hastily when she heard agitated sounds from Simon. "Kane, stop choking him."

"I want to kill him." Kane's handsome face was wearing a fighting grin that held no humor and would have been familiar to a berserk Viking howling his way into battle.

Simon's well-made shoes were dangling off the floor, his fingers plucking at the iron hands encircling his throat, and the noises escaping him were growing desperate.

She knew Kane was honestly furious, not the least because Simon had nearly killed her. But she had seen him almost this angry in the past, and had learned to deal with his very rare but killing rages by being matter-of-fact and even humorous about the situation. It occurred to her only now that if she had stopped to consider her ability to calm him down in the past, she would have realized he had cared more about her than either of them had realized.

Tyler tucked the gun into the waistband of her jeans, brushed Simon's hands away and began prying Kane's fingers loose. "Well, you can't kill him."

"Why not?" Kane demanded fiercely.

"Because your friend with Interpol wants to arrest him," she replied calmly, still working his fingers loose. "And because I love you, and I don't want to have to bail you out of jail."

Kane looked at her for a moment, then dropped Simon onto the floor. He glanced down at the villain who seemed unable to do anything except cough and gasp, then returned his wistful gaze to Tyler.

"Can't I break at least one of his arms, Ty?"

"No, but you can tie his wrists together." She looked down at Simon thoughtfully. "Tightly."

Kane's chuckle started deep in his chest, emerging in a sound of utter delight. He pulled her into his arms and kissed her. "I love you," he said huskily. And added, "What's that poking my stomach?"

"The gun," she answered cheerfully.

He kissed her again. "Oh. Find a piece of rope or something, will you, baby?"

Simon didn't even struggle.

chapter twelve

"HE WAS A good boy when he was small," Elizabeth Montegro said sadly. "But . . . unaffectionate. Cold. I could never get close to him. After his father died and I married Stefano, Simon chose to spend most of the year in a boarding school. Then he grew up and . . . I'd barely seen him in years when he married Erica and they moved in here. It was only a few months later that I realized he was still cold. And that he was cruel, as well."

They were in the sitting room, all tired after the long day behind them. Elizabeth, Tyler and Kane. Erica was in bed and under a doctor's care, though her hysterics had worn themselves out hours before. Officers from Interpol had arrived late in the afternoon and had taken Simon away; two of them were still down in the cellar making an inventory of the valuables.

Vincente's list had been found in one of the jewel boxes and, along with his journal, had provided the officers with the story behind Simon's activities on the black market. The contessa knew now, and though she grieved, she was hardly surprised.

Tyler stirred slightly as she sat close behind Kane on the low sofa. She was exhausted, but she wanted all the loose ends tied up. "You let them stay here because of Erica, didn't you?" she asked the old lady gently.

Elizabeth nodded. "By the time they moved in with me, I'd already heard she . . . she was known to chase after other men. But once they were living here, I realized that Simon was behind that. He used her, had her get information from other men. Then he used that information. I'm sure there were stock tips and advance warning of business mergers and the like. Perhaps even blackmail. I thought—I hoped—I could protect her, at least a little."

"Why did Erica stay with him?" Tyler asked. "Love?"

"She wouldn't confide in me. But I thought that was her reason. She does love him, I think, but . . . I was blind to what was really happening. The doctor told me this afternoon that she'd been using drugs. Simon was giving them to her, I'm sure."

Quietly Kane said, "Don't blame yourself, Elizabeth."

The contessa managed to smile at him.

Tyler decided it was time to change the subject. "Elizabeth, I remember you said that Stefano had known about the hidden valuables. But if he didn't know where they were hidden . . ."

"He didn't." She seemed to welcome the change. "Vincente was something of a tartar, according to Stefano, and he was very secretive. I'm sure he intended to tell his son about the existence of the room, but he died before he could. He'd written to Stefano and said only that the family valuables were hidden on the grounds of Villa Rosa. When Stefano returned here, his father was in a coma. The entire area had been bombed heavily, and a number of outbuildings here had been destroyed. Stefano assumed the valuables had been lost."

"Why didn't he read his father's journals?" Kane asked.

"He couldn't find them at first. The old devil—" She smiled quickly, honestly amused. "His description of his father. Vincente had hidden them away. Stefano found them years later when he was searching for something else; they were in a trunk in the attic along with other journals. He took one look at the jumble of half a dozen languages, and just put all the journals in the library."

Tyler looked at Kane. "Simple enough."

"Once you have the answers," he agreed. "Then Simon read the journals a few years ago. And found the valuables. All those art objects, virtually untraceable because they'd been missing since the war years. Most of the records had been destroyed; he knew that. As long as he disposed of them gradually and cautiously, he stood to make a fortune."

"Thank you," Elizabeth said suddenly. When they looked at her, she smiled gently. "Someone had to stop Simon and I—I didn't have the strength. I'm grateful the two of you did. Erica will be all right; I'll see to that. She'll get the help she needs."

"You'll be able to renovate the villa," Tyler said with an answering smile. "The majority of those things in the cellar are yours, Elizabeth. You'll have private collectors and museums beating a path to your door."

"The way the two of you did?" She laughed in genuine pleasure at their startled looks.

"You knew?" Tyler said blankly.

"That you were searching for something specific here? Yes, my dear, I knew. After I talked to Keith Dutton, I called a few of the friends I had made over the past few years—friends involved in historical preservation. They knew of both of you."

Kane winced. "Then I'm surprised you invited us here."

"On the contrary. I was told in no uncertain terms that you were scrupulously honest people." Elizabeth's green eyes were twinkling. "In addition to being fascinating to observe. I was told to expect fireworks of one kind or another."

Tyler laughed a little. "Lightning rods, both of us. But thank you for trusting us, Elizabeth."

"I am curious," the contessa admitted. "What brought you here?"

Kane and Tyler exchanged looks, both of them remembering the final bit of helpful information that silly

Melina had provided in her diary; Tyler had discovered it just a few hours before.

Papa is so angry! That ugly cup he lent the church in Florence has come up missing. He has the other one, the one with the odd mark on its bottom, but he says it's worthless now. I think it's an ugly thing anyway, but he says Alexander was poisoned with one of them and that makes the pair valuable. And they were a gift to the family. . . .

Tyler leaned forward to open the flight bag on the floor by the sofa. Elizabeth, who had hardly noticed they'd come into the room with it, watched now as a heavy chalice was placed on the coffee table between them. She looked puzzled.

"This," Tyler said. Quickly she explained how she and Kane had come into possession of the chalice, and how Drew Haviland had put them on the trail that had led to Villa Rosa and the Montegro family. Then she explained what they'd found in Melina's diary, finishing with, "So it's yours, Elizabeth. We haven't had it authenticated, of course, and it'd be worth far more if we'd found the other chalice with the valuables, but Kane and I think it could be one of Alexander's. I suppose the mate was sold somewhere along the way, or—" She broke off, because Elizabeth was laughing weakly.

"Are you telling me that cup is priceless?"

"It's an antiquity," Kane said slowly, puzzled by her reaction. "Valuable for that, and the gold content. If it's Alexander's, it certainly is priceless. Elizabeth—"

The contessa rose to her feet, still smiling with an

odd, rueful humor. "It's late, and we're all tired. But before we retire, I want to show you something. Kane, please bring the cup."

He obeyed, and they followed the contessa up to the second floor and to her suite of rooms. They were baffled, even more so when they stood in her sitting room and she faced them with a smile.

"Look around."

They did, still puzzled. It was a warm room, decorated in bright colors and modern furnishings. Sturdy shelves held books and framed photos and knickknacks; there were a few landscapes on the walls; wildflowers from the villa's garden were arranged in two chipped porcelain vases.

Elizabeth laughed softly at their bewilderment. "I don't feel so bad now," she said dryly. "If you two experts missed it." She pointed to one of the bookshelves silently.

Tyler saw it then, and gasped. It stood in the center of one of the shelves, books leaning against it on either side, and since no light fell directly on it, there was no way of guessing that it was made of solid gold.

Kane set their chalice down on a table near one of the chairs and went to lift the second one from its shelf. He turned it in his big hands for a moment, then upended it and studied the bottom of the pedestal base. Slowly his mouth curved. He carried the cup back to Tyler and silently showed her the faint but visible mark pressed into the base.

She touched the cool metal softly, thinking of a dying

king trying to leave evidence of possible treachery. "It's Alexander's," she murmured, and she felt no doubt of that.

"Alexander's," Kane agreed. He placed the chalice beside its mate on the table.

Elizabeth shook her head ruefully. "I suppose I assumed it was made of brass. I never lifted it. It's been on that shelf as long as I can remember. How absurd . . ."

It was absurd, and Tyler started to laugh. Kane and Elizabeth both joined in, all of them thinking about a priceless chalice squatting peacefully on a shelf for years, a missing piece of history.

"Take it," Elizabeth said softly when their laughter had finally died. "Take them both. If the two of you hadn't come here . . . I owe you so much. Take the cups, please."

It was an incredibly generous offer. Kane looked at Tyler, then put his arm around her as she smiled up at him. He returned his gaze to the contessa. "Thank you, Elizabeth, but we can't. We brought them together—we won't be responsible for separating them again."

"I don't understand."

Quietly Tyler said, "If the cups were ours, Kane and I would be . . . honorbound to turn them over to our respective employers. Two men who are bitter rivals. The chalices deserve better than that." She smiled suddenly. "However, we *do* know of a man who would give them both a good home. And give you a good price for them."

* * *

HALF AN HOUR later as they got ready for bed in their room, Tyler said sleepily, "I don't know about you, but I'm in hock with my expense account. I'll have to pay Robert back. It's a good thing my bank account's healthy. I hate to think what he's going to say about losing the chalice."

Kane grinned a little. "I'm more interested in hearing what both of them say when they find out about us. Maybe we should accept Elizabeth's invitation to stay here for a few weeks, at least until they cool down."

"I'd like to stay here for a while," Tyler agreed, crawling into bed. "And we can help Elizabeth, run interference for her when the collectors and museums start calling."

Sliding into bed beside her, Kane said conversationally, "Just how many of these sexy nightgowns do you have?"

Tyler smiled up at him, her arms lifting to wreathe around his neck. "A few. I was hoping you wouldn't be too tired to take this one off me."

"Aren't you tired?" he murmured, nuzzling her neck.

"Not that tired."

"Good," Kane said huskily, and took the nightgown off.

KANE STOOD ON the balcony of their hotel room and gazed out over the city of Venice. After spending three weeks at the villa, they had returned here a few days ago; they both loved the city and had wanted this time to explore—and to be with each other. Kane found himself smiling as he remembered these last weeks, and wondered how he had ever survived without Tyler in his life and his bed.

Once they had each gotten over the fear of being thought too possessive by the other, everything had been just fine. In three years of battles they had learned to know each other with a depth and certainty that few lovers ever achieve, and with the barriers between them gone their love was absolute. Not peaceful, however; since they shared intense passions—about everything including each other—the fights had been as glorious as the loving.

And Kane knew it would always be that way. It wouldn't suit some people, but it suited them perfectly. They had promised each other that they'd never go to bed angry—which was something that seemed utterly impossible anyway—and that left them free to enjoy their fights.

"Are you still sulking?" she called out sweetly, and Kane grinned to himself as he turned to go back into their room.

Fights, indeed.

"Of course I'm not sulking," he told her as he came inside. "It's undignified."

"That's what I thought," she said with a nod. She was sitting cross-legged on the bed, bright-eyed and beautiful, and only wearing one of his shirts. "Besides, I said I was sorry."

Kane sat down on the edge of the bed and stared at her. "I heard you."

"I wasn't sure," she murmured. "You were yelling so loudly I thought you might not have heard me."

He laughed despite himself. "Damn it, Ty, next time will you just *tell* me before you go haring off?"

"Look, Drew was leaving Italy and wanted to talk to one of us, and you were gone off on some mysterious errand you wouldn't tell me about—"

"—I came back to find you gone, not even a note—"

"—and I wasn't away more than an hour—"

"—scared the hell out of me—"

"—you didn't give me a chance to explain—"

They both stopped and stared at each other.

"I'm sorry," she said meekly.

Kane, knowing only too well that his Tyler was about as meek as a star going nova, burst out laughing. "Sure you are."

Her amber eyes were dancing. "Cross my heart. I didn't mean to worry you, really. Forgive me?"

"Yes, damn it," he growled, and leaned over to kiss her.

"Good." She slipped her arms around his neck. "Now I can tell you what Drew said."

"He has the chalices?"

"Yes, he bought them. But that isn't it. He'd heard about Sayers and Phillips firing us, and then about them meeting by chance in Westminster and screaming at each other."

"How'd he hear that?" Kane asked curiously.

Tyler giggled. "It made the papers. Apparently they stood there toe-to-toe accusing each other of base treachery at the top of their voices, and a very confused reporter who happened to be there took notes. He wrote an article."

"God help the reporter," Kane murmured.

"I know. Anyway, Drew wants to hire us."

Kane stared at her. "He what?"

She nodded. "He says it's more fun to watch us than to do it himself. A funny little man in Calcutta sent him a message about a jade bull, and—"

"No," Kane said.

Her eyes were dancing again, but her voice remained solemn. "It sounds really fascinating."

"We're going to be busy," Kane said firmly.

"Doing what?"

"Making a baby. The winters in Montana are long and cold; we'll be spending a lot of time in bed."

Her laughter vanished, and she looked at him gravely. Her disappointment at learning that she wasn't pregnant had surprised her; until then she hadn't realized how much she wanted to carry Kane's child inside her.

He kissed her a bit roughly. "Damn it, look what you made me do," he muttered. "I was going to propose tonight in a gondola." He reached into his pocket and brought out a small black velvet case. Inside was a beautiful diamond solitaire.

"Kane . . ."

He slipped the ring gently on her finger, then held her hand against his cheek and gazed at her with warm, inexpressibly tender eyes. "You're a beautiful, maddening, vile-tempered woman, Tyler St. James, and I can't live without you. Marry me."

"Yes," she whispered. "Oh, yes." She went into his arms, her face glowing. "I love you, Kane."

"I love you, too, baby."

A LONG TIME later, the afternoon sun shone through the open balcony doors and onto a tumbled bed where two lovers lay in each other's arms, temporarily sated.

"Can you ride a horse?" he murmured drowsily.

She yawned and rubbed her cheek contentedly against his broad chest. "I can ride a camel," she reminded. "There can't be that much difference."

He chuckled, wondering what a horse would have to say about that vague statement. He rubbed his chin against her soft hair. Beautiful, wonderful Tyler. He'd have his hands full for the rest of his life, and he was looking forward to every second of it.

Drifting slightly, he was barely aware of saying, "A jade bull?"

"Mmm. Stolen from a temple, supposedly."

"In Calcutta?"

"Uh-huh."

"Odd."

"Yes, it is." Tyler smiled secretly and cuddled closer

to his warm, muscled body. So what if their route to Montana took them east instead of west; the world was round, after all.

They'd get home eventually.

author's note

THE FACTS CONCERNING Alexander the Great's life and death are accurate. I have speculated that his death, believed to be caused by malaria, might instead have been due to poison; however, that is pure speculation on my part.

The two golden chalices exist only in my imagination, and in the pages of this book.

Now Available

Kay
New York Times
Bestselling Author
Hooper

Enchanted

Together for the
first time—three
beloved romance
classics: *Kissed by
Magic, Belonging
to Taylor,* & *Eye of
the Beholder*

A Jove
Paperback

0-515-13714-6